Other novels by André Swartley:

THE ISLAND OF MISFIT TOYS*

AMERICANUS REX**

LEON MARTIN AND THE FANTASY GIRL***

*Indiana Book Award Finalist (2006)
**Next Generation Indie Book Awards Fiction Finalist (2010)
***Dante Rossetti Award First-Place Category Winner (Urban Lit) (2013)

Published by Workplay Publishing
Newton, KS 67114
workplaypublishing.com

Copyright © 2015 André Swartley

andreswartley.com

ISBN 0-9842122-9-9
Cover design and interior layout by André Swartley
Cover artwork "Spooky Old House" by Margaryta Yermolayeva
(www.artbyryta.com)

PRINTED IN THE UNITED STATES OF AMERICA

THE WRETCHED AFTERLIFE
OF ODETTA KOOP

BY

ANDRÉ SWARTLEY

Workplay Publishing

For Bill & Matty

The night has a thousand eyes,
  And the day but one;
Yet the light of the bright world dies
  With the dying sun.

The mind has a thousand eyes,
  And the heart but one;
Yet the light of a whole life dies
  When love is done.

Francis William Bourdillon

Sometimes one feels that it would be merciful to tear down these houses, for they must often dream.

H.P. Lovecraft

PART I: HOMECOMING

Show Me

Grover Solomon Yoder returned to New Canaan, Iowa when he was twenty-four years old, and he came alone. The big house where he'd grown up sat empty now, sullen and restless and waiting for its new owners, a family with the decidedly un-New-Canaan-ish name of Escobar. His parents had moved out the previous winter and made for their new condo in the suburbs of Atlanta, but this house hadn't sold until a couple weeks ago, at the end of May. The closing deal included an inspection of the premises, a tedious, symbolic responsibility that fell to Grover Solomon now that he lived closer to Iowa than his parents did.

He parked and exited his Honda with grimace that had little to do with stiff muscles from the morning's drive. He was thinking about the second task before him—a task that would never be written on any piece of paper. It was down to Grover Solomon to deal with Odetta Koop. If she was still there.

He tugged open the hatchback and peered into the cargo space. His backpack, containing his laptop and a few books, lay propped against a plastic milk crate. Until yesterday the crate had sat beside the futon in his apartment in Chicago, stacked high with the entirety of a nonfiction book series called *Haunted Nation: True American Ghost Stories*. Now the crate held a more eclectic scattering of objects, most of which he'd purchased at a dumpy little occult shop in central Chicago. At the top of the pile rested a thick, plain and rather gnarly pine crucifix that Grover Solomon had made himself as a child in his dad's woodshop. One of its arms was noticeably longer than the other, and the central shaft had warped.

He stuffed the cross into his back pocket, thinking of Bart Simpson and his trusty slingshot. Next came a silver dagger in a black faux-leather scabbard, which he buckled at his right hip, next to his cell phone. A tiny glass vial of holy water went into his front pocket, and he rounded out his arsenal with a drawstring pouch of rock salt, which he knotted to a belt loop at his left hip. He'd dropped a full head of garlic into the salt pouch for good measure before leaving Chicago, and the heavy tang of garlic rose from it, making his eyes water. In for a penny, in for a pound, as his old friend Lazarus might have said.

Thus armed, he slammed the hatchback and trudged up the front walk to the house. It was the oldest house still standing in New Canaan and, at three stories high, one of the largest. A brass plaque hung to the right of the front door, marking the house as a historical landmark. Grover Solomon stared into the dim eye of the plaque, a cowboy reluctantly squaring off for a high-noon duel. The plaque stared back, dull and spiteful.

"I can't do this," he said. He inserted the key his parents had mailed him last week into the lock on the front door. "I *can* do this," he argued with himself, and he twisted the knob and stepped inside the entry room.

The smell of old wood rolled over him in cloud, yellow and sweet and cloying. The entry room was a mismatched forest of wooden fixtures: walnut front door, oak flooring and trim, long cherry staircase and banister, and a mahogany credenza set against the far wall. The coat closet in the entry room was also lined with cedar to keep moths away. The sharp, red scent of cedar on top of all the other wood made the room feel more like wilderness than civilization.

Welcome home, he thought morosely.

As he latched the front door, his eyes kept flicking to the cedar closet. How many times had he and Lazarus played Show Me—a variant of Go Fish they had invented themselves—in that closet while Grover Solomon's mother believed they were playing outside? Because they had needed to hide the game. Naturally, all manner of playing cards had been forbidden in the Yoder household, and this particular deck had not been regular Hoyles or Bicycles. They were covered in *nudie* pictures. Or at least that's how Grover Solomon thought of them. The cards were cheap, generic things with black and white burlesque photos of ladies wearing sheer, loose flapper dresses or holding up feathery fans in coy arcs to hide their naked-ness. The only card to show a completely nude woman had been, fittingly, the Queen of Hearts.

Neither the cards nor the photos had impressed Grover Solo-mon much, except in the frankly alarming amount of danger they represented if they had ever been discovered. Lazarus, on the other hand, couldn't get enough of them. "Gad, look at those knockers," he said whenever the Queen of Hearts came up in their game. He always spoke in a world-wise tone that suggested he had no real idea what the words meant. Indeed, Grover Solomon remembered Laz once pointing to the naked woman's fleshy knees, clearly be-lieving them to be her "knockers."

But Laz had lost the card at some point, and Grover Solomon doubted he would ever forget the tense weeks that followed. Laz couldn't be sure whether he'd last seen the card at his own house or at Grover Solomon's, and so the boys simply waited, sick with dread, for the moment when one of their parents would find it. But that never happened. Either the Queen of Hearts had been well and truly lost, or she had been found but not connected to the boys.

Even now the scent of cedar still filled Grover Solomon with that same childish, giddy panic that came from doing something mysterious and wrong and exciting all at the same time. Something forbidden in other words.

He amused himself by imagining Mr. or Mrs. Escobar drawing the missing Queen of Hearts out of a heating vent, perhaps while they were deciding where to place a sofa or dresser. But the thought of the Escobars reminded him of where he was and why. His amusement, feeble to begin with, swept out of him as if blown away by an icy wind. All of this would have been so much easier with Lazarus at his side. Laz hadn't ever seen grinning gargoyle faces materialize from patterns in the carpet. He had never spent a sleepless night listening to the relentless ticking of a clock that did not exist.

Laz hadn't been afraid of anything in the world, and so had opened this house to Grover Solomon in a way that no one else had ever been able to. When Laz let loose his high, rolling belly laugh, as he was prone to do at the punch line of even the lamest joke—particularly if he told it himself—any resident boogeyman would run for the hills.

But of course there was no such thing as the boogeyman. There was only Odetta Koop. She of the stomping feet and ticking clocks.

As for the house itself, this dusty old barn had outlived Laz by almost fifteen years now and would probably continue earning historical plaques long after Grover Solomon was so much dust in the wind himself.

He sighed and drew a ballpoint pen and a folded sheet of paper from his pocket. His father's checklist for the inspection was, much like the man himself, straightforward but thorough. Even so, Grover Solomon's gaze snagged on one of the notations like cloth on a jutting nail. His father had scrawled the word *Crawlspace* under the heading for the third floor.

Grover Solomon gave himself a little shake and returned to the top of the page. He would worry about the third floor when he got there. He flipped on the light switch in the entry room—the Escobars had reconnected all of the utilities in anticipation of their arrival on Monday—and the antique globe in the center of the ceiling flared to life. He switched it off again, drawing a check on the page.

The cedar closet came next on the list, but the memories of that place were suddenly too fresh. Maybe later, maybe at the end of the inspection he would force himself to enter that dark, cramped space where he had spent so much time with his now-dead best friend. Then again, it might be easier to enter the closet than the crawlspace on third, but that was like saying it would be less painful to fall fifty feet onto asphalt than onto cement.

Bypassing the closet for now, he moved through the rest of the first floor rapidly, opening cupboards and closing them, squinting up into corners of rooms to check for cracked plaster or stains that could mean leaky pipes or faulty roofing, switching lights on and off to check for electrical shorts or light bulbs that might need replacing. By the time he came to the kitchen and found the lighting, garbage disposal, and range vent to be in working order, he thought the inspection might not be so bad after all. His parents really had kept the old place in great shape.

They had even put in a new gas range before they moved out, and now Grover Solomon turned the four knobs to activate the burners. At once the kitchen filled with a silvery hiss of gas and the rapid click of electric ignition sparks. Blue flames tipped with yellow sprang in fluttering circles from each of the four burners. Grover Solomon made another checkmark on his page and spun all the dials back to off. The flames disappeared, but the clicking continued.

Frowning, he bent over to look under the burners, expecting to see a white-blue spark still snapping somewhere. The burners were all dark. The clicking sound began to grow louder and slower, louder and slower, until the clicks came about a second apart and they were less *click-click* and more *tick-tick*.

What was more, they were not *about* a second apart, but *exactly* a second apart. Like the ticking of a clock.

He backed away from the stove, casting aside the pen and paper and scrabbling for the pine crucifix in his back pocket. He raised it in one hand and drew the silver knife with the other, brandishing them like a feeble sword and shield.

"You're not welcome here!" he bawled at the empty kitchen. This was a tactic several books and websites had agreed upon for banishing a house spirit—telling the invading spirit that you, the living occupant, did not want it in your space.

For a wonder, the ticking began to fade. Several hitching breaths later, the sound might never have existed. He jammed the cross into his pocket with trembling hands and sheathed the knife before irritably snatching up the pen and paper from the floor. He was an adult, for crying out loud, and this was still his house. He couldn't allow himself to be turned out of it by something that couldn't even rightfully be called a memory.

Yet Odetta Koop was real. The genealogy book stashed in the trunk of his car proved that. She had been a real person who lived here and maybe even died here. And if some part of her lingered, well, why else had he brought weapons?

But first things first. He was going to complete this absurd inspection. A feeling of recklessness stole over him, not dissimilar to the way he'd felt as a child whenever he and Laz had played Show Me. He strode from the kitchen to the entry room, directly to the cedar closet, yanked open the door, and...

Empty. Of course it was. What else had he been expecting?

The two side walls of the closet were lined with panels of rough, unfinished cedar. The bare lath ceiling angled steeply downward from the doorway toward the back of the closet, following the slope of the staircase that ran behind and above it to the second floor. The closet had no back wall, but terminated where the slanted ceiling met floor. The only light in here was a single bulb, which Grover Solomon switched on by tugging a white string above the doorway.

Nothing happened. The bulb stayed dark and dead. Something like an electric current, but cold, arced from the crown of his head down his shoulders. This precise scenario was how most of his nightmares started. He'd be enjoying a normal dream about attending a work meeting in his underpants, or flying over the Chicago skyline like Superman, and *pop!* There he'd be in his old house, flicking broken light switches, one after another, as Odetta Koop's footsteps thudded toward him in the dark.

Momentarily paralyzed, he clutched at that brave and reckless feeling from before, seized it, and stoked it with memories of his and Lazarus's forbidden card game. This was no dream, after all. And what did it matter that one light bulb had burned out? If anything, he should be surprised that this was the first one he'd encountered considering that his parents had moved out last winter.

He felt himself beginning to calm down, and he peered determinedly at the ceiling for cracks, following his father's checklist. Some light spilled in past him from the entry room, and now that his vision had adjusted to the dimness, he could make out the even spacing of the lath.

His eyes traveled down toward the back of the closet, and he saw that the room wasn't completely empty after all. Something small and white and triangular stuck out between the lathing, bright against the dark wood floor.

Grover Solomon peered at the triangle without moving. Was it his imagination or could he hear ticking coming from the kitchen again?

"I am an adult," he told the half-lit closet in a voice that had slid upward into the voice of the child who had spent so much time in here. He dropped to his hands and knees, salt pouch banging softly against his left thigh, the pine cross in his back pocket taut against his rear, and crawled deeper into the closet until he could reach the white whatever-it-was.

The ticking grew in volume, not from the kitchen but from the entry room, just outside the open closet door. He forced himself to focus on the triangle, which he now saw might be the corner of a piece of paper stuck between the boards. When he pinched it between his thumb and forefinger, it pulled free easily. The ticking sound abruptly amped up into a thud so loud that little puffs of plaster dust were expelled rhythmically from the seams in the wood like blood from an open artery. Every hair on Grover Solomon's body suddenly stood on end. The thing in his hand was a playing card.

It was the Queen of Hearts.

"You're not welcome here," he said again, but the words came out in a hoarse whisper.

As if in answer, the door began to swing closed behind him, cutting a straight, sharp shadow across the interior of the closet like the blade of a guillotine. All thoughts of silver, salt, and holy water fled his mind in an instant. He whipped the card out of his hand and it spun like a ninja's throwing star, striking the downward slope of the ceiling perfectly between two strips of lath. The card sank into the wall as if pulled from the other side. The closet was almost pitch dark now.

Still on his hands and knees, he launched himself backward toward the door. When the soles of his sandals connected with the door it swung outward, but slowly, resisting the motion. He righted himself and threw his back against the door with all of his strength, emitting a low groan of effort that was inaudible beneath the thunderous ticking emanating from nowhere and everywhere all at once.

Abruptly the resistance on the other side of the door vanished. Grover Solomon spilled out of the doorway into the entry room, landing painfully on the pine cross, which snapped in half with a loud *crack* like a breaking bone. He barely noticed. He scrambled to his feet and pelted out of the house.

So now he knew. Odetta Koop was still there. And she remembered him.

Retreat

His first instinct was to hop in the car and drive back to Chicago with the radio blasting and the speedometer pegged. Never mind what had happened to Laz all those years ago. Never mind what was still happening to *him*, Grover Solomon, after a quarter century of life. Had he really believed a few gimmicky trinkets would be any use against the thing that had terrorized him throughout his entire childhood?

Instead of running away, Grover Solomon opened the hatchback of his car with deliberate slowness and began repacking his "weapons," including both pieces of the now broken cross, into the milk crate. The knot on the drawstring pouch required several minutes of fumbling before his shaking fingers managed to untie it, but he got there in the end.

At last, sweating with heat and terror in the empty street, he pulled his cell phone from his belt dialed his parents' realtor. The receptionist picked up on the second ring. Grover Solomon gave his name in what he felt was a steady and, yes, adult voice.

"I am afraid—" he told the receptionist, and had to clear his throat. "I'm afraid I won't be able to complete the inspection of my parents' house today. Got into some traffic outside Chicago."

This was a lie, of course, but Grover Solomon did not expect the girl to challenge him on it, and she did not. She told him brightly that they would be closed tomorrow, but he could return the key to a drop box outside their office any time before Monday.

A day and a half, then. Maybe as long as forty hours if he went without sleep. Because he understood now how woefully he had underprepared to face Odetta Koop. He could try to collect himself and march back inside right now, but she would just chase him out again. Or worse. Much, much worse.

After his parents had dropped the bomb that they were pulling up stakes and moving to Georgia, he had developed something of a fever about the house in New Canaan and the thing that denned there. Every minute outside his job (and increasingly over the last few weeks, *during* his job as well), he pored over any piece of literature he could find that might tell him something useful about taking the fight to an angry spirit.

Yet despite months of research and preparation, he hadn't lasted a single round. Odetta Koop had thrown him against the ropes, slapped him around, and tossed him out of the ring in all of twenty minutes. Obviously he'd missed something. But what?

He reached back into the trunk and tugged his backpack free. He unzipped it and pawed through the books he'd brought with him. There was a commercial hardcover called *Spiritual Warfare in the Twenty-First Century;* a musty old paperback he'd picked up at the occult shop in Chicago titled *Ghosts' Stories: Listening to What Spirits Have to Say;* a pocket Bible he'd received from the Mormons who made the rounds in his apartment building every month. Colorful sticky notes protruded from various pages of the books like tiny neon signs, marking passages that made any mention of spirits.

But he did not open any of those pages now. He merely tossed each book into the milk crate until he came to the one he wanted, a slim volume with a plain white cover and fading lilac colored lettering that read *Koop Genealogy: 1850-1950.* More pamphlet than anything, this book had resided on the living room bookcase for as long as he could remember. It had shared shelf space with the family Bibles (one each, leather bound and embossed, for all three of the Yoder family), the illustrated children's versions of Bible stories his mother read him every night before bed, and dog-eared devotionals that comprised his family's library. The genealogy book had told him the least of any resource he'd investigated in the last few months—only that Odetta Koop had been a real person who had lived in this house. Yet it had given him a place to start. It had given him, as the old expression went, a name for his pain.

He opened the book to the page he'd marked with a bright yellow sticky note back in his apartment. The entry on Odetta was as brief and utilitarian as the rest of the book. No picture accompanied the text.

Koop, Odetta Wilfrieda (Mueller) b.1886 d.1947
Third daughter of Sebastian and Hestia (Brock) Mueller of Sagatuck County (IA). Marriages to Eli Koop (1914-1928) and Zebulon Koop (1928-1930). Founder and Headmistress of New Canaan Mennonite Academy (1920-1939). Owned and maintained the dormitory and grounds until her death.

Grover Solomon had known since he was a child that this house had once been the academy's main dormitory, and the description in this little book sure made it sound like Odetta Koop had died here. Today's inspection had been the final test of his theory, and after his encounter in the cedar closet, there could be little doubt that he'd been right. At least, little doubt to him. No one else would believe him, obviously.

He closed the genealogy and set it slowly back into the trunk. He *had* missed something in his research. He needed to know more about the person Odetta Koop had been, and no published book or website would ever tell him that. His mind ran through the short list of people he knew from his parents' old church here in town. But none of those people were historians. Worse yet, they would undoubtedly tell Grover Solomon's parents that he had come to them inquiring about Odetta.

And then he had it. He knew who he could ask.

With a purposefulness he rarely displayed in his non-professional life, Grover Solomon stuffed the rest of the books into his backpack once more, slammed the Honda's hatchback, and leapt into the driver's seat.

On a map, New Canaan appeared as a roughly diamond-shaped blot of homes and locally owned businesses. A few fast food restaurants and the abandoned husk of an old Walmart languished near the city limits, the last soldiers of a corporate siege that never managed to penetrate the town proper. Grover Solomon's house sat near the geographical center of New Canaan, meaning that most places in town fell within a three mile radius of his home. His destination, the New Canaan Public Library, was less than a two-minute drive away. As he drove, he passed not one but two grain elevators, and his car rumbled across the town's only set of railroad tracks, begrimed with rust and overrun with ragweed and cockleburs.

Throughout Grover Solomon's childhood the public library had been a magnificent thing. It was a relic of the old robber baron days when the Carnegies and Rockefellers of the world, in fits of competitive philanthropy, had tossed money into the Midwest like farmers scattering seed. But the library had fallen into disuse before Grover Solomon had left New Canaan for Chicago. He half expected to see boards across the windows and a glum sign reading, *Closed forever due to the existence of the internet.*

It therefore pleased him as he strode through the main entrance to find the library not only open, but renovated and bustling. Sometime in the last few years a bank of computers and audio/video booths had been erected in the center of the main room, and every station was currently occupied by visitors whose ages spanned at least three generations. One corner had been walled off into a windowed classroom where a young woman was parsing English sentences on a white board for a group of adult language learners. In another corner, a cluster of wide-eyed children sat cross-legged on floor cushions while a high school student read a Harry Potter book aloud. Even the layout of the stacks had been altered, and everywhere Grover Solomon looked he saw cozy little nooks furnished with puffy armchairs or beanbags.

In spite of all of the changes, Grover Solomon saw with a surge of relief that the most important fixture of the New Canaan Public Library remained firmly in place. The head librarian, a middle-aged widow with the unlikely name of Althea Gibson, perched on her customary stool behind the circulation desk, straight-backed as a soldier. Unlike the tennis champion and civil rights activist for whom she had been named, she was white as a cavefish and waifishly thin, with lank gray hair. She had always dressed in coarse gray wool that she wove on her own very own loom—she gave regular demonstrations at the library—making her resemble nothing so much as a malnourished escapee from a medieval dungeon.

None of this had changed, Grover Solomon saw, except that she had evidently started accessorizing. She wore a pair of hot pink spectacles on a gold chain, and she had adorned a single ratty braid of hair with colored beads that swung against her cheek. When Grover Solomon approached she glanced up and broke into a sunny, if skeletal, grin.

He couldn't help smiling back. "Hello, Mrs. Gibson."

After Laz had died, and with no school friends to fill the gap, this wispy scarecrow of a woman had become something like a friend. Or at least the only person he knew who always seemed happy to see him, including his own parents. Unlike his mother, the librarian had hugged Grover Solomon goodbye when he had left New Canaan for the last time.

"Grover Solomon Yoder," she declared in a stage whisper. A lifetime of working in a hushed space had left her sounding like she had chronic laryngitis. "I never thought I'd see you back here after your parents moved."

"I'm only back for the weekend, ma'am."

"Call me Thea, for heaven's sake," she hissed, reaching over the desk to swat his wrist. "I'm not a schoolmarm and you're not a little boy."

"Okay, Thea," he mumbled awkwardly. "I—" He broke off before the words that had leapt into his mind could come tumbling out: *I've really missed you.* No need to make this interaction any weirder. "I'm afraid I don't have time to do any catching up. I need some information."

"Then you'll have it." At once she laid down the book she had been reading, a slim hardcover called *Obscene Gestures for Women,* and swiveled to face her workstation. "Lay it on me, daddy-o."

"Are you sure? If you're busy…"

She swatted his wrist again and motioned for him to get on with it.

"Well, you know my parents are selling our house. And I'm trying to learn more about the old place before the new family moves in. For a…a genealogy project," he invented. "But I haven't been able to—"

She nodded smartly, fingers already clacking across the keyboard. "New Canaan Mennonite Academy main dormitory," she rattled off, staring at the screen. "Built in 1910 by Eli and Zebulon Koop."

"That's a start." So Odetta Koop's two husbands—brothers who also appeared in the Koop Genealogy—had built the house together. Not earth-shaking news, but still new information. He leaned across the desk to look at the monitor too. "Did you find that online? I thought I looked everywhere."

Thea shook her head. "Historical archives. I've been cooperating with Kurt Martin and Dorcas Hershberger over the last few years to convert them to digital, but they're not accessible from any external website without a password."

"Kurt Martin?" he repeated. "Like, *Pastor* Kurt Martin?" The man whose congregation Grover Solomon's parents had left to start their own? The man whose name they had not so much as mentioned since the last time they'd walked out of New Canaan Mennonite Church all those years ago?

Thea looked up from her monitor. Her normally buggy eyes had gone soft, full of understanding behind the hot pink spectacles. "That's right. He's the archivist for the Iowa regional church conference."

For a moment Grover Solomon could say nothing, unexpectedly poleaxed by the Martin name. Returning home had acted upon his memory like a tiller through an old forgotten graveyard, and more than one restless skeleton had been turned out with the emotional debris.

"So," he cast about, struggling to rediscover the thread of his investigation, "if the archives aren't available online, can I access them here? Maybe on one of those library computers over there?"

Thea's expression soured. She glanced around guiltily and dropped her voice even further so he had to lean in to hear. "The truth is I shouldn't be showing you any of this. It's a locked archive. Everything is password protected. Some of the families mentioned in the records still live in town, and…" She peered conspiratorially over the pink rims of her glasses. "*You know.*"

He *didn't* know. That was the problem. "What about the other person you mentioned? Dorcas somebody."

"Hershberger," said Thea. "Yes, she has been very helpful. She actually attended the academy as a student."

Grover Solomon whistled softly. "And she's still around? She'd have to be almost a hundr—" He stopped suddenly. "Wait, does that mean she knew Odetta Koop?"

Thea nodded. "Dorcas even held some kind of leadership role at the academy until she and Odetta had a falling out." She paused, as if catching herself. "Not that I can talk about that either."

Grover Solomon tried not to roll his eyes. "Look, is there anything else you can tell me? I wouldn't ask if it weren't important."

The librarian was watching him closely. "About your house."

"Yes."

"Not the people who lived there."

"I…I guess not."

She seemed to weigh something in her mind before turning decisively back to the monitor. "I can tell you that the house functioned as the New Canaan Mennonite Academy dormitory from the time it was built until the school closed in 1939. After that it was the residence of Odetta Koop until she passed away in 1947. It looks like the place was owned by another local family for a few decades until your parents bought it."

Grover Solomon's palms had gone slick on the surface of the help desk. He chewed his lip, struggling to recall everything he had read about why a spirit might attach itself to a certain building or location. "You said Odetta Koop stayed in the house another eight years after the academy closed. But why?" he mused, more to himself than to Thea. "Both her husbands were gone. She had no students left to teach. It had to be lonely there, so why stay? Maybe she wanted to finish something. Or maybe something bad happened."

He hesitated, but it was time to test out his theory with another person. "Did Odetta Koop die *in* the house? She did, didn't she? I know you said she lived there right up to her death, but I just—I need more details."

Thea's friendly smile had vanished. She shrank away from him as if afraid he might whip out a knife and start slashing at her.

"Please," he begged. "Anything. Unfinished business. A betrayal. There's got to be *something*."

Instead of answering, she reached up and switched off the computer monitor. "I'm sorry, Grover Solomon. There's bending a rule, and then there's snapping it over your knee. I just can't discuss people's personal history. Maybe if you asked Kurt Martin…"

He made a frustrated noise in his throat. "Look, I have to know this stuff. It's not like I can just go ring the Martins' doorbell and—"

He broke off again. Why *couldn't* he visit the Martins? Because of some old family feud that he had never really understood? Kurt Martin had always been kind to him, and Kurt's son, Leon, had been Grover Solomon's very first friend before…whatever it was had happened. Besides, if anyone could help exorcise Odetta Koop from his old house, it was a pastor. A man of God.

He stepped away from the desk. "Thanks, Mrs. Gibson. Thea. It was good to see you again."

"Grover Solomon—" she began in her huskiest library whisper, but he made for the door before she could say anything else.

Reinforcements

The Martins lived on Jackson, two blocks over and one up from Grover Solomon's old house. After his parents had left Pastor Martin's church, Jackson Street might as well have been the dark side of the moon. His parents had avoided any interactions with the Martin family with an almost obsessive determination. They knew when Kurt and Cynthia Martin went to work and came home, where they shopped, what kind of cars they drove. And they employed that information to make sure they never crossed paths, which was not terribly easy in a town like New Canaan.

Grover Solomon had watched his former friend Leon grow up in odd, uneven leaps of time, catching glimpses of him riding his bike up the street or playing in a park, almost always alone. At first Grover Solomon had asked permission to go play with him, but his parents' stony silence on the matter discouraged such questions quickly. And he'd still had Lazarus to play with. But then Laz died, leaving Grover Solomon just as alone as Leon Martin.

The homes in this part of town had not changed one jot in the six years since Grover Solomon had moved away. True, the house on the corner of Taylor and Jackson appeared to have been painted recently, but its owners had repainted it in the same color it had been all of Grover Solomon's life: beige. The drive through the old neighborhoods soothed him somewhat, and by the time he parked and hiked up the steps to the front porch of the Martin's little Cape Cod, that icy, electric feeling of having exposed nerves all over his body that had been with him since visiting his house had mostly faded.

Cynthia Martin answered the door when he pushed the doorbell. Other than a bit more gray in her brown hair, she looked just as he remembered.

"Hello, Mrs. Martin," he began, "I'm—"

"Grover Solomon Yoder," she said at once, stepping onto the porch and giving him a brief, motherly hug.

His hands come up automatically, more in surprise than to reciprocate the hug. The pastor's wife had always struck him as being a closed and severe woman. As a child he'd been a little afraid of her.

When they broke apart she was smiling, and Grover Solomon realized she didn't look quite like he remembered after all. Her slender face seemed softer, less pinched than it had all those years ago. In fact, aside from the gray hair, she actually looked younger than she had then.

An orange tabby cat with a sharp, triangular head and eyes like shining yellow moons peered up from between her ankles. "This is Clementine," Cynthia Martin said, indicating the cat. "He loves visitors."

"Hello," said Grover Solomon apprehensively. He had never been allowed to play with animals.

The cat yawned and licked its chops without taking its eyes off him.

"Come in out of the heat," said Cynthia, ushering him inside with a hand at the small of his back. "Are you here to visit Leon?"

"No, ma'am, I—"

Kurt Martin's head appeared from the kitchen doorway. "Grover Solomon Yoder! No kidding!"

Like his wife, Kurt Martin now had a great deal more salt than pepper in his hair, and his square face was craggy and grandfatherly from years of smiling benevolently behind a pulpit. Stocky as his wife was lean, Kurt wore a long apron over what must have been shorts, because his legs were bare under the apron's hem. He looked like he'd been baking with no pants on.

"Wonderful surprise." He wrung Grover Solomon's hand firmly and clapped him on the shoulder, kicking up a little cloud of whitish dust that might have been baking flour or pulverized plaster from the cedar closet.

"Thank you, sir, I—" he began again, but stopped short when he turned the corner into the kitchen and saw three more people sitting around the table. This was turning into quite a party.

The person in the middle was surely Leon. He was trim and dark haired like his mother, with his father's welcoming smile. The boy Leon had been was still visible in that face, though with two new features. First, a long, thin scar ran up from the bridge of his nose almost to his hairline, white against his summer tan. Rather than marring his features it suited him, made him seem worldly and somehow more handsome than he would have been otherwise.

Second was a new hardness to his expression. Grover Solomon had heard from his mother—one of the few times she'd deigned to mention the Martins at all—that Leon had developed severe arthritis in high school, and this hardened expression struck Grover Solomon as the look of a person who spent a lot of time in great physical pain.

Two unfamiliar women sat on either side of Leon. The one on the left had straight black hair held up in barrettes and dark, almond-shaped eyes—Grover Solomon guessed she came from a Japanese or Korean background. Like Leon, she wore a permanently haunted expression on her otherwise smooth and pretty face.

The second woman was almost absurdly beautiful, with piercing green eyes and blonde hair tied back in a ponytail. Leon's arm was slung casually across the back of her chair.

For some reason the three of them made Grover Solomon felt less like an adult than ever.

Leon stood and held out his hand. "Hey, man, great to see you. What's it been, like fifteen years?"

"More." He shook Leon's hand gingerly in case the rumor about arthritis had been true. Leon's grip was firm.

The two women also stood and Leon made introductions all around. "This is Autumn," he said, indicating the blonde. "Autumn, this is my old friend, Grover Solomon Yoder."

"That is a killer name," Autumn said, also shaking hands.

He thought she might be poking fun—it certainly wouldn't be the first time he'd taken ribbing for his name—but her smile appeared open and friendly, and no one laughed or seemed uncomfortable.

"Thanks."

"And this is our friend, Shin," Leon went on.

Grover Solomon shook with the shorter woman, whose hands were smallest but by far the strongest. She too bore scars, spaced at odd intervals across her slim neck. Grover Solomon had no guess as to what might make such scars, and he decided he could go his whole life without finding out.

"Please call me Alice," said the woman in a soft, lightly accented voice that did not at all match her steely handshake.

"Shin—Alice, I mean," Leon corrected himself, "is the acupuncturist up at the chiropractor's office. We met during the summer I lived in Germany. She gave me my hands back after I wrecked them in high school."

He raised his hands and wriggled all ten fingers. Grover Solomon noted that the ring finger and pinky on the left hand did not move with the same dexterity as the others. Scars were visible on those fingers too, almost as if they'd been severed and reattached at some point. What on earth had happened to these people?

Introductions completed, Kurt dusted his hands on his apron and drew out the last vacant chair, inviting Grover Solomon to sit. "So, to what do we owe the pleasure? Surely you didn't come all the way back to New Canaan just to say goodbye to the old homestead."

"Yes," said Grover Solomon. Then, "No."

Kurt's eyebrows rose politely.

"Your parents are down in Georgia now, aren't they?" Cynthia asked.

"Atlanta, yes."

"Last I heard, you were in Chicago doing…" she trailed off expectantly.

"I work at a consulting firm in urban planning and engineering."

"So you time traffic lights and stuff?" Autumn asked.

"That's part of it," he agreed, looking down at the table instead of at her. She unnerved him somehow. Her eyes were much too green, much too smart.

He turned back to Kurt. "The new family moves into the house on Monday. My parents asked me to come back here and make sure nothing needs repairing. Things tend to deteriorate when you leave an old house empty for six months."

"Has it really been that long already?" Cynthia murmured to herself.

"And you decided to stop here to say hello," Kurt beamed. "Our good fortune to have so many friends visit today."

"Actually, I can't stay," said the woman who had asked to be called Alice. She rose once more. "I have two more appointments this afternoon. It was nice to meet you, Grover Solomon."

Kurt loaded her up with two linen-wrapped parcels containing cookies and a loaf of bread that had been cooling on the counter. Cynthia followed her out, and Grover Solomon heard Alice shouting down an invitation to dinner all the way to the front door. The whole production had an air of familiarity that suggested Alice was a frequent visitor.

"You said your parents are selling an old house?" Autumn asked. "Which one is it?"

"Grover Solomon grew up in the old New Canaan Mennonite Academy building," Leon answered. When she looked blank he added, "You know, that giant place a few blocks from here."

She brightened. "My dad always said that if his practice made it big he'd buy that place. He's a lawyer over in Sagatuck, where I grew up," she clarified to Grover Solomon. "And he never made it big."

Be glad he didn't, Grover Solomon thought but did not say.

"Can we come with you?" she asked.

With a soft chirruping noise, the orange tabby—Grover Solomon had already forgotten its name…Kermit?—leapt lightly into her lap and stared at him with its ears pricked, as if also eager to hear his answer.

"Come with me?" he repeated blankly.

"To your house," she said. "You said you have to go there, right? I've always wanted to see what it's like inside."

A frown creased the scar in Leon's forehead. He laid his hand over hers. A gold ring set with a small diamond glinted on one of her fingers. "Actually, we've got plenty to do here ourselves," he said apologetically to Grover Solomon. "We're only in town for a couple days."

The look Autumn gave Leon made up Grover Solomon's mind in an instant. The next time he entered his old house, he wanted someone by his side capable of delivering look like that. It was the look of a person who could not be chased away by an invisible dead lady.

"Sure, I'd love to show you around. Anyone else who wants to come is welcome, too," he added to the others. "It won't take long."

Cynthia seemed ready to take him up on the offer, but Kurt said, "You kids have fun catching up. Be back for supper in a couple hours. That goes for you too, Grover Solomon. We want to hear all about what you do in Chicago."

"Yes, sir. Thank you." Grover Solomon still wanted to ask Kurt for help dealing with Odetta Koop, but he did not know how to bring up the topic without doing a lot explaining he didn't want to do in front of the others. And maybe with Leon and Autumn tagging along, he could finish the inspection for the realtor. Then his remaining time before Monday could be spent worrying about Odetta Koop.

So the three younger people stood—Grover Solomon, his oldest friend, and his newest one—and they went together to see the house.

Inspection

Thirty minutes later Leon and Autumn followed Grover Solomon out of the kitchen. No threatening ticking accompanied the gas stove demonstration this time. They had already toured the basement, which was as gloomy and full of spiders and field crickets as ever, but structurally sound. Now they filed through the dining room on the way to the second floor.

"This place," Autumn murmured, staring up at the chandelier holding court over the now empty dining room. "It feels more like a museum than a house."

Grover Solomon nodded tightly. He eyed the ancient, yellowing lace curtains that shrouded the room's long bank of windows. Why hadn't his parents taken those curtains down when they'd moved out? Dry heat boiled through them all summer—as was happening now even though it was still only June—and the hotter it became, the more they stank of dust.

And there's a face, Grover Solomon suddenly recalled. As if performing a long-remembered trick, his eyes resolved the old face in the teardrop lace design—a three-pronged crown atop two eyes with deep circles beneath them and a diamond nose and grinning mouth at the bottom. The face comprised only five of the repeating teardrop designs, so it could appear in any one of a thousand different places across the surface of the curtains.

As a kid he'd thought of that face as belonging to smug old monkey king. Once he had spent an entire morning laboriously sketching it out in chalk on the blackboard in his room when his mother insisted she could not see the face he was talking about. She had been so delighted with the drawing that she had hauled out the camera to take a picture for his photo album.

The face leered down at him now, as if sardonically welcoming him home. *Faces in the laces,* he thought, only barely restraining himself from sticking his tongue out at the curtains the way he'd done as a child when he'd been home alone and needed to feel brave.

Leon was glancing around the empty room too. Despite the heat, he gave a little shiver. He was standing very close to Autumn. "Man, I don't even remember the last time I was here."

Autumn slid her arm around his waist, green eyes troubled and unsure. All of a sudden she and Leon looked as young as Grover Solomon felt, like Hansel and Gretel must have looked the moment they understood that their father meant to leave them in the woods to starve.

They feel her too, he realized, and by some miracle the idea comforted him.

Autumn frowned up at Leon. "I thought you guys were friends as kids."

"We were," said Leon. "We played together whenever our parents were working on church stuff. Something happened, though." He turned a quizzical look on Grover Solomon. "One day my mom told me your parents didn't want me coming over here anymore. I never figured out why."

"I'm not sure either," admitted Grover Solomon. "It was all tied up in us leaving your dad's church." A sort of strained silence descended. Perhaps the Martins still carried some hard feelings too. Not wanting to offend Leon, he added, "You were also starting kindergarten. You kept talking about how you were going to go to school in the fall, and you made it sound so exciting that I asked Mom if I could go too. I was old enough to be going into first grade by then."

"Homeschooler?" Autumn asked.

"My parents were protective when I was younger," he answered, and left it at that.

Autumn snorted. "By the time I was in first grade my parents only talked to me when they were fighting and wanted me to choose a side." For some reason she threw Leon a dirty look.

He seemed not to notice. "Yeah, I guess I was about five. Well, I'm sure our parents had their reasons, but I'm sorry it ended like that."

"Me too," said Grover Solomon, once again recalling his glimpses of the boy Leon, riding his bike or playing in the park by himself.

"Okay!" Leon declared suddenly, in a let's-get-down-to-business sort of way. Grover Solomon and Autumn both jumped. "Not to cut this party short or anything, but what do we have left, Grover Solomon? I'm not even sure what we're supposed to be doing.

Just walking through and looking for cracks in the walls?"

"Yes, pretty much," said Grover Solomon. "We need to cover all three floors, so we can head up—"

Before he could finish, heavy footsteps thudded across the floor above them. Five steps up, five steps back. All three of them turned up toward the sound.

"I thought you said the other family couldn't move in until Monday," said Leon, frowning.

Grover Solomon closed his eyes and took a breath. So much for Odetta Koop letting him finish the inspection just because he'd brought guests. Still facing away from the other two, he voiced what he believed to be the truth. "This house is haunted."

Neither one said anything. Grover Solomon tried to look out the window while they decided how to respond, but found the leer of the monkey king too upsetting. He stared at the floor instead. The yellow light filtering in through the curtains glinted dully on the uneven oak slats like mortician's wax slathered over a cadaver's sunken ribs.

He hated this place.

At last Autumn spoke. "You don't strike me as the kind of guy to make jokes, Grover Solomon."

He turned back toward them. "I'm not," he said earnestly.

Autumn burst out laughing. It was a wonderful and surprising sound in this unbearable sarcophagus of a room.

The thudding sound came again, louder this time, as if to tell them to knock off all the noise.

Autumn's smile faded. "Who is it?"

Grover Solomon hesitated again. But he'd already said too much to hold back now. "I think her name is Odetta Koop," he said. "From what I've been able to find out, she was one of the founders of New Canaan Mennonite Academy."

"The school that used to be in this house," Autumn said, clarifying the point for herself.

"The first school in town," Leon agreed, nodding.

"Is this why you really came home?" asked Autumn. "Because of this—" She glanced at Leon. "This ghost?"

"She ruined my life."

She nodded slowly, as if digesting his answer.

"So," Leon said, clearly off balance, "is this person part of the inspection? Is there a box for you to tick on that paper from your dad that says 'Patch up any floorboards Odetta Koop kicks out'?"

"Nothing like that. My parents either don't know about her or won't admit that they do. I didn't even start to suspect who she was until recently, and I still don't know as much as I'd like to."

"Well," Autumn said, rather too brusquely. "I've heard weirder stories. Someday I should tell you who Leon thought our friend Alice was the first time we met her."

Leon took her cue and nodded. "Yeah, okay. How do we tackle this thing?"

Grover Solomon didn't answer right away, thrown by that casual "we." Yet he didn't argue either. On the topic of Odetta Koop's ghost, they both seemed ready to take him at his word. For the moment, at least.

"I don't know," he admitted. "I guess I haven't thought that far ahead."

Autumn's brows rose. Those too-smart eyes flashed. "The guy who decides when Chicago's stoplights turn green doesn't have a plan?"

And just like that, he had it. A new idea, startling in its simplicity, shot into his mind and stuck there, quivering like an arrow loosed from an archer's bow: *She's not afraid. Whatever she thinks about Odetta Koop or me, she's not afraid.*

He thought he might finally have his plan.

The second floor of the house contained six bedrooms connected by a long hallway and a landing at the top of the stairs. As with the first floor, wood was the order of the day, with heavy oak baseboards and trim around seven foot high doors of solid walnut.

An antique store in Iowa City had once offered Grover Solomon's father three thousand dollars for the six doors on this floor alone. He had refused, of course. Ethyl Yoder was a woodworker by trade and knew the doors were irreplaceable for any amount of money. Grover Solomon had always been glad his father hadn't sold them. He liked the doors, with their sturdy height, dark stain, and smooth grain. They were the only fixtures in the whole house in which he could see no faces.

The rooms behind the walnut doors were in fine shape too, and the inspection of the second floor passed with no surprises. Autumn and Leon seemed more relaxed now, even daring to unclasp hands while they peered into different rooms.

"I can't believe how well your parents maintained this place, Grover Solomon," said Leon.

"Dad's a carpenter."

"Sure, but—" Leon began, then seemed to catch himself. He reddened. "I figured a house like this would be too much even for a carpenter to keep up with."

Grover Solomon thought he knew what Leon had been about to say. Something along the lines of, *But he's a* lousy *carpenter.* He let the abridged version of Leon's comment pass. He had no desire to stir up any further emotional dust today. And besides, it was true. The mutant fossils of his dad's botched projects had lain scattered across the third floor for as long as Grover Solomon could remember.

Not today, though, he realized. The whole third floor must be cleared out like everywhere else. He wondered what it would look like empty.

Autumn emerged from a doorway at the end of the hall. "Everything is ship-shape in here. What else have we got?"

"Top floor." Grover Solomon gestured at a door next to the one she had just exited. "It's through that—"

Several sharp thuds from the ceiling cut him off. After her pacing episode earlier, Odetta had kept her peace while they examined the second floor. This new sound suggested she would not do so for much longer. It had a definite air of a territorial dog firing off a few warning barks before it started using its teeth.

Autumn glanced up at the ceiling before her eyes flicked over to Leon. Something seemed to pass between them.

Leon turned to Grover Solomon. "I'm sorry, man, but this isn't a joke, right? There's not some dude stomping around up there in a Frankenstein mask, waiting to jump out at us?"

Grover Solomon felt a stirring of anger. "I didn't even know you were in town," he reminded Leon. "Do you think I went to your parents' house for the first time in over a decade to invite them over for a prank?"

"No, I just—"

"You guys asked to come."

"Does that mean you want us to leave?" Autumn asked.

Grover Solomon closed his eyes and consulted the solemn, emaciated creature that served as the emotional center of his mind. Did he really mean to carry out his new plan? He discovered that he did, and to do so he needed Leon and Autumn. "I promise you I don't have any friends upstairs in masks." He barely refrained from adding, *I don't have any friends at all.*

He moved past Autumn to open the door to the third floor. Unlike the big, open staircase between the first and second floors, this one was a claustrophobic hallway, more tunnel than stairwell. The three of them clumped upward in single file. Their footfalls on the tile steps—hard green ceramic shot with flecks of red and gold—sounded unnaturally muffled and dull in the enclosed space.

The stairway ended in a closed horizontal trapdoor. For as long as Grover Solomon could remember, the door had been held open by a pair of thick metal hook-and-eye fasteners screwed into the third-floor wall. In fact, until this moment he had never actually seen the trapdoor closed. Yet it rolled open easily enough when he pushed upward with his shoulder. He offered Autumn a hand as she mounted the last step, and the two of them fastened the trap door to the wall while Leon climbed out behind them.

The third floor seemed smaller than the others due to a low, angular ceiling that mirrored the roofline. Even so, Grover Solomon had never appreciated just how large a space it was, having only seen it crammed with storage boxes and crooked wooden sculptures. The entire level comprised only a single open space with kitchen, dining, and living room areas delineated by boundaries of linoleum and carpet instead of walls. It was by far the warmest part of the house, with bars of late afternoon sunlight sprawling across the dusty carpet.

"My dad had no idea what he would have gotten himself into if he'd bought this place," Autumn said. If she felt any residual anger about their argument downstairs, none of it showed in her voice. "He's got a little two-bedroom condo in Sagatuck that he can hardly keep clean."

Grover Solomon barely heard her. Across the sea of brown carpet stood the half-door with the iron padlock—the entrance to the room that Grover Solomon's dad had so casually labeled "Crawlspace" on his checklist.

A thick iron key that Grover Solomon had only seen one other time in his life jutted from the lock. His father must have left it there for the inspection.

Autumn followed his gaze to the half-door and wrinkled her nose. "Creepers. Do we need to go in there?"

"Hang on," said Leon sharply, head cocked. "Do you guys smell smoke? We didn't leave the stove on downstairs, did we?"

Autumn shook her head. "I remember seeing Grover Solomon turn off the burners."

"There was a fire up here," said Grover Solomon. He could smell smoke too, and he also remembered switching off the stove. "When I was a kid."

And then, without any idea that it was going to happen or any way to prevent it, Grover Solomon screamed.

Behind the Half-Door

Lazarus Beachy dies on the last day of September. The miniature forest of elm trees surrounding the Yoders' house—a three-story mono-lith that old timers in New Canaan still refer to as "the Academy"— succumbed to Dutch elm disease in the preceding summer. Their bare branches writhe at the sky like crooked fans, gray and dead as stone. Lazarus thinks they look like props in an old horror movie, and Grover Solomon has to take his word for it. Horror movies are as forbidden in the Yoder household as Laz's deck of burlesque playing cards. Grover Solomon doesn't have the stomach for horror movies anyway. He is already scared most of the time.

He is scared right now, in fact. He huddles amid the clutter of the third floor while Laz searches for a new place to play Show Me. The cedar closet where they normally play is torn up for what Grover Solo-mon's father generously calls "renovations."

The fourth of seven brothers who all make their living at carpentry in the way of their risen Lord, Ethyl Yoder suffers the threefold malaise of having what many consider to be a woman's name, being a true middle child, and, worst of all, possessing no natural talent as a woodworker. His left thumbnail grows in a dented and warped claw from being whacked repeatedly with a hammer over the years, occasionally blackening and falling off to regrow even harder and more stunted than before. He has joked that if his aim doesn't improve, someday his nail will be so hard he'll be able to open soup cans with it. Grover Solomon's father has little more skill in humor than in carpentry.

But like his own stubborn thumbnail, Ethyl Yoder has a Puritan's work ethic, and he has become a serviceable carpenter through an admirable combination of practice and willpower. He can build a spice rack that does not lean on its braces, and by God he can replace the paneling in a cedar closet. So what if the cuts he makes do not align precisely to the slope of the ceiling? The closet is oddly shaped and tragically off-square to begin with.

In the meantime Grover Solomon and Laz must find somewhere else to play their favorite game, and the hunt has led them to the third floor. Everything up here is redolent of disuse, if not outright decay. Once while reading a National Geographic *magazine at the library, Grover Solomon came across the term "elephant graveyard," and immediately thought of the third floor of his house: a grim, dusty space with his father's leaning, jutting creations scattered about like elephant bones. The boys are surrounded by boxes of old clothes, books, and Ethyl Yoder's unsalvageable woodworking projects. They stand side by side before a closed half-size door that Laz believes will serve their purposes very well if they can open it. The door matches perfectly the huge walnut doors on second, but in miniature. An ancient padlock hangs in an assembly that connects the door to its frame.*

In the days of the school, this floor functioned as Odetta Koop's private residence. That might be why she's still here now. Invisible, she slouches behind the boys. She stands six and a half feet tall—larger in death than she ever was in life—and she is blind. When she died the mortician stitched her eyelids shut, as was the custom at that time. But he did it poorly. The man was a drunk, a worse undertaker than Ethyl Yoder is a carpenter, and the stitches meander across her eyelids in a row of uneven black X's. Normally—if anything about the situation in which Odetta Koop finds herself can be considered "normal"—such a disfigurement would not carry over from body to spirit. But Odetta, like the doomed king Oedipus before her, has chosen blindness. She has, as the expression goes, seen enough.

She can still smell, however. She noses at the air the way a prowling cat might scent out a nest of baby rabbits. Hot, stinking vitality bakes off of the boys like heat shimmers from desert sand. Her gorge would rise at it, had she but a gorge and bile to fill it.

The boys are going to play their disgusting card game again, and they are going to play it in the small room behind the half-door. In the later days of the academy, her students called that room the Cave. They thought she didn't know, but she knew everything that happened in her school. Undoubtedly the students would have been surprised to learn that she approved of their nickname for the room. But approve she did, and heartily. Did she not teach Plato's Allegory of the Cave in her theology lessons?

"Let's just go outside," says Grover Solomon, trying to sound nonchalant. If Laz hears any fear in his voice, it will only make the game more fun. Laz is not cruel, but he thinks scary things are fun rather than, well, scary. Moreover Laz is wearing jeans today despite the unseasonable heat, which can only mean one thing. Short pants will not hide his current crop of bruises. Grover Solomon knows too well that the more bruises his friend has, the more eager he is to misbehave.

Laz waves him off, as Grover Solomon knew he would. "Outside? Puh-leez. It's hotter than a pig's a-hall out there."

Grover Solomon thinks the real swear is "a-hole," but he finds the image of a pig's bottom extending inward like a long, broiling hallway evocatively repellant. He also elects not to point out that it is just as hot up here on the un-air-conditioned third floor as it is outside. What would be the point?

Laz rummages in his pocket. "Besides, lookie what I found in your mom's underwear drawer."

It also does not surprise Grover Solomon that Laz has been digging in his mother's dresser. Grover Solomon has caught him there before, and when he asked why, Laz only gaped at him. "Are you kidding? Your mom's got the best under-things. All that slippery cloth in one place, it's like dipping your hands into the very clouds of paradise. If the drawer was a little bigger I'd go swimming in it."

Laz draws out the thing he discovered in the underwear drawer. It is a black iron key as big around as Grover Solomon's pinky. Grover Solomon has never seen this key before, yet there is no question it will fit the lock on the half-door. The lock and key are so old and huge that they look like they were drawn for a cartoon about castles and dungeons.

Like everything else in this house, the padlock has a face. Rounded bolt heads for eyes and a gaping keyhole for a mouth. Grover Solomon has thought before that if he stuck his finger in there he would not feel old, rusty tumblers, but sharp iron teeth. He would just have time to register their ancient points before they chomped together, taking off the end of his finger all the way to the first knuckle.

Laz turns to the door and rams the key into the big padlock. Grover Solomon has time to hope that there really are teeth inside the lock and that they will bite off the key rather than grant him and Laz entrance to the old forbidden room—Grover Solomon will not realize until he is an adult just how often he applied that word, "forbidden," to objects, places, and behaviors during his childhood—but the key turns smoothly. The lock clicks free, and Laz tugs it out of the assembly with some effort.

"Gall-damn, this thing weighs more than a jar of lead pennies. Catch!"

He tosses the padlock to Grover Solomon, who leaps backward to avoid it and crashes into one of his father's homemade sawhorses. The rough end of a two-by-four pokes him between the shoulder blades hard enough to leave a rectangular patch of red, raw skin through his t-shirt. The lock thunks to the floor with the key sticking out of it. The locking bar juts up at an angle like a cocked, disapproving eyebrow.

Laz lays a hand on the doorknob and grins back over his shoulder at Grover Solomon. He is straight-backed and handsome, delighted to be breaking a new rule. You would never know to look at him now how it feels to wear jeans over the welts that crisscross the backs of his knees in purple stripes. On the other hand, his grin suggests that the bruises never reach the deepest part of him. That even if Lazarus Beachy knew these were the last moments he had to live, he would believe his life had been a fine thing worth the living.

The knob twists with a squeal of old springs and Laz yanks open the door. Both boys peer inside, their faces twin masks of eagerness and dread. The room is windowless, about eight feet deep with a peaked, triangular ceiling like that of a pup tent. Suspended from the ceiling on heavy duty sewing thread are dozens of strips of paper about one inch wide and eight to ten inches long, curled and brittle and yellow with age. They papers rustle with the opening of the door like the feathers of some ancient hen whose coop has been disturbed for the first time in a century.

Laz fumbles in one of his other pockets and pulls out a cigarette lighter. He flicks the spark wheel with a practiced motion of his thumb—Grover Solomon suspects that Laz sometimes smokes his father's cigarettes—and steps through the door, hunched over with the lighter held out ahead of him like a torch. In the flickering yellow light, Grover Solomon sees writing on the slips of paper. He cannot make out any words from here.

Fully inside the room, Laz cocks his head and squints at one of the papers. His grin, which has faded slightly, returns. "Well shut my mouth and paint me red. Get a load of this, Grover Solomon. They're

Bible verses. 'For this is the will of God, even your sanctification, that ye should abstain from fornication: That every one of you should know how to possess his vessel in sanctification and honour.'" He giggles. "I know how to possess my vessel, all right."

He moves to the next one. "'Therefore put to death your members which are on the earth: fornication, uncleanliness, passion, evil desire, and covetousness, which is idolatry.'"

And the next. "'Even as Sodom and Gomorrah, and the cities about them, in like manner giving themselves over to fornication, and going after strange flesh, are set forth for an example, suffering the vengeance of eternal fire.'"

He turns back to Grover Solomon, more pleased with himself than ever, light flickering across his delighted features. This is how he will return to Grover Solomon in dreams, grinning endlessly in the play of shadow and flame.

"Well I don't know about you, buddy, but this place seems perfect to play Show Me. I'm just sorry we didn't find it sooner."

Grover Solomon hears two familiar—terribly familiar—thudding footsteps behind him before he is knocked aside by something like wind. The side of his head collides with another of his father's angular wooden creations. Tiny blue sparks explode across his vision and dance there like electric midges. He will have a black eye for the next week.

He has no way of knowing that this is one of only two occasions in his life when he will be physically touched by Odetta Koop, and the next time will be much worse.

He regains his feet and staggers toward the half-door.

Laz's voice drifts out through the doorway, "Grover Solomon? What happened out there? You trip over your own shoes aga—"

His voice is cut off by the sharp slam of the door. Grover Solomon reaches it a moment later and wraps both hands around the knob. It rattles in his grip but does not turn. Smoke begins to curl out from under the doorway, caressing the toes of Grover Solomon's sneakers in soft, *coy tendrils. The metal doorknob feels too warm. Yet he does not let go, not even when the heat begins to sear his palms.*

He hears screaming now. It is coming from behind the door. It is coming from him.

It is coming from the house.

The Joker and the Queen

For several moments Grover Solomon was completely lost in time, the hot bite of smoke still filling his nose and lungs. He wasn't even sure whether he was the child or adult version of himself. A floorboard creaked somewhere behind him and he flinched.

Then his eyes focused and he saw Autumn crouching in front of him on the floor. He had no memory of sitting down. Her thumbs were pressed to his wrists, feeling his pulse.

"Do you take any medications?" she asked, her eyes flicking back and forth between his with clinical coolness.

"No medication, never."

"Just like Leon," Autumn grumbled. "Sometimes I think 'Mennonite' is actually just Dutch slang for 'teetotaler.'"

"I'm not Mennonite," he said, feebly brushing her hands away so he could stand. "Let me go. My heart is fine."

"Stay there," Autumn commanded. "It's not your heart I'm worried about."

She dropped his wrists, laid her hands on either side of his face, and planted the tips of her thumbs into the shallow bone indentation between his eyes. At once a strange, cool lightness seemed to spread into his head, clearing it as if she had released an emergency pressure valve inside his skull.

He stared back into her green eyes, no longer attempting to stand. "What are you doing?"

"Life-changing, isn't it?" Leon asked from somewhere behind and above Grover Solomon. He sounded shaken.

Grover Solomon turned to look at him but Autumn held his head fast. "If you think this is something, you should see what Alice can do."

"The acupuncture lady? Is this acupuncture?"

"Acupressure," Autumn corrected. "Same idea but without the needles. Now be quiet." She continued to clasp his head in silence for another thirty seconds. The cool, blissful, empty sensation spread down his neck and shoulders and into the hollows of his knees, making him feel almost like a different person. At last her hands dropped away. "Feel better?"

"Yes," Grover Solomon said, although this was such an understatement that it felt like a lie. Leon reached down and hoisted him to his feet. Grover Solomon thanked him without taking his eyes off of Autumn. "Where did you learn to do that?"

She shrugged. "Mostly from Alice. I got certified a last year to make it official. Leon's better at it than I am."

"Hardly," said Leon. He still looked pale, concerned. "What was that just now?"

"Tell the truth," Autumn added, as though she could tell he were spinning a lie in his head. Which of course he was.

Oddly, he found it easier now to meet her eyes. How could he have thought she was scary? He thought hard for several moments, deciding where to begin.

"Leon, do you remember the Beachys?"

"Sure. They made life pretty tough for my parents for a while before…" He trailed off again, as he had done to avoid disparaging

Grover Solomon's father's ability as a carpenter.

Grover Solomon nodded. "Before they helped my parents separate from your dad's church and start their own," he finished. "Well, after that, their son Lazarus became my best friend. My only friend. We were the only two kids in the new church."

"I never knew Lazarus," Leon said. "His folks were even less interested than yours in having their son mix with my family. I guess you two stopped being friends when the Beachys moved away?"

Grover Solomon stared at him in disbelief. Surely Leon knew what had happened to Lazarus. This was New Canaan, after all. The accidental death of a child should have set the gossip mill churning for months. He would have been surprised if the news had not made it to Autumn and everyone else over in Sagatuck, too. However, the blank looks on both their faces were answer enough.

And, he supposed, who would have told them? He had never discussed Lazarus's death with anyone besides his parents. In fact, after he told them that Laz had been playing with a cigarette lighter in that little room filled with old paper, they had seemed to draw their own conclusions about how the fire had started and never spoken of it again. Not to Grover Solomon, at least.

Never.

Only now did he realize how odd that was.

"We didn't hear too much about what went on at your parents' church," Leon said, obviously choosing his words with care. "The people who attended it kept to themselves. I mean, the reason they left our church was because it was too open. Too accepting. Right?"

Actually Leon had missed the mark rather badly, but now was not the time to correct him. "Laz died. In this house. In that room." He pointed to the half-door with its oversized iron padlock.

"*What?*" Leon said, wide-eyed shock making him look like the little boy Grover Solomon had once known. "How?"

"If you feel comfortable telling us," Autumn added.

He found that he did. He told them everything. How Laz had

discovered the key in his mother's underwear drawer, opened the door and read the hanging scraps of old paper in the stuttering glow of his dad's cigarette lighter. How he, Grover Solomon, had been shoved aside by something he could not see in the instant before the door had slammed on Laz's grinning face. How smoke had seeped out from under the doorway while the doorknob grew hot under his hands.

The only thing he left out was the fact that he and Lazarus had been looking for a new place to play Show Me. Of the card game he made no mention at all.

"Jesus," Autumn whispered when he had finished.

"Is that why we smelled smoke a minute ago?" Leon asked. "Is it still in the walls or something?"

Grover Solomon frowned. "No. My parents said they had the whole house fumigated after the fire. I've never caught so much as a whiff of smoke until today."

"But you guys smelled it too," Leon persisted.

"Yes," said Grover Solomon at the same moment that Autumn said, "No."

The three of them stood in silence for several seconds, the two men gazing toward the half-door while Autumn continued to watch Grover Solomon.

"I was going to ask you to open the door for me," he said without looking at her. "That was my big plan. Even after what happened to Laz, I was going to let you go inside that room in my place because I thought maybe…maybe if Odetta came after you, you'd be able to fight back somehow. You're not afraid of anything." His chin jutted in what might have been defiance or a severe pout. "I'm afraid of everything."

Autumn seemed to have nothing to say to this. Grover Solomon stepped past her and strode across the room—five paces that kicked up dust from the carpet and drew squeaks from the floorboards. He knelt before the half-door and laid his hand on the black key. More squeaks behind him suggested that Leon and

Autumn had followed. That someone had followed him, anyway. He elected not to turn around.

The black iron key spun smoothly and the lock released with a loud click. He pulled the long bar from the locking ring and threw the whole thing aside. It thudded to the carpet just as it had all those years ago, raising another swirl of dust motes that hung lazily in the sunlight.

"Leon, do you still smell smoke?"

Leon drew in a deep breath through his nose and let it out. "Not anymore."

"Me neither."

He turned the knob and pulled the door open. All three of them bowed low to see inside. The room was just as he remembered it. Tiny and windowless with a peaked ceiling like a pup tent. And—

"Oh, no." A wave of gooseflesh erupted on his scalp and washed down his back and arms like icy water.

The room was *just* as he remembered it. Strips of yellowing paper that could not have survived any fire hung like old flypaper from every inch of the ceiling.

Grover Solomon squeezed his eyes shut. This was nothing but an illusion, just like the ticking he'd heard earlier in the kitchen. A spiteful trick by an angry spirit determined to terrorize him one last time.

I am an adult, he thought with a fervency that bordered on prayer.

He opened his eyes. The strips of paper were still there.

"Fine," he said aloud.

He dropped to his hands and knees—gone were the days when he could simply duck his head to enter as Laz had done—and crawled inside. The room was cooler than the rest of the third floor and did not smell at all of smoke. The fumigators had done their job well.

Autumn crawled in behind him while Leon waited outside.

There wasn't space for three adults to enter. She squinted, head tilted to one side to read one of the hanging strips. "Bible verses?"

"Yes," said Grover Solomon tightly.

"Yeah, that's not creepy at all." She hugged her knees and peered around the gloomy space. "Why is that one different?" she asked, pointing to a shorter, wider strip of paper hanging near the far wall.

"Different?" Grover Solomon reached out and plucked it off its string. Even as his fingers brushed the glossy surface, he knew what it must be. Another wave of goosebumps cascaded down his back.

Autumn peered upward toward the short peak of the ceiling above her head. "There's another one here."

He was barely listening. The thing Autumn had seen was a playing card, but not the Queen of Hearts as he had feared. The word *Joker* appeared on both edges in vertical print, and a photograph in the middle depicted a nude man with long, smooth muscles that might have been carved from marble. He beamed up with a rather roguish grin.

Grover Solomon's stomach gave a swoop as if he'd had just leapt from an airplane.

It was Laz's grin. The grin that had compelled Grover Solomon into a hundred different (admittedly enjoyable) misdeeds during his childhood. Even now it seemed to light up some corner of his mind that had long since gone dark. Here on this card stood his best friend, all grown up but still inviting him on some new forbidden adventure as though they were not separated by fifteen years and the harsh, ragged curtain of death.

Autumn hissed suddenly behind him. "*What the fuck is this?*"

Grover Solomon spun guiltily, heat blossoming in his cheeks. What must he have looked like, staring longingly at a photo of a naked man? But Autumn's attention was fixed on another playing card in her own hand. Even in the dim light he could see it was the Queen of Hearts, naked and posed coyly for the camera. Except something was different…

Bright pink spots had risen in Autumn's cheeks too, and her

hair suddenly looked thicker, as if standing on end. "Where did this come from?"

"I don't—" he began.

"Look at this!" she snarled, shoving the card not at him but at Leon, who still hunkered outside the door.

Something about seeing Leon framed in the doorway reminded Grover Solomon irresistibly of Laz's final moments of life. That electric feeling crackled through his whole body again, slowing his mind, dulling it. Everything was happening too fast.

Leon stared down at the card in Autumn's hand, nonplussed. "It's you." He frowned. "But—"

"Get out!" Grover Solomon bawled, dropping the Joker card and lunging forward, nearly knocking Autumn on her face.

Too late. The half-door had already begun to swing shut. Still crouched outside, Leon saw it closing too. Rather than getting out of the way, he thrust his hands into the narrowing gap. The door rebounded off his knuckles and began to swing closed again, faster this time.

"No!" Autumn cried.

Leon collapsed to his knees when the second blow landed, but he kept his hands firmly in place so the door could not latch. The sharp edge ground into his skin as if someone were leaning against the door, trying to force it shut from the outside.

"Move out of the way!" Autumn ordered, and Leon scooted as far out of the path of the door as he could while maintaining his protective grip.

She launched herself forward, crashing into the door with her shoulder. It flew open and struck the wall, only to bounce back and begin swinging closed yet again. But Autumn scrambled out and sprang to her feet. She raised one powerful leg and kicked out, planting her heel above the knob like a cop busting down a door on TV. The door flew back and hit the wall again, hard enough to crack the plaster.

Only when Grover Solomon had also scuttled from the room

did Leon sink back, cradling his hands to his chest. The others pulled him into a standing position and half-carried him to the trapdoor leading down to the lower floors. The last thing Grover Solomon saw as he descended the stairs was the half-door, its knob powdered with plaster, swinging purposefully closed.

The Secret Renovation

"You're just lucky that wasn't one of the big doors on the second floor," Autumn told Leon for the third time in in less than two minutes as they embraced in the street beside Grover Solomon's car. She sounded angry and scared. "You would have lost more than just two fingers this time."

Grover Solomon dug through the milk crate for his first aid kit while simultaneously attempting to hide the contents of the trunk with his body. He needn't have bothered. Autumn had eyes only for Leon. She squeezed him around the middle, her face buried in his neck. Grover Solomon heard her whack Leon's back in temper. "What were you thinking?"

His arms enfolded her as well, though his hands dangled limply between her shoulder blades, red and scraped and swollen. "I could ask you the same thing. Why did you go in there in the first place?"

Grover Solomon tensed. Autumn had entered the crawlspace because of him. Not only that, he had already admitted that he'd meant for her to go inside instead of him. His memory replayed the image of Leon shoving his hands into the path of the closing door, thoughtlessly putting himself in harm's way to protect others.

Grover Solomon had never felt like such a coward in his life.

In hot-faced silence, he freed the first aid kit from the bottom of the milk crate, fumbled open the clasp, and drew out an instant cold pack and a roll of gauze. "Here you go."

Autumn disengaged herself from Leon and accepted the supplies. She twisted the ice pack in her hands, shaking it for several seconds until the chemicals inside mixed and became slushy. Then she laid it on the back of Leon's right hand—the more mangled of the two—and wrapped it with a tenderness Grover Solomon would not have believed her capable of.

He turned away, that curious and unwelcome jealousy rising in him again.

"Do you know how to use any of those things in your trunk?" Leon asked over the top of Autumn's head.

He winced. So Leon had seen after all. "Sort of. I don't think they do much of anything."

Autumn strode past him and peered into the trunk for herself. "You had all this stuff just sitting out here? Why didn't we take it with us? Maybe Leon's hands wouldn't have been turned into hamburger if we'd had some way to defend ourselves."

Leon laid his non-bandaged hand on Autumn's shoulder. Blood welled in a straight, shallow wound where the edge of the door had cut into his skin. A purple welt was already rising around it. "This isn't his fault" he said gently.

But that was a very poor lie. What had happened was entirely Grover Solomon's fault, and he suspected all three of them knew it.

"No matter what," Leon went on, "I think we should talk to my dad before we go inside your house again."

Grover Solomon had to replay Leon's words in his head before he allowed himself to believe he'd really heard that word "we" again. Didn't Leon realize how much danger all three of them had been in just now? If Odetta had managed to lock them in her little closet, it would certainly have ended in something worse than a few bloody knuckles.

He shook his head. "Autumn is right." His voice sounded high in his ears, but firm. "I shouldn't have gotten either of you involved. This isn't anyone's business but mine."

Autumn snorted. Those pink spots had returned to her cheeks. "It's way too late for that. Even if your lady friend upstairs hadn't tried to take a bite out of Leon, that playing card I found up there makes this my business."

"Right," said Leon a bit tentatively. "That card…you're sure it wasn't—"

"I'm sure."

"Wasn't what?" Grover Solomon asked.

"Never mind," Leon muttered, reddening.

"When I turned eighteen I created a website to sell nude photos of myself to strangers on the internet," said Autumn. Unlike Leon, she seemed to find no reason that this information should make her blush. She cocked an eyebrow. "You never saw the pictures? Everyone else in this town did."

"Wait, you're Autumn *Springer?*" Grover Solomon said before he could stop himself. He had heard plenty about the high school girl who had become an internet celebrity a few years back, although he'd never actually seen the pictures. He remembered his mother getting very sniffy about it, claiming the scandal proved she had made the right choice in performing his schooling at home.

"Knew we'd get there eventually," said Autumn dryly. "Anyway, the photo on that card…" An almost imperceptible shiver ran through her, more a flutter of eyelids than anything else. "It didn't come from my site, and I've never posed for any photographer besides myself. What about yours?"

"My what?"

"Your card," she said impatiently. "The one you were holding before everything went to hell. Was it another picture of me?"

"Ah. No, that was…"

The adult version of Lazarus swam into his mind—the broad, mischievous grin; the long arms and legs wrapped in lean ropes of muscle.

"It wasn't you," he said lamely. Now he was the one blushing, though he didn't for the life of him know why. He cleared his throat. "We should go somewhere to patch up your hands, Leon. I'll drive."

Leon nodded. To Grover Solomon's surprise, so did Autumn. He'd felt sure she would press him about the second playing card. But when he saw the expression she turned on her fiancé, so full of care and concern, he realized he should have known she would never delay while Leon was in pain.

"Let's go back to my parents' house," said Leon. "I'll clean myself up and then we can ask Dad about this Odetta person."

The drive took all of three minutes. Autumn ushered Leon out of the car and into the house as soon as Grover Solomon pulled up to the curb. He was halfway up the walk when his cell phone buzzed. He lifted it from his belt and saw with some surprise that the caller was his father. He tapped the green button to answer.

"Grover Solomon," Ethyl Yoder's voice said in his ear. "I guess you're back in town."

"Yes, sir," said Grover Solomon. "I haven't been able to finish the inspection yet. Bad traffic out of Chicago."

"I heard. The realtor phoned."

"Ah."

A brief silence fell across the line.

"Is it warm there?"

"Yes, sir," said Grover Solomon uneasily. This was very unlike his father. The man hated telephones. Whenever he was forced to use them he spoke directly and tersely in the hope of ending the call as quickly as possible. The idea of him making idle chat about the weather over the phone was almost too surreal to believe.

"Is something wrong, Dad?"

"No. It's—well, your mother doesn't know I'm calling." A sigh. "Have you been in the crawlspace on third yet?"

"Yes." And then, before he could stop himself, he burst out, "Those Bible verses are still hanging from the ceiling in there. They should have burned up in the fire, but they're back."

"I thought they might be," his father said gruffly. "I asked her to take them down."

Grover Solomon blinked. "Her?"

"Annette. She doesn't like me going into that room, or I would have done it myself. She promised she would do it, but I…well, I had my doubts."

"Wait, you mean Mom put those papers up?"

Another silence, longer and more hesitant this time. Grover Solomon knew exactly why, too. A year ago any discussion that broached his parents' personal lives or Lazarus's death would have been impossible. But the rules had changed, and Grover Solomon needed an answer.

When Ethyl spoke again it was in a careful and slow voice. "Those papers were—ah, the original ones I mean—they came with the house. But like you said, they burned up. Annette spent a lot of time in that room after…Well, you may have been too young to notice, but things were very difficult for your mother in the years after we started our church."

Grover Solomon could practically hear sweat running down his father's face in an anxious waterfall.

"Look, son, as far as I know, the new family hasn't been inside that room yet, and I would be grateful if you could just take those papers down before you give the key over to the realtor. I'd rather not have anyone know that room had any purpose besides storage. You know how gossip spreads in New Canaan, and people wouldn't understand."

"*I* don't understand," Grover Solomon said bluntly, though he now had at least a partial answer as to why the big iron key had been stored in his mother's dresser all those years ago. "What did Mom do in that room? And what does that have to do with us leaving the church?"

Yet more silence, this time with an edge of shock. Never mind the rules changing. Grover Solomon had just shattered one of the biggest rules of all. The topic of their family's departure from Kurt Martin's church had always been, like so many things in Grover Solomon's childhood, absolutely forbidden. He may as well have been asking his dad to deal him a few hands of blackjack with Laz's old burlesque cards.

But now it turned out that his mother had "spent a lot of time" in Odetta's little cupboard? So much that she had made the effort to write out and rehang all of those Bible verses? He couldn't just ignore this new connection between his mother and Odetta Koop.

His father did not speak for so long that Grover Solomon actually checked the phone's glossy screen to make sure the call had not cut out. Seconds ticked by on the digital timer. The line was still active.

Sudden anger coursed through him. Anger at his father, anger at his mother, at his house, at Odetta Koop, at New Canaan. Anger at his own fearful and lonely existence.

The phone rose back to his ear in a shaking fist. Gone was the pleasant, hollow feeling that had filled his head after Autumn's acupressure treatment. "Never mind," he said. "I'll ask Pastor Martin instead."

A sharp hiss crackled through the earpiece like a burst of static. "What did you say?"

"I'm at the Martins' house now. They were really happy to see me. Mrs. Martin gave me a big hug when she answered the door."

"Now you listen here, young man—" Ethyl Yoder began, sounding plenty angry himself.

"*No!*" The word exploded in the lazy afternoon heat like a firecracker. "Remember Pastor Martin's son, Leon? My first friend? He's got a fiancé now. He's been to Europe! He…he has interesting friends. I mean, do you have any idea what it feels like to be almost twenty-five years old and realize you stopped growing up when you were ten?" He did not wait for an answer. "Don't worry, I'll have the key back to the realtor Monday morning. Goodbye, Dad."

He jabbed the button on his phone to end the call and then switched off the phone entirely.

Leon had been right. It was time to talk to Kurt Martin.

Pastor Martin's Mistake

When Grover Solomon let himself back into the Martins' home, Kurt had evidently not finished his baking for the day. He greeted Grover Solomon in the entryway, still wearing the long, flour covered apron. His forehead was creased with concern.

"I guess there was some trouble at the house? Leon and Autumn were in too much of a hurry to give any details. Cynthia's with them now."

"Yes, sir, trouble."

The crease in Kurt's forehead deepened to a canyon as he took in Grover Solomon's expression. "Why don't we have a seat in the kitchen?" He pulled the apron over his head and hung it on a peg by the stove before drawing out two chairs from the kitchen table. "Please."

Grover Solomon lowered himself into the offered seat. "Pastor Martin, I need to know the real reason my parents left your church." He steeled himself for a quick, decisive *No*, perhaps tempered by that old standby, *You can know when you're older.* But regardless of how he felt on the inside, he was still 24 years old, and the look Kurt sent him across the table was one that might pass between two men on serious business. Between equals.

Cynthia entered the kitchen behind him. "Leon's hands are pretty banged up," she announced. "Doesn't look like anything's broken though."

"That's very good news," said Kurt, smiling. "Can you ask Leon and Autumn to give us a minute in private, please?"

Years of being a pastor's wife must have acclimated her to moments like this. She simply said, "Of course," and retreated from the room.

Once her footsteps had receded down the hall Kurt turned back to Grover Solomon. "Did your parents and the other members of their church never talk about their motivations with you?"

He considered his answer. "I gleaned that they disagreed with your church's stance on sexuality. They didn't talk about it much around Laz and me."

"Our church's stance on sexuality," Kurt repeated. He set his elbows on the table and rubbed his face in a gesture of long weariness. "That's one way to put it."

"Once I got older," added Grover Solomon, watching Kurt carefully, "I assumed it had something to do with homosexuality, given how many passages in the Bible speak against it. I don't know how many sermons I heard about that growing up. At least one a month."

Kurt rubbed his face a few moments longer before he surfaced. Dark circles had materialized under his eyes. Granules of flour stuck in his hair, making it appear even grayer than it was. "Your parents left our church," he said heavily, "because I made an awful mistake."

"What do you mean?"

"Actually, that's not true," Kurt corrected himself as if he had not heard. "I won't be so arrogant as to make my role seem larger than it was."

"Your role in *what?*" pressed Grover Solomon, a bit impatient now.

"There was a rich man," Kurt said gravely, sounding for all the world like he was about to launch into a parable. "Rich and powerful. I won't tell you the man's name. But he gave money to good causes. Thanks to him, there is still a yearly scholarship fund for young people at our church. Over time, though, he evidently began to see himself as being above reproach, as if the normal rules didn't apply to him. Worse yet, when the chips were down, many people agreed. Myself included."

Another connection sparked in Grover Solomon's mind, similar to the revelation about the iron key in his mother's underwear drawer. He was thinking of the very first sermon delivered at his parents' new church. His mother had spoken about multiple passages in the Gospels when Jesus says it is easier for a camel to pass through the eye of a needle than for a rich man to get into heaven. His mother had wept as she spoke. As a child, Grover Solomon had believed she was sad about leaving the old church.

"What did he do to my mother?" he asked after a moment. "This rich man."

Kurt's lips spread in a humorless smile. "You're a sharp guy, Grover Solomon. Maybe you don't remember, but both your parents actually worked at our church."

"I remember."

"Well, your dad participated in most Sunday services, but your mother put in more hours during the week. She preferred to work behind the scenes, coming and going at odd times of day. One evening it transpired that both she and this rich man arrived in the church office at the same time. I don't know if they had worked together before, or if this was just a coincidence. He may even have planned it, though such a thought is enough to give me nightmares."

"What did he do?" Grover Solomon demanded again. His brain seemed to be a bonfire of connections now: the skeleton key in his mother's drawer, all those Bible verses about the evils of sexuality painstakingly hung in the crawlspace...

The pastor's shadowy eyes locked onto his. "He tried to rape her. In the church office."

"Tried to..." Grover Solomon repeated.

"We might never even have known, except your mother fought back. The next morning the office was a mess. My assistant found paper and supplies scattered all over, the lid of the photocopier was cracked, hanging off its hinges..." he trailed off. The mixture of pain and sadness and desperation on his face made him look positively ancient. The eyes of a thousand-year-old man stared from under his salt-and-pepper hair. They bore an expression Grover Solomon knew well. After all, how many times had he seen it on his mother's face? How many times had he seen it in his own mirror?

"What was your mistake?" he asked. He thought he might already know the answer, but he wanted to hear the pastor say it out loud.

Kurt flinched as if Grover Solomon had cracked a bullwhip over his head. "I asked your mother to keep quiet. I don't mean I asked her to forget about the attack or pretend it never happened. I wasn't so foolish even then to ask such a thing. I just thought we could handle the matter quietly, through confidential mediation and therapy."

"And that's when my parents left," said Grover Solomon, slumping back in his chair. He felt as exhausted as Kurt Martin looked.

"Not at all," said Kurt, surprised. "Your parents agreed to the mediation. But the man who assaulted your mother became furious at the suggestion that he should face his accuser. He and his wife left town shortly after that."

"He was married?"

"They usually are," Kurt sighed. "Worse yet, I very much doubt Annette was the first or last woman he took advantage of. I can't guess how many more lives I damaged with the choices I made during that week."

"But if the guy left, then why—"

"Don't you see?" Kurt interrupted edgily. "I insisted on secrecy. I was more concerned about a scandal disrupting my congregation than providing your mother with the healing she needed. Eventually she couldn't set foot in the church at any time of day or night without suffering severe panic attacks."

Grover Solomon stared past him, past the pies cooling on the counter, and into the half lit passages of his imagination. He imagined his mother kneeling in the tiny room with the half-door, those hanging strips of paper drifting across her scalp like ghostly fingertips.

At last he said, "If you were so bent on keeping this secret, why are you telling me now?"

"The worst thing I've ever done in my life is keep silent about what happened to your mother. And if pain or harm has come to you because of it, you deserve the chance your mother never got— to face at least one of the people who caused that harm. Grover Solomon, I beg your pardon."

Grover Solomon had never heard that last phrase spoken quite this way, as an earnest, literal request rather than a rote phrase to be muttered to a stranger after brushing shoulders on the sidewalk.

Kurt laid his flour dusted hands on his thighs and pushed himself into a standing position. "I think I'll check on Leon now."

Grover Solomon stood too. He clenched his hands into fists to stop them shaking. He couldn't tell whether he was angrier with Kurt Martin or his parents for never telling him about this.

"You're wrong."

Kurt stopped in the doorway. "I'm sorry?"

"You said you didn't have a big role in this, but so much of it is your fault. *So* much. How can you not see that?"

At last Kurt rotated slowly to face him. He didn't seem to know what to say, and Grover Solomon hated him for it.

"My parents sleep in separate beds. It's been almost twenty years and she still can't stand to be touched. She doesn't even hug me when I come home to visit. Just today I found out she had a secret room in our house filled with Bible verses about how sex is evil and wrong. You want to beg someone's pardon, Pastor Martin, go see my mother. You go beg *her,* on your knees."

"I've tried, Grover Solomon," Kurt said wearily. "I can't tell you how many times. But at some point I realized that I wanted to give my apology more than she wanted to hear it. The only thing she truly wants from me is space."

He held Grover Solomon's furious gaze a moment longer, then his eyes dropped to the floor. He looked lost, tired, and older than ever. "We'll be ready to eat in about twenty minutes. You're still welcome to join us. For all my other faults, I do make a good pizza."

On the Nature of Spirits

No one else entered the kitchen for some time. Grover Solomon suspected Kurt had corralled the others in the most distant part of the house to give him space to recover. In his mind, he stormed out of the Martins' home a dozen times, sometimes shouting at Kurt as he went, other times shouting at his father over the phone, and still others simply fuming in silence. He did so much imaginary storming and shouting, he was surprised to discover that, when Cynthia Martin entered the kitchen, he had been sitting alone for nearly fifteen minutes. He further surprised himself by saying yes when she asked if he could help set the table for supper.

They had all sat down and Cynthia was just dishing out thick slices of Chicago style pizza to everyone's plate when the woman who had asked to be called Alice returned to the house, much to the Martins' collective surprise and delight. Autumn, it transpired, was unsatisfied with Leon's increasingly ill-tempered insistence that his hands were *"Fine,* dammit," and had secretly phoned Alice to request a professional opinion.

Alice gave a polite little bow as she entered the kitchen. She wore a colorful outfit that looked to Grover Solomon like a cross between nursing scrubs and a martial arts tunic, a messenger bag slung over one shoulder. She knelt in front of Leon, taking his large, mangled hands in her tiny ones.

"You here to chew me out too?" growled Leon. But he yielded to the inspection, taking it in turns to glare impotently between Autumn and Alice. Obviously he didn't dare refuse either woman's wishes outright.

By the time Kurt and Cynthia had prepared a sixth place at the table for Alice, she was ready with her pronouncement. "There doesn't seem to be any lasting damage," she said, frowning slightly. "Autumn said your hands got slammed in a door?"

"It was an accident," Leon muttered. "Can you pass the olive oil, please?"

Alice's frown deepened. "An accident? I see two different injuries."

Leon glowered.

At first Grover Solomon didn't understand why Leon would lie, but he also didn't mind. With everything that had happened today, he had no real desire to talk about Odetta Koop or the half-size room where Lazarus had died. But then he realized that Leon must be lying for just that reason—to spare Grover Solomon the pain of retelling Lazarus's death.

A confusing rush of gratitude, respect, and affection for Leon flooded him, causing him to blush quite as much as the playing card with Lazarus on it. Luckily none of the others were paying attention.

"You are the absolute worst liar," said Autumn, patting Leon's thigh. She seemed more relaxed after the positive prognosis from Alice, though still distracted.

Probably, Grover Solomon thought, because she and Leon had been dragged into his lifelong nightmare and now couldn't think of a way to back out gracefully. He thought too of the call from his father. *Things were very difficult for your mother in the years after we started our church.*

But thinking about that only made his anger surge once more. How could his parents never have told him why they left the Martins' church? How could they have kept something so horrific and life-changing from him, their only son?

The way you've kept Lazarus's death a secret for fifteen years? suggested a small voice deep inside him, the voice of a child drifting up out of a dungeon.

Suddenly it all seemed too much. Images old and new flashed through his mind: the black iron key jutting from the mouth of the lock; the yellow curl of the Bible verses hanging in their silent crypt; Lazarus's face lit from below by the flame of a cheap cigarette lighter; Kurt's visible anguish as he begged Grover Solomon's pardon; Leon's hands and scarred forehead; Alice's old neck wounds and haunted eyes...

That one word summed it all up, didn't it? All of them at this table were *haunted* people, living haunted lives. And Grover Solomon was sick of it.

"The ghost of Odetta Koop attacked us," he heard himself say loudly. "She's the one who slammed the door on Leon's hands."

Now the others around the table did stare at him. He felt no embarrassment. He was telling the truth.

Kurt regarded his son. "You just said it was an accident."

"And Autumn called me a liar," answered Leon, throwing a quick look at Grover Solomon as if seeking permission to talk about what had really happened. "There's definitely something in that house, Dad."

"Something," Kurt repeated.

"Something nasty," Autumn agreed. She glanced down toward the floor and made little kissing noises at the Martins' cat, Marbles or whatever its name was. It hopped into her lap and nosed hopefully at a string of mozzarella hanging off her plate.

"Cats!" said Leon suddenly, making Alice, Grover Solomon,

and indeed the cat, all jump. "Aren't cats supposed to be able to sense spirits or supernatural things?"

"And then what?" Autumn said with that little giggle she seemed to reserve for occasions when Leon said something kind of dumb. "Can they scare them away too? Can you scare away a ghost?" she asked the cat, who turned up from the cheese to rub its head on Autumn's chin, purring loudly, eyes closed in ecstasy. Autumn's giggle bubbled into a bright and delighted laugh. "Aw, who's a fierce kitty?"

Only Alice and Grover Solomon failed to smile at this rather sickening display of affection. Maybe Alice didn't like cats either.

"I've heard of Odetta Koop, of course," Kurt told Grover Solomon diplomatically. He seemed determined not to let their earlier conversation color this one. "But first I'd like to hear why you think your home has a spirit."

Grover Solomon grimaced, not in temper but in concentration. How could he convey the terrible weight and dread of simply being in Odetta Koop's presence to someone who had never experienced it?

"She stomps," he began. "She paces up and down the third floor. You can hear it all through the house, even when nobody's home. And she makes clocks go crazy. Sometimes you can hear loud ticking in rooms that don't have any clocks at all."

"Ticking," repeated Kurt. "Have you ever seen this…spirit?"

"Have you ever seen God, Pastor Martin?" asked Autumn, now scratching the cat between its ears.

Leon and his mother stiffened, but Kurt only chuckled and raised his hands in surrender. "Point. You know, I'm sure some men would balk at the prospect of having such a quick thinking daughter-in-law, but I wouldn't trade it for the world."

Autumn gave him an eye roll any thirteen-year-old would have been proud of. His smile only widened.

"I haven't seen her," admitted Grove Solomon, "but I know she's real. She killed someone." He wanted nothing less than to have to go down this road again—Laz's death seemed terribly fresh today—but he also needed Kurt to believe him. "There was a fire."

Kurt's smile faded. "Yes, there *was* a fire. But I've never heard anyone suggest it was started by Odetta Koop. Frankly I'm surprised you know about it."

This was the last response Grover Solomon could have imagined. He felt his mouth fall open stupidly.

Evidently Leon was just as confused. "Wait, *you* know about the fire, Dad?"

Kurt shrugged. "It's mentioned in multiple historical records. Even back then, two men dying in a fire made headlines."

"What are you talking about?" Autumn asked, frowning. "There was a second fire?"

The conversation had gotten away from all of them. Everyone, not just Autumn, was frowning now. Alice stared broodily down at her plate, clearly wishing she had just gone home instead of returning here.

"Why don't we start over?" Kurt suggested. "Grover Solomon, you said someone died in a fire."

"My friend Lazarus. He got trapped inside a room on the third floor when a fire started in there. I was right outside the door, but I couldn't get to him." A wave of remembered panic surged in his belly. Yes, Laz's death was much too fresh today. "I heard him screaming."

"Walt and Cora Beachy's son?" Cynthia asked, horrified. "That's impossible."

"I promise you it happened," said Grover Solomon. "Fifteen years ago. I was surprised that Leon hadn't heard about it either. I guess my family knows how to keep a secret," he added, and took guilty satisfaction in seeing Kurt wince.

"We would have heard," Cynthia insisted. "There would have been memorial services."

"What did you ever really know about what went on in my parents' church?" Grover Solomon countered.

Leon held up his puffy and bandaged hands. "The same thing almost happened to us today. We went up to that same room, and someone or something was very unhappy about it. If that door had actually closed instead of just banging against my hands, it would have been me outside that door, with Autumn inside…" He swallowed.

Autumn took one of his hands in both of hers and held it so tightly her knuckles turned white. It must have hurt, but Leon didn't pull away.

Cynthia refused to give up. "At the very least we would have seen an accident record from the fire department."

"The fire put itself out," said Grover Solomon. "Mom and Dad came running when they heard me screaming. Mom pulled me downstairs while Dad stayed to put out the fire. But he said when he finally got the door open the flames were gone. He never even pulled the pin on the fire extinguisher. He only saw…"

But he didn't finish the thought. The truth was that his father had never spoken of what he'd found inside the charred room.

Cynthia didn't argue this time. She only watched Grover Solomon, her dark eyes large and round and moist. "I don't know what to say. I'm so sorry."

Grover Solomon shook his head. "I'm not telling you this for sympathy. I just want to make sure it doesn't happen to anyone else. I want Odetta Koop out of that house. I want her gone, to wherever it is she's supposed to be."

"I suppose," Kurt said slowly, "that ours is one of the only cultures in the world that habitually denies the existence of ghosts outside of religious contexts."

Relief swept through Grover Solomon. Pastor Martin seemed ready to listen at last. "Yes, sir. I've been researching exactly that kind of thing."

"For example, everyone knows the German myth of the poltergeist," said Kurt. He seemed much more enthusiastic now that the conversation had turned in a more academic direction. "Although they haunt a specific person rather than a location, if I remember correctly. Alice, is there any Korean folklore about ghosts?"

Alice, on the other hand, looked less pleased than ever that she hadn't simply gone home after work. "The *gwishin,*" she said reluctantly. "A spirit who wants revenge for something."

"That sounds about right," said Leon. Autumn was still holding his hand, but in a gentler grip now. The cat pawed lightly at the little diamond on her left hand, attracted by the sparkle. "How do you get rid of them?"

Alice shrugged. "I have never fought one."

For some reason Autumn snorted with laughter, startling the cat out of her lap. Alice smiled too, and a bit guiltily.

"Alice gets to play the Asian mystic all day at work," Autumn explained to Grover Solomon. "Fielding questions about healing cancer with dragon blood or whatever."

Alice nodded. "Last week the chiropractor asked if I could speak with a Chinese accent while I'm at work. He said research shows that patients are more comfortable with the idea of acupuncture if the person performing it has a thick 'Oriental'—" She made little quotation marks in the air with her fingers. "—accent."

"He did not say that," said Leon, appalled.

"Of course he did," Autumn grunted. "Same thing happens in Asian restaurants, doesn't it?"

"At the Korean restaurant in Iowa City, only one of the waitresses is actually from a Korean family," agreed Alice. "She grew up in the States and can't speak a word of Korean, but she said she makes much better tips when she fakes an accent."

"Fascinating," said Kurt, actually leaning forward now.

Grover Solomon felt the conversation slipping away again. "Sorry, I don't mean to bring us down or anything…" he interrupted.

The others fell silent, cautious smiles that had begun to grow with the lighter conversation—and it did not escape Grover Solomon that everyone at the table regarded racism as a "lighter" topic than his ghost—winking out like stars behind storm clouds.

"Of course not," said Kurt. He sighed heavily. "You'll want to know about the other fire. The one that killed Zebulon Koop."

Autumn's Little Secret

The kitchen had grown very quiet, all eyes on Kurt. "You can keep eating," he invited with a wave toward the half consumed pizza at the center of the table. "There's not all that much to tell. The fire occurred a long time ago, but we do have a couple records of the incident. The simple version is that the academy woodshop, which was a large shed off the main dormitory, caught fire one night while Zebulon Koop and another man were working inside."

"They couldn't get out?" asked Leon, looking sickened.

"Well, like I said, it was a big old shed made of wood, full of dry lumber and sawdust and who knows what else. Witnesses said the whole place burned to the ground in a few minutes." Kurt made a little hand gesture like the *poof* at the end of a magician's disappearing act.

"Witnesses?" Grover Solomon asked.

"Odetta Koop and some of her students. By the time the town fire brigade arrived, the shed was basically gone. They focused their efforts on keeping the fire from spreading to the dormitory. No students were hurt," Kurt added. "They evacuated as soon as they knew about the fire. Odetta herself suffered slight burns when she ran too close to the shed, presumably to rescue her husband and the other man trapped inside."

"How do you know all this?" Leon asked. "Surely that last part isn't in the archives."

"The *New Canaan Gazette* was in its first year of publication, so we actually have a written account of the event and its aftermath. No evidence in any source," he added gently to Grover Solomon, "ties Odetta Koop to the fire."

Grover Solomon stared right back at him. "I have a genealogy that says Zebulon Koop was Odetta's second husband, and that her husbands were brothers. Both men died after they married her."

"She bumped off her first husband so she could marry his brother?" Autumn mused. "Twisted."

"Let's just cool our jets here," said Kurt, clearly agitated. "We're leaving the realm of speculation for outright conspiracy. The school's records show that Odetta's first husband, Eli Koop, died of pneumonia, and that she and Zebulon were legally married according to the law of Levirate Marriage."

"Which is?" said Autumn.

"A childless widow marries her husband's brother to produce an heir," Grover Solomon explained automatically. "Historically, a widow had to remarry so she could retain possession of any property that had belonged to her husband, because women could not own land."

Autumn and Alice exchanged a grim look.

Kurt nodded. "After the fire, the loss of Odetta Koop's second husband in just two years seemed to affect her deeply. The school's motto became *Erweiterung durch Evangelismus allein.*"

Leon squinted. "'Expansion by evangelism alone'?" he translated, cocking an eyebrow at Autumn as though for confirmation.

She shrugged. "The only German I remember is *pack dich!*"

Kurt favored her with an indulgent smile. "Isn't it amazing how rudeness is the first part of a language we learn and the last part we forget?"

"You should hear what I can do in English," said Autumn cheerfully. Even Cynthia laughed.

"I don't get it, though," said Leon. "Every religion uses evangelism as a means of growth."

Kurt shook his head. "The official translation read 'Expansion *solely* by evangelism.'"

Alice raised her hand as if asking a question in a classroom. "Evangelism?"

"Going out into the world to share your beliefs with others," Leon clarified.

"You know, like people who go door to door selling steak knives sharp enough to cut tin cans," said Autumn.

No one laughed this time.

"You're on fire tonight, honey," Leon murmured, patting her leg.

Kurt seemed to decide that no response was the best response, and he simply went on as if Autumn had not spoken at all. "The implication in the case of Odetta Koop's school being that growing the church by sexual reproduction had become antithetical to Odetta's belief system. She revised her curriculum into a sort of anti-sexual education. She taught her students that sexuality in any form, including between two married, consenting adults, was repellent in the eyes of the Lord. Her ideas caused quite a stir in the wider church leadership at the time, I can tell you."

He paused while they all digested that. "On the other hand, not everyone disagreed. Enough parents thought she had the right view that she was able to keep her school open almost another ten years."

"And how did those parents produce the children they sent to her?" Autumn asked moodily. Before anyone could answer she muttered, "God, what does marriage *do* to people?"

"Excuse me?" Cynthia said.

"Autumn, not now," Leon begged softly, squeezing her hand. "Please."

She pulled free of him. "If not now, when? After we're married, and our relationship has turned to garbage and it's too late to do anything about it? I haven't felt right about this from the beginning, and you just keep saying, 'Not now, we'll figure it out later.' How about we figure it out now. We came back to New Canaan to talk to your parents, right? So let's go. Let's grab this motherfucker by the horns."

Cynthia turned to her husband, plainly terrified.

Grover Solomon glanced at Alice, the only other extra-familial interloper at the table. She seemed as tense as the others, but her expression betrayed a sort of unsurprised resignation. Clearly she had known something like this might happen. Either way, it appeared the topic of Odetta Koop had just been tabled indefinitely.

"Lay it on me, Pastor Martin," Autumn invited. "I love this man next to me more than anyone else on the planet, and I want to spend the rest of my life with him. What possible reason could we have for getting married?"

"That's—But—" Kurt stammered, clearly wrong footed. He cleared his throat. "Maybe I don't understand the question, because it seems like you've answered it already. If you both feel the same way, why would you *not* get married?"

"Marriage is bigger than just the two of you," added Cynthia, pink spots rising in her cheeks. "It's about declaring your love and commitment before friends and family."

Autumn didn't miss a beat. "I just did."

"Yes, but—" Cynthia spluttered.

"There are legal reasons too," Leon said, his cheeks burning like his mother's.

"That's true," said Kurt. He seemed to be recovering more quickly than his wife from the dramatic turn the conversation had taken. "Taxes and finances and so forth."

Autumn laughed. It was not a nice sound. "You realize my dad is a divorce lawyer, right? You think I don't know all the legal implications of marriage and separation?"

"Of course I—"

"And as for finances, do you know how rich I am? Do you have any idea just how goddamn much money I have? Leon and I could never work another day in our lives and still buy our kids their own polo teams."

"Well, you've just named the best reason right there," Kurt countered. "If and when you have children, marriage is a concrete, easily explainable way to show them what a responsible commitment between two loving adults looks like."

"Like my parents did?" asked Autumn.

The atmosphere at the table changed instantly. Kurt leaned back and said, "Ah," as if he'd just solved a riddle that had been vexing him.

It was the wrong response. Leon's brown eyes widened in dread as Autumn's green ones narrowed.

"Don't you dare try to reduce this to some simple psychological block I've built up because my parents got divorced. Leon and I have already seen two sets of friends who got married after college split up. One couple didn't even make it a year. And look at what you've just told us about Odetta Koop, for God's sake. She married two brothers—because the Bible told her to, no less—and it wrecked her mind so badly that she spent the rest of her life teaching kids that sex is ugly and unnatural and wrong. And whatever you say, it sure sounds like she torched at least one of her husbands, especially when you put it alongside what Grover Solomon told us about his friend Lazarus."

"I'm sorry, I don't see how—" Kurt began.

Autumn cut him off coldly. "Your son is the most wonderful person I've ever met. Our relationship is the best thing that's ever happened to me, and I refuse to risk it by signing a pointless contract that just ends up driving wedges between people."

"It's a symbol," insisted Cynthia. "Like the ring you're wearing.

It's a way for other people to recognize the power and beauty of your relationship. You could even argue that it gives others a hopeful example to follow in their own relationships."

Up to this point Leon had let Autumn carry her side of the argument alone, but now he fixed his mother with an odd look. "Would you be saying that if Autumn already had a kid, by me or some other guy? Or if I had brought home a man instead of a woman? Would you be so excited for us to get married then?"

Grover Solomon squirmed. Suddenly his supper wasn't sitting too well.

"Of course we would," said Kurt at once. "Love is love."

Cynthia only stared at her son, apparently struck dumb by his question. After several seconds of very uncomfortable silence she found her voice. "I'm sorry, but I don't understand why we're even having this conversation. Autumn, you're still wearing the ring, so I take it you intend to marry our son. And we wouldn't say no to grandchildren riding polo horses, either," she added, attempting a joke.

Autumn stood. She slid the little diamond off her finger and set it at the edge of Leon's placemat. "You'll get your grandchild, and Leon and I will raise her together. But she was the wrong reason for me to start wearing this thing."

"*She?*" asked Kurt sharply.

Autumn ignored him. She turned to Grover Solomon, who felt a sudden urge to dive under the table. A fierce, elemental power seemed to crackle in the air around Autumn like an electrical corona. She reached into her pocket and slowly drew out the playing card she had found in the room with the half-door. "I believe you when you say that Odetta Koop killed your friend, and I will do everything in my power to help you destroy her."

She held the card out to him, fingers shaking slightly. Grover Solomon accepted it warily. He remembered thinking when he'd glimpsed this card in the half-light of the crawlspace that it had looked different than the Queen of Hearts from his childhood, and now he understood why. The woman on the card possessed Autumn's face and, he assumed, Autumn's body as it might appear without any clothes on. Except that on the card, her belly bulged outward, round and smooth below the globes of her breasts.

"Your ghost knows I'm pregnant," Autumn said stiffly, "and I think this afternoon she was trying to kill me and my baby."

PART II: AWAKENING

Gwishin

Fifteen rather awkward minutes later, Grover Solomon found himself descending the Martins' front steps beside Alice. After Autumn's pronouncement, she and Kurt had pressed bravely on with the conversation, covering such topics as how far along she was—fourteen weeks—and whether she and Leon had picked out a name—they hadn't—while Leon and his mother glared determinedly in opposite directions, identical pink patches high on their cheeks. Everyone at the table understood that the real conversation would begin after the guests had left.

And so when Alice rose to excuse herself, the pie and coffee Kurt had prepared for dessert resting untouched on the counter, Grover Solomon nearly knocked over his chair in his haste to join her. It was only as he and Alice stepped onto the sidewalk together that he realized he'd landed himself in a position almost as awkward as the one he'd left. Making small talk with strangers had never been his strong suit.

"So, how did you and Leon meet?" he asked as naturally as he could manage, as though he regularly spent his evenings chatting with intelligent strangers from other countries. "You didn't grow up in New Canaan, right?"

"I was born in South Korea. I met Leon and Autumn five years ago. Leon believed I was…someone he had known before."

"And you guys hit it off, I guess. Since you came all the way to Iowa."

"We were both in trouble," said Alice curtly. "We helped each other."

"He might be in trouble again." Grover Solomon nodded toward the house and, by extension, the familial argument they had just escaped.

Alice shrugged. "He is with Autumn." It was difficult to tell from her tone whether she meant that Autumn protected Leon from trouble or created it.

They came to the end of the walk, where the main sidewalk split in two directions. Alice turned right. "Good night."

"Wait!" called Grover Solomon, dropping all pretense of coolness. "Please."

She stopped and faced him expectantly.

"Autumn did this thing back at my house. She kind of poked me right here." He pointed between his eyes. "It felt like, I don't know, like she unlocked something in my brain. She said she learned it from you, and I…I wondered if you could explain it to me."

Alice seemed to relax. Grover Solomon remembered what Autumn had said about Alice not wanting to be an "Asian mystic." Good thing he hadn't asked her about the *gwishin*.

"What I do is not quite the same. Autumn uses her fingers, as you said. I use these."

She rummaged in her bag and drew out a shiny black box, wooden and lacquered, covered in symbols Grover Solomon could not read. The box opened on a vertical hinge, and inside were perhaps two dozen needles, short and so thin they were almost invisible except for the way they glittered in the light from the Martins' front porch. Each needle sat in its own little velvet recess, accessible by a circular ornamental grip painted and lacquered to match the box.

Grover Solomon cared little for needles, and he must not have hidden his alarm very well, because Alice smiled. "It is not like getting a shot. My needles are very thin."

"Yes, well," said Grover Solomon bravely.

"You believe a dead woman's spirit inhabits your house?" asked Alice. She did not close the box.

"Yes."

"And if you believe that, then you must believe that the woman's spirit once lived in her body. Made it alive."

"Y—Yes," he said more uncertainly.

"And," she persisted, "that a similar spirit is living inside your body to make it alive too."

Grover Solomon blinked. "I—Yes, I suppose so."

"Give me your hands."

He obeyed. They shook quite as badly as Autumn's had done when she'd passed him the card back in the kitchen.

With her free hand, Alice probed gently at his palm, his knuckles, his wrist. "You said before that you work with traffic lights?"

"There's more to it than that, but—"

"Then you will understand this. Imagine that your body is a city with traffic lights spaced all over it. But instead of changing from red to green to yellow, the lights should always be green. When one of them turns red, your spirit—your *qi*—can no longer flow through that part of your body, just like a red traffic light stops motorists from moving toward their destinations."

Grover Solomon's heart was pounding, and not just because the bare needles seemed to be leering at him like the grin of some horrible steel gremlin. Every part of his upbringing rebelled at this conversation. His parents would have cried heresy the moment Alice used the word *qi*.

He licked his lips. "And then what?"

"Illness. Depression." At last she looked up. "Trouble."

He made himself stare straight back into those dark eyes. "I'm in trouble, aren't I?"

To his surprise, Alice smiled. "No more than Leon was in when I met him."

"What do you mean?"

"Leon's body was full of red lights. His *qi* was trapped away in little compartments, unable to go anywhere."

"Then he met Autumn and everything opened up, right?" Grover Solomon said, puzzled at the sudden bitterness in his voice.

"Not at all. Leon didn't have the strength to love Autumn when they met. He spent the whole first summer I knew him reconnecting every point of energy he had so that he could love her as much as she loved him. It was sweet." Alice smiled again, obviously reminiscing. "Actually, they were both kind of idiots back then."

"What about me?"

"I don't know if you are an idiot."

He snorted so hard that he had to wipe his nose. "No, I mean how is my—you know, *qi?* Red or green lights?"

"Are you asking for my help?"

His eyes flicked from the box back to her face. "Yes."

She seemed to weigh some decision in her mind. "I told a lie before, because I didn't want to talk about *gwishin.*"

He waited.

She drew out one needle, holding it by the lacquered head while she closed the box and slid it back into the top of her bag, easily accessible. Next she spread apart the webbing between the index and middle fingers of his left hand. The needle slid into his skin with scarcely a prick. He'd felt more painful mosquito bites. At once a slow current, alternating between hot and cold, began to trickle up his arm from the tip of the needle. She retrieved a second needle and repeated the exercise with his right hand, speaking all the while.

"My parents died when I was young. My grandmother moved to Seoul to raise me. Before that she was a healer. An acupuncturist in a small village."

"Is that where—" He winced as the webbing between his fingers grew abruptly hot. His body felt simultaneously light and full, like an over-inflated zeppelin. He closed his eyes and focused all of his mental energy on keeping his body firmly attached to the sidewalk. He experienced several more tiny pricks in each hand as Alice continued her story.

"A man came to my grandmother because he wanted her help to banish a *gwishin*. She treated him for several days, and afterward, for the first time, he was able to see the physical form of the spirit he wanted to fight. But *gwishin* become more powerful the longer they stay on earth, and this one had been in the village for as long as anyone could remember."

Grover Solomon barely understood any of this. His breath came in such deep gusts that he felt sure his chest must be expanding like the throat of a bullfrog with every inhalation. A complicated fire filled his hands, freezing and burning, burning and freezing. The points where she had inserted the first two needles blazed hard and bright in his mind, pulsing like tiny neutron stars in the darkness behind his eyelids.

And then, seconds or perhaps minutes later, the heat and light began to recede. Grover Solomon opened his eyes and saw two swirling green-orange blobs at the center of his vision as if he had indeed been staring into bright lights. These too faded, but the night seemed brighter, clearer than it had before. The stars seemed closer.

And, in fact, never mind the stars. He could *see* the buzzing song of the cicadas in the trees, drifting among the leaves and swirling on the humid air in lazy, yellow-golden eddies of sound. He could sense the earth spinning on its axis, feel it barreling around the gravitational basin of the sun like a beach ball bobbing along the outer arc of a whirlpool. Never before had he felt so connected, so awake to the furious energies of the cosmos.

Then a new thought: what would he see if went to his house right now and opened the crawlspace? What bright torrents of old prayer and terror and shame would he see coursing between the hanging slips of paper?

But like the bright orbs in his vision, all of this began slipping away too, draining from his mind like a dream on waking.

He gulped warm night air. "Autumn wasn't kidding about you, was she? I remember reading about people in the Bible who had power in their touch, but I never understood what that might actually mean."

Alice didn't smile. "The man in the mountain village decided to fight the *gwishin* by himself. He entered the house and stayed inside for one hour before he reappeared and fled down the central road, screaming words no one understood. The road curved around a pass, but the man ran straight off the edge and fell two hundred feet. My grandmother said the other villagers heard him shouting all the way down."

She tore open a little packet from her bag and drew out a small white cloth to wipe down the needles before replacing them in the box. The scent of rubbing alcohol lingered, sharp on the heavy summer air.

"Are you saying that if I try to fight Odetta Koop I'll go crazy and throw myself off the nearest mountain?"

Alice shook her head. "My grandmother told me that story when I was a child because she wanted me to understand that sometimes people must try to do impossible things. After that man died, people from three nearby villages came together to banish the *gwishin*, and they succeeded."

"So it wasn't impossible," Grover Solomon mused. "Your grandma's friend only failed because he went in alone."

"Who said he failed?" Alice countered. "Perhaps he weakened the spirit to the point where others could finally defeat her. The tools my grandmother gave that man enabled him to see and confront the *gwishin* in a manner he could not have accomplished on his own."

"The tools she gave—Hang on, are you talking about whatever you just did to me?" Grover Solomon demanded, both excited and terrified at the prospect. "Did you give me the same tools just now?"

She stared up at him, and he could almost see the path of her gaze the way he had seen the cicadas' song, as precise and penetrating as the beam of a laser boring into his mind.

After a moment she said, "Do not go back to your house tonight."

"What about tomorrow? I'm in sort of a time crunch here."

Alice shrugged. "Like I said earlier, I have never fought a *gwishin*. Goodnight, Grover Solomon."

"Oh," he said, taken aback at the sudden close to their conversation. "Yes, goodnight. Thank you."

She turned and headed up the sidewalk, disappearing into the night she and her needles had brought to new life.

The DTs

Grover Solomon disobeyed. The moment Alice disappeared around the corner at the end of the block, he leapt into his car. He had to visit his house before whatever she had done to him could wear off completely. But during the brief drive between the Martins' house and his own, something began to happen inside him. As Alice put it, red lights were turning green throughout his body and mind, and traffic that had sat stationary for a long time was beginning to roll.

He parked under the single arc sodium streetlamp that painted the patch of street in front of his house a harsh orange-pink tinge. But he did not exit the car. He huddled in the driver's seat, squeezing the bejesus out of the steering wheel and bracing himself against a rising wave of rage and horror and grief and shame. Had Alice known this would happen? Was this why she'd warned him not to come back here?

The same raw, animal instinct that had driven him out of his house earlier today was telling him to run now too. Run for his *life,* because once all this stuff hit, there would be nothing to do but ride it out and hope he didn't drown. This wasn't red lights turning green; it was the collapse of a dam.

And when the flood finally crashed over him, it literally slammed his body backward against the seat. He quaked and convulsed while tears ran in salt streams into the corners of his mouth. He opened his jaws and roared at the windshield until he tasted something like metal on the back of his tongue. His sobs became so ragged and violent that they sounded like desperate, unhinged laughter.

A tiny part of his mind remained curiously awake and detached during all of this, and it wondered clinically whether this might be what it felt like to die.

Sometime later, after he was able to stop sobbing and the shakes had subsided into occasional shivers, he finally saw the clinical detachment for what it was: he was in shock.

And why not? that same small part of him asked coldly. He had never been allowed to work through Lazarus's death. For God's sake, his only friend in the world had been burned alive and then deliberately forgotten. And as if that weren't bad enough on its own, now he learned that some nameless rich man had tried to rape his mother, prompting her to suffer panic attacks which had also been covered up, first by Kurt Martin and then by Grover Solomon's parents themselves.

How could they never have told him? He was their son.

He thought too of Lazarus's parents sitting in the front row of church every Sunday, Bibles open piously across their laps as though they did not regularly lay their own son across those same laps with his back, butt and legs bared for the belt.

Maybe Autumn was right, he thought savagely. Maybe marriage and religion really did screw people up forever. He recalled the sensation of his old warped pine crucifix snapping in half in his back pocket and thought, *Good.*

Then he opened his door, leaned out of the car, and vomited

a thick column of half-digested pizza onto the pavement. Grimly wiping the back of his hand across his lips, he started the car and pulled forward several feet, away from the puddle of sick. As he braked again, a half-empty water bottle rolled into sight down in the passenger side footwell, a relic from who knew how long ago. He snatched it up and drained the warmish water before at last stepping out into the street. His head and fingertips still buzzed from the episode inside the car, but otherwise he felt cleansed. It was like the blissful, hollowed out sensation he'd experienced when Autumn had touched his forehead, but magnified a thousand times. Yet he also felt weak and frail, as if he were recovering from the flu.

"I'm growing up," he mumbled, and staggered slightly with another bout of shivers.

He halted at the head of the walk leading up to his old front door. The house stared down at him, quiet and mundane, framed in black sky. Except...

Grover Solomon spun on the spot, attempting to peer in every direction at once. Aside from the pink-orange cone of light from the streetlamp down on the corner, the night remained as still and dark as ever. But when he faced the house he could see...what?

He reached up and jammed his thumbs against the spot between his eyes where Autumn had touched him earlier. His nails dug painfully into the skin, but he held them there for a full thirty seconds.

This is nuts, he thought. *Forget shock, I'm completely delirious.*

What he saw when he opened his eyes only strengthened this notion. Something like heat shimmers drifted lazily around the house, so subtle as to be nearly invisible. The shimmering things looked like a warren of mole tunnels carved through the air. Grover Solomon watched them roil and whirl for several minutes before he could convince himself he wasn't imagining them.

He walked forward and dipped his arm into one of the shimmers. At once he heard a very familiar high, delighted belly laugh.

An icy breeze puffed across his legs in two quick gusts as if two children had just sprinted past him. He leapt backward, but more out of reflex than fear. Because sticking his arm into the shimmer had felt *great*. For one instant he'd actually experienced the delight he'd heard in that high laugh.

Before he could talk himself out of it, he stepped forward and plunged his whole body into the shimmer.

Lazarus tears around the corner of the house, yellow rubber boots kicking up sprays of snow. He wears a red winter parka with matted grey fur lining the hood. A snarl of yellowish stuffing floofs out from a rip in one shoulder. Under the coat he wears a pair of lavender snow pants with Care Bears stitched into the elastic suspenders. The winter has been unusually frigid, and the coat and pants were the only items the local Goodwill had carried in Laz's size. But whatever the clothes look like, they are warm, and Laz's parents, possibly feeling guilty for making their son wear girls' clothing, have been uncharacteristically permissive lately. Laz doesn't have a mark on him.

Perhaps this is why he is in such a tremendous mood today. He is especially delighted with himself right now for having drilled Grover Solomon right in the kisser with a snowball a moment ago.

Ten paces behind Laz, Grover Solomon chugs into view, face red and stinging, crystals of snow clinging to his hair. His snowsuit is black and gray and fits better than Laz's, but he still can't keep up with his friend. Then Laz stumbles and Grover Solomon is on him. He scoops up great mittenfuls of snow and stuffs them down Laz's collar—revenge for the snowball.

Laz howls with cold and glee and shoves Grover Solomon off him. "Oh, you're gonna get it so bad now!"

Switching instantly from predator to prey, Grover Solomon pelts off back in the direction he came from, squealing with happy terror. Lazarus scrambles to his feet and lunges after him, going nearly horizontal in the air, arms stretched out like Superman. He catches Grover Solomon at the knees and both of them go sprawling again, rolling around, giggling like maniacs and cramming as much snow as possible into each other's clothes.

"Grover Solomon!" a voice shouted. Feet pounded up the cement toward him and he felt a warm hand at the small of his back.

His struggle back into his adult mind came more quickly and naturally than it had this afternoon. And as before, when his eyes finally came into focus, Autumn's concerned features filled his vision.

"You okay?" she asked.

"Yes," he said thickly. At some point he had sat down on the sidewalk without realizing it. With Autumn's help, he staggered upright. "What are you doing here?"

"Getting some air," she said evasively.

"Leon didn't want to come along?"

Autumn's eyes seemed to flash like strobe lights on some kind of emotional alarm system. "He knows me better than that. But what are you doing here? After everything that happened today I assumed you'd want to steer clear of this place tonight."

Grover Solomon looked away, scanning the air around the house for the swoops and whorls of…whatever had been swooping and whorling around his house. Sure enough, those shimmery tunnels still encircled the house, lazy and innocuous as motes of dust in an afternoon sunbeam.

"Something's changed," he said. "I think something's wrong with me."

"Why?"

"Your friend Alice used her needles on me, and now I'm seeing things I've never seen before."

"Is it your old pal Odetta? Because if she's here right now, just hook me up with those ghostbusting weapons in your trunk and point me in the right direction. I've got a whole industrial boiler full of steam to blow off, and punching a ghost in the face sounds like a terrific way to start."

He shook his head. "Not Odetta. It's—I don't know how to explain it."

She cocked her head and gave him that appraising stare she was so good at. "Show me."

His entire body erupted in gooseflesh. He wouldn't have been more startled if she'd socked him in the gut. He reached out and took her arm. "What did y—"

Her free hand crashed down on his forearm and she twisted out of his grip. In an instant she'd put six feet between them and her posture suggested she was ready to make a fight of it if he came at her again. He suddenly recalled how she'd kicked the half-door hard enough to crack the wall behind it.

"I'm sorry," he said, cradling his wrist. The spot where she'd struck him throbbed. "You just surprised me."

"Ditto," she said coolly. A dark red ring was forming around her bicep. Evidently he'd grabbed her much more forcefully than he'd realized.

"I'm sorry," he said again, retreating a step back himself. "When you said 'show me,' I just…that was the name of a game Lazarus and I used to play."

"So naturally it made you want to rip off my arm."

"No, I—" How could he explain? "Okay, Laz had this deck of cards with naked ladies on them, like the card you found up on third. Our game, Show Me, was like…Did you ever play Go Fish?"

Autumn eased herself into a normal stance again, although Grover Solomon felt a new, rather chilly barrier between them. "Of course."

"Show Me was like that. You know, 'Do you have any fours?' 'No, go fish.' Except in addition to pulling a card out of the pile we also—" Grover Solomon cleared his throat. "We removed a piece of clothing too."

"Okay…?" said Autumn. She seemed to be waiting for something.

"I've never told anyone about it before. Our parents would have killed us." He paused. "Actually, Laz's parents really might have killed him for it."

"God, I'm so sick of this!" Autumn exploded. "Religious peo-ple and sex. It's Odetta Koop and her weird coed nunnery all over again."

When he didn't reply, she made an impatient *tch!* sound. "Little kids are always trying to figure out their bodies, aren't they? Take this little boy I used to babysit. He was two years old and he never quit playing with his penis. When you changed his diaper or put him in the bath—anytime his pants were down he was poking at it and tugging on it and just…figuring out how everything worked down there. And it was *fine*. He wasn't weird or perverted." She glowered, silently daring him to contradict her. "And neither were you guys. You think you and Lazarus were the first boys ever to huddle around pictures of naked women or play strip poker and compare boners?"

Grover Solomon turned away. If his face got any hotter his hair would surely burst into flame. "Playing Show Me is how I found out that Laz's parents hit him so much. After a while it seemed like Laz only wanted to play when he had really bad bruises. I think he just wanted someone else to know."

"Did you ever tell anyone?" Autumn's voice had grown much quieter all of a sudden.

He nodded miserably.

"Your parents?"

He nodded again.

"They already knew." It was not a question.

The two of them stood in the shadowy front yard with cicadas buzzing ceaselessly around them, she watching him, he the glowing currents wafting around the house.

"Thought I'd find you guys here!" a new voice called.

Grover Solomon jumped. Autumn merely craned her neck around. A tall, lumpy figure was approaching on the sidewalk, still mostly hidden in the shadow of one of the remaining elm trees on the corner of the property. As the figure emerged into the orange glow of the streetlamp it resolved itself as Leon, laden with very odd cargo. He wore a camping backpack with rolled sleeping bags strapped to the top and bottom. In one hand he carried a third sleeping bag, and in the other a small duffel.

"You going on a trip?" Autumn asked mildly.

"Nope." Leon set the duffel bag gently on the ground as if it contained something fragile. "My parents just need time to work some stuff out."

"What happened?" Autumn demanded. Her eyes narrowed. "What did your mom say?"

Leon shrugged out of the backpack and set it down too. "*One of them made a comment that he or she will feel very lousy about in the morning. But until then, we're not spending another minute in that house. I made an executive decision.*"

"What did she say?" Autumn persisted, hands rising dangerously to her hips.

But Leon shook his head. "They need time." Suddenly he frowned, looking between them. "Is everything all right? Did something happen here?"

Before either could answer, the duffel bag at Leon's feet meowed.

This time Autumn jumped. "What in the world…?"

Looking down, Grover Solomon saw that the sides of the duffel bag were made of a fine black mesh. It wasn't a regular bag at all, but a pet carrier. A triangular face with shining yellow eyes peered out from behind the mesh.

Autumn hunkered, unzipped the bag, and pulled out the Martins' cat—Penelope or Bart or whatever its name was. Its eyes and ears flicked wildly around. Autumn gaped at Leon like he'd lost his mind.

"Our canary in the coal mine," declared Leon in a satisfied sort of way.

Autumn obviously didn't understand, but Grover Solomon thought he might. And if he was right, Leon really had lost his mind.

Sleepover

They set up camp in the living room, the only carpeted space on the first floor. By unspoken consensus, they all seemed to conclude that: one, sleeping any closer to the third floor would be a bad idea; and two, they should all spend the night in the same place. For staying the night was indeed Leon's plan. He had brought quite a lot more with him than a few sleeping bags and the family cat. His backpack contained a broad mix of toiletries, bedding and extra clothes, as well as a few tins of cat food. When Grover Solomon asked—striving to keep the revulsion out of his voice—where the cat would do its business, Leon assured him that it would let them know when it needed to go out.

"And why exactly is it here at all?" Grover Solomon asked, unable to help himself. "You said something about a canary?"

"Well, we've only got about thirty-six hours to evict your ghost, right?" Leon reasoned. "And if cats really can sense spirits better than people can, we'll want Clem around to let us know if and when Odetta is creeping up on us."

The cat, which had settled itself in Autumn's lap again, stared insolently up at Grover Solomon as if it knew exactly how little he wanted it around.

"Does this mean you're planning to live here until we figure out how to get rid of Odetta?"

"That's the plan, Stan."

"So," Autumn cut in irritably, "we're *not* staying here to give your mom time to retract whatever awful thing she said about me. Glad that's settled."

Leon ignored her. He unzipped two sleeping bags and laid them out one on top of the other, making a large padded square the size of a double bed. Clearly he and Autumn were going to share a bed despite the fact that she had shed his engagement ring less than an hour ago.

Grover Solomon felt himself redden. Neither Leon nor Autumn seemed embarrassed in the slightest. It must be culture shock, he decided. As he'd told Kurt Martin, his parents had slept in twin beds for as long as he could remember. He'd learned about the birds and the bees from his father during a particularly squirm-inducing "health class" in fifth grade. But even after this lesson, he had assumed all other married couples slept in separate beds too, only crossing into one another's sleeping spaces—briefly and joylessly if his father's description had been anything to go by—to produce offspring.

Yet here was Leon, unabashedly laying out a bed for himself and Autumn *with Grover Solomon in the room.*

He had been managing to feel more or less like a grown man ever since he'd hung up on his outraged father. Now he felt like the mortified, maroon-faced twelve-year-old whose dad had enlightened him about the "biologically interlocking parts" of man and wife as though explaining how to dovetail two hunks of wood together.

Beds made, Leon reached into his pack and pulled out two books. "I borrowed these from my dad's study. Either of them duplicates of yours, Grover Solomon?" he asked, indicating the haphazard pile of paranormal literature sticking up out of the milk crate over by the wall.

Grover Solomon accepted the books and read the titles. One was a paperback called *Fire with Fire: Human Soldiers in a Demons' War*. It showed a man's silhouette wreathed in bright orange flames. The other was simply titled *Spirit War*, with the T of *Spirit* elongated in the shape of a cruciform sword.

"Nope, don't have these," he said unenthusiastically. Then, feeling he should express more gratitude for Leon's efforts, he added, "They look pretty good though."

But five minutes' perusal confirmed his suspicion that they wouldn't be much help. Both approached the subject of spiritual warfare with a focus on demon possession, and Grover Solomon doubted Odetta was a demon—at least not in the way the books used that word—and she definitely wasn't possessing him. She had remained behind in this house when he moved to Chicago, which suggested that she was tethered here somehow.

Maybe Kurt had been on the right track when he suggested a poltergeist. Then again, maybe not. Poltergeists typically made their presence known by sending knickknacks flying off shelves or tipping over furniture. Simple mischief, in other words, that could hardly be compared to burning a child to death.

He sighed and rubbed his eyes. Leon and Autumn had both dug out their phones to search online for ideas, but he didn't bother. Not only had he already been scouring the internet for months, he didn't feel much like turning his phone back on and seeing ten missed calls from his parents.

"This website says we can burn herbs to banish a spirit," said Leon thoughtfully. He scrolled with his finger. "But it doesn't say which herbs. Why would they leave that part out?"

"Probably because whoever wrote it is only burning *one* herb," said Autumn, "and they don't feel like sharing it."

Leon gave a soft snort of laughter. "Hey, here's something a little more helpful. Grover Solomon, have you tried forcefully telling Odetta Koop that she's not welcome here?"

Now it was Grover Solomon's turn to snort. "Yes."

"And?"

"It didn't go well."

After another five minutes of silence in which Grover Solomon stared vacantly at Leon and Autumn's bed, Autumn clicked her tongue in annoyance. "Am I the only person in the world who hasn't seen *The Exorcist*?"

"I haven't," said Leon and Grover Solomon together.

"Jinx," said Autumn, still looking at her phone. "You both owe me a Coke."

"I don't think that's how you play that game," said Leon.

Yet again Grover Solomon felt himself gripped by jealousy. These two spoke to each other so easily, with such comfortable familiarity, that he supposed in another few years they wouldn't even need to talk at all. They would just sit and think at each other, with bright threads of understanding flowing between them until they were fused, mind to mind and soul to soul by blinding white-hot ropes of thought and love and life. Would he, Grover Solomon, ever get to experience that kind of—

"The power of Christ compels you!" Autumn said loudly toward the ceiling.

Grover Solomon nearly fell over. He blinked rapidly, wondering if he had fallen asleep. For a moment he actually *had* seen bright threads connecting Autumn and Leon, slow and shining and fibrous.

Leon frowned at Autumn. "What was that about?"

She stared upward a bit longer as if expecting something to happen, then shrugged. "It's a quote that keeps coming up. I'm telling you, people love that *Exorcist* movie."

"Well, it was weird," said Leon gruffly. "Freaked me out."

As if to punctuate his statement, several hard raps came from somewhere above. All three of them looked expectantly upward.

The cat lifted its head off Autumn's lap, ears pricked toward the sound, but nothing more came. It laid its head down again and closed its eyes.

Autumn tossed her phone fitfully onto the nearest sleeping bag. "This is pointless. Leon, let's just go back to your parents' house and talk all this crap out with them. What can we possibly gain by hiding here?"

Grover Solomon felt a little thrill of terror. Surely they wouldn't leave him here alone.

"We're helping Grover Solomon," said Leon mulishly.

"Hardly," she countered. "And I don't think Clementine is going to be much use either."

"No." Leon scowled at the snoozing cat. "I sort of thought he'd, I don't know, go sniffing around for Odetta Koop. Find her den or something." He lifted the cat out of Autumn's lap and set it on the floor. It stood, hunched and annoyed, ears laid back, before crawling right back into Autumn's lap and settling itself into a tight ball, tail curled around its nose.

"Pathetic," said Leon. One yellow eye glared briefly back at him before closing once more.

"Look," said Grover Solomon, trying to sound as calm as possible, "it's late and we're already here. If nothing happens tonight, I'll drive you back home in the morning and you can forget about this whole thing. I know you have stuff to work out."

Autumn seemed to be x-raying him with her green eyes. Leon merely said, "You got it, man," and sat back down with his phone. After several seconds Autumn leaned forward and retrieved her phone too.

More as a show of solidarity than in any real hope that he would learn something new, Grover Solomon pulled out his own phone and switched it on. As he had feared, a record of missed calls from his parents scrolled down the screen, each one accompanied by an angry little red icon. He deleted the notifications and started typing search phrases.

Leon pointed. "What's your number, Grover Solomon?"

"Why?"

Leon shrugged. "Autumn and I have been to Chicago a couple times. Maybe we can hang out."

"Oh," said Grover Solomon stupidly. "I mean, yeah." He gave the number, painfully aware that it was the first time he had done so for anyone who wasn't from his family or job. Leon typed it in and then jabbed a final button. A moment later Grover Solomon's screen lit up with an incoming call.

"There you go," said Leon. "That's me."

"Thanks."

Almost immediately his phone lit up again.

"Me," said Autumn. She gave Grover Solomon a slight smile, full of understanding and a soft sort of kindness that might have come across as pity on someone else's face. But she said nothing, and soon all three of them were absorbed in their own little screens.

Twenty minutes later Leon finally stood and stretched. "I'm out. Time to hit the hay."

He gathered up his toiletries and headed for the restroom. He hadn't been typing or reading much on his phone anyway. He was probably worrying about the fight with his parents. Grover Solomon could identify. That long list of missed phone calls nagged at him, the mental equivalent of pebbles in his shoe.

Autumn got up as well, depositing the cat in the middle of her bed before shuffling off to join Leon. It mewed feebly after her and then began a vigorous grooming process that involved chewing rather violently at the tufts of fur between its toes. After a full minute of this, it abruptly leaped off the sleeping bag and trotted through the kitchen to the back door, where it began yowling obnoxiously.

"I think Clem wants out!" Leon called from the bathroom. "Do you mind, Grover Solomon?"

Grumbling, Grover Solomon heaved himself to his feet, made his way through the dark kitchen, and opened the back door. The cat slipped out and spent a good ten minutes sniffing around the back patio and trees. Grover Solomon squinted into the darkness for a sign of those wavering, glittering trails he'd seen earlier. Either they had vanished or he could no longer see them.

By the time the cat finished its business and came back inside, Leon and Autumn were chatting in bed. Leon lay on the upper sleeping bag, wearing a ratty old Hawkeyes t-shirt and gym shorts, one arm propped behind his head. Autumn was hidden under the covers except for one bare arm that lay between her and Leon. They were holding hands.

Grover Solomon had never felt lonelier in his life. He retreated to the bathroom, but couldn't even bring himself to brush his teeth. He laid his forehead miserably against the mirror, breath fogging the glass. At last he drew away and stared into his own eyes. "What am I doing here?" he asked. No answer came to him or his reflection. When he returned to the living room, the other two were asleep.

Midnight in Purgatory

He woke sometime later with a vague awareness that he had slept deeply but that morning had not yet come. He rolled onto his side and swept his arm clumsily across the floor for his phone to check the time. But the phone didn't seem to be there. He blinked a few times and eased up on his elbow, coming more fully to his senses. The living room was too dark to see anything. Impossibly dark, in fact. He waved his hand an inch in front of his face and saw only unbroken blackness.

He sat up, but threw himself immediately back to the floor when something skittered across his face. As the back of his head collided with the floor—not carpet, but hardwood—he heard rustling above him as though his movements had stirred a pile of old leaves.

Adrenaline surged through his body in shining silver estuaries. He knew exactly where he was.

Rising into a half crouch to avoid the slips of paper, he clawed madly at the air around him for the doorknob. But he felt nothing.

No door, no walls. Just empty air in every direction. Still crouching, he crawled forward ten feet...twenty. Still the slips of paper rustled above him, and still he met no door or wall.

His outstretched hand fell to the floor in relief. This was not the first time he had dreamed of being trapped in the crawlspace up on third. True, this dream seemed rather more real than previous ones, but perhaps Alice's treatments had affected his unconscious mind as well as the conscious one.

Who knew green traffic lights could cause so much trouble? he thought wryly, and congratulated himself for staying cool in the face of this new nightmare. He *was* dreaming, of that he could be certain. If there had been any doubt, he could also feel—even if he could not see—that he was naked.

He eased back onto the hardwood, hugging his knees to his chest, and waited for the dream to change, as dreams do. Maybe next he would be delivering a presentation to one of his clients in Chicago, naked as a jaybird and pointing to diagrams on a whiteboard.

But after several minutes of claustrophobic silence, it became clear that the dream wouldn't let him off so easily.

"Fine," he said. He rocked forward, putting his weight on the balls of his feet, and suddenly leapt upward into the whispering, slithering mass of hanging papers. He scrunched his eyes against the inevitable crack of his head on the ceiling. Maybe a good thump to the noggin would wake him before anything really awful happened.

His head and shoulders parted the sea of papers without resistance, and then gravity brought him crashing back down to the wood floor, rattling his teeth. Frowning, he lifted his arms over his head. The peaked ceiling should be slanting downward on either side of him. Once again, he felt nothing. The hanging slips of paper might have reached upward for infinity.

And then he heard it—very distant, a metallic rattling sound. He stopped moving and listened hard. The rattling stopped. There came an unmistakable squall of metal on metal, as of a great iron gate rolling open on disused hinges. This was followed by a soft, rapid thudding that sounded like Odetta's heavy pacing sped up to a run. And it was growing louder. Drawing closer.

Never mind that this was a dream. Never mind that he'd lost his clothing and he couldn't see where he was going. He flung himself in the opposite direction from the sound, swatting the hanging papers out of the way. He knew running would only make panic worse, but screw what he knew. He was *not* going to let Odetta Koop catch him in this pitch-black cave with its paper stalactites.

The thudding behind him grew louder, overlaid by the slap of wide, bare feet on hardwood.

"Wake up!" he commanded himself as he ran. "Wake up! Wake up!"

Now he heard breathing too, heavy and labored and somehow masculine, which only made the panic worse.

"*Wake up wake up wake up wake up!*" he shrieked. Paper sliced at his hands, covering them in minuscule, shallow cuts.

Suddenly he recalled what Alice had said about the man who had fought the *gwishin*. The way the man had fled the spirit and run to his death screaming nonsense words.

No. His life would not end that way.

Without thinking, without knowing what he meant to do next, he stopped dead and spun around. Something huge crashed into him, but he met the impact on his feet and shoved back hard. Whatever had collided with him flew backward and hit the floor, wheezing.

"Get away from me!" Grover Solomon bellowed. "I've got friends now, and I'm not afraid of you!"

Several paces ahead, a tiny orange ember of light sparked feebly to life. Surrounded by complete blackness, it looked oddly distant, like a lantern carried by someone on the far side of a lake. The ember split apart and hovered—two orange eyes dancing in the dark. A drawn, stubbly face materialized around the eyes, and Grover

Solomon could finally make out the features of the thing that had chased him. He'd seen them once before, this very afternoon on a playing card. It was Lazarus Beachy, gaunt and mature and weary, with skin the color of cold, dead ash.

If shock could have yanked Grover Solomon out of his dream, this would have been the moment. He staggered backward, ever more hanging slips of paper slithering against his neck and shoulders like desiccated fingers. But he didn't wake. Time spun mercilessly onward as he and the Lazarus who would never be stared at one another across a chasm of life and death.

"God, no," the adult Lazarus croaked glumly from the ground. "Not you too."

A ghostly hand appeared, dark gray against the ubiquitous black, and reached out to be grasped. Helplessly, Grover Solomon took it and hauled his friend upright. Lazarus pulled him into a brief, fraternal embrace. He felt solid enough, and Grover Solomon noted that his old friend also seemed to be naked.

When they broke apart, Lazarus was frowning. The flames in his eyes intensified, throwing the angles of his face into sharp orange and black relief. "Something's wrong. How did you get here?"

A short, involuntary bark of laughter escaped Grover Solomon. Something was wrong, all right.

"You're not dead," Lazarus persisted.

Grover Solomon reached up and patted his torso, which he could feel but still not see. "I sure hope not."

"You think you're dreaming."

"Yes," he agreed, even though he didn't. A paranoid intuition came to him. What if this *was* a dream, just not *his* dream. What if he didn't exist at all? What if his nearly twenty-five years of life and memories were only a fabrication of someone else's dreaming mind?

"Stop being so dramatic," Lazarus said dryly, as if he had heard Grover Solomon's thoughts. He raised a dim, ashy finger and poked Grover Solomon hard in the shoulder. "See? You're as real as I am."

Not at all comforted, Grover Solomon said, "How did you get here, then?"

A sigh seemed to ripple through the hanging strips of paper. One of them drifted like a shadow across Lazarus's face and he batted it away. "Let's sit. I doubt we have much time, and we'll be harder to spot down below."

"Harder to spot?" Grover Solomon asked uneasily. His eyes raked the unbroken darkness around them as he hunkered beside Lazarus.

"I don't know how you found this place," Lazarus said in a low, urgent voice, "and maybe you don't either. But the hell with any of that. What matters is that your friends are right."

"My friends? What do you—"

"They didn't know I died. No one knows I died. You have to realize how insane that is."

"I do," breathed Grover Solomon.

"The only way—and I mean *only* way—our parents could have kept the fire a secret is if…" He raised his eyebrows expectantly, as if waiting for Grover Solomon to compete the thought for him. When it became obvious that wouldn't happen, he said, "…there never *was* a fire."

Another sigh rustled through the papers, louder this time.

Laz's orange eyes flicked upward and then back to Grover Solomon. "There's so much to say. So many things I've wanted to tell you for so long."

"Like what?"

Laz seemed to be organizing his thoughts. "Do you know what your dad found when he got the door open that day?"

"He never told—"

"Nothing," Lazarus cut him off. "Well, no body anyway. Didn't you ever wonder why your dad didn't have to use the fire extinguisher? My clothes were just lying there, empty, but laid out in the shape of a person. Along with my dad's cigarette lighter. My belt was still buckled in my jeans, my socks still tucked into my shoes.

It was like I'd just been beamed out of my clothes like frigging Star Trek. And your dad, blessed moron that he is, thought I'd laid them out like that."

"That doesn't even…Why would he think—"

"Your parents and my parents agreed on one thing: they believed I'd run away. My parents insisted that you laid out those things and made up a story about a fire so they wouldn't come looking for me."

"That's—You—I was—" Grover Solomon stammered, outraged.

"*Your* parents," Laz went on, "thought I planted the clothes myself and tricked you into thinking the house had eaten me or something. They knew this place terrified you, even then. At first they agreed to help my parents search for me, but after about a week, my mother suggested that she would be able to get you to tell her where I'd gone if she could talk to you alone, maybe with one of your dad's belts."

"*What?*" A very real shiver ran across Grover Solomon's dreaming body.

"I know. Super classy lady, my mom. That sort of ended their friendship. Your parents had always known that mine got pretty, ah, physical with punishments. But I don't think they ever knew or believed the extent of it."

Grover Solomon gave his head a little shake. "But wait, if you didn't die, I mean, if you aren't dead, where are you? Why haven't I seen you in fifteen years?"

Lazarus's eyebrows rose. That familiar little smile Grover Solomon had seen so many times curled Laz's stubbly upper lip. "What makes you think I'm not dead?"

Without warning the floor around them trembled with several hard impacts, as though an army of lumberjacks had just swung their hatchets into the floorboards.

The embers in Lazarus's eyes flared like torches, casting a circle of amber light around himself and Grover Solomon. The two of them were caught in a tight cage of paper strips that had been driven deep into the wooden floor, straight and rigid as fence posts. Laz's body was now fully visible, long and lean and coiled into a defensive crouch. Grover Solomon looked down at where his own body should be, but still saw nothing. He didn't even cast a shadow.

"It's her," Laz said matter-of-factly. His burning eyes bored in to Grover Solomon's. "Listen, if you've come this far, maybe you can find me for real. *Please* find me. I don't want to be here anymore."

"But—"

Booming footsteps echoed around the paper prison. They sounded nothing like the soft patter of Laz's earlier pursuit. The air itself had changed, had become heavier, textured somehow. It grated against Grover Solomon's invisible skin like a coarse, dry sponge. He'd never felt anything like it, yet it could mean only one thing: Odetta Koop was coming. And in this oppressive, stygian dreamscape, she would have him at last, consume him in ways he couldn't even imagine.

"You have to get out of here," Laz whispered urgently. He spun around and grasped one of the rigid strips of paper that had become the bars of their cage.

"What do you mean find you 'for real'?" Grover Solomon asked desperately. "You're right here."

The hardened paper came free with squeal that sounded like metal on wood. "Yeah, I'm here, all right," Laz grunted. "But you're not."

He swung the paper like a broadsword in a wide arc. Grover Solomon jerked backward, but too late. The paper caught his throat just above the Adam's apple and he cried out against a burst of hot pain. White-gold light splashed out from the cut. Laz raised a forearm to shield his eyes, and…

The Seduction of Grover Solomon, Part 1

...he awoke with a gasp, the sleeping bag soft and warm under his back, Lazarus's voice still echoing in his ears.

Please find me.

This time when he opened his eyes he saw the ceiling of his old living room, but the sight brought him little comfort. The whole room was illuminated with a ghostly peach-colored light that reminded him forcibly of the embers in Lazarus's eyes. But a glance out the window revealed that the light originated from the very mundane source of the streetlamp outside.

To his left he saw Autumn's profile, rimed in shadow, lips parted, chest slowly rising and falling. At some point she had emerged from under the sleeping bag. She wore a tight halter top and very short shorts, both of which made her pregnancy much more noticeable. The subtle mound of her belly strained at the shirt and the elastic hem of her shorts. Her sleeping form made such a peaceful, angelic image after the nightmare that he could have stared at her until sunrise.

A pair of triangular ears and glowing yellow eyes rose from Autumn's other side to regard him haughtily, as if making sure he was behaving himself, before sinking back down out of sight.

He lay back too, doing his best not to dwell on the upsetting dream but dwelling on it all the same. The image of Lazarus's glowing eyes and stubbly cheeks as he begged to be set free seemed carved into Grover Solomon's imagination like a wound.

As quietly as he could, he lifted his phone off the floor to check the time. "*Ow!*" he hissed. The pad of his index finger stung suddenly as he pressed the button to activate the screen. In the harsh white-blue light, he saw dozens of tiny, shallow cuts across his fingers and palm. Paper cuts.

Find me.

A shiver wracked him so hard that the cat stirred again and gave a perturbed little mew. Grover Solomon slipped out of his sleeping bag and crept past Autumn, Leon and the cat, whose glowing eyes followed him all the way out of the room.

Ever since he'd begun to suspect the existence of Odetta Koop's ghost, Grover Solomon had believed her to be the sole architect of his childhood misery. Something about this house had always sat on his chest like a stone, suffocating him and stunting his emotional growth. If not for Lazarus Beachy, he might not even have known what life felt like without it. But Lazarus's charismatic presence had always kept the extra emotional weight at bay, had freed Grover Solomon to breathe in his own home.

Yet it appeared that Lazarus hadn't been able to fend off Odetta forever. She'd caught him in the end, snatched him up in a gout of ghostly flame, and now he needed Grover Solomon to repay the favor. And if Odetta really did have Lazarus trapped somewhere in this house, she would use only one place as her prison.

Find me.

Instead of banishing Lazarus's haunted, orange-eyed face from his mind, Grover Solomon fixed it there, carried it before him like a beacon. Clad in his white t-shirt and boxer shorts, he crept past the cedar closet in the entry room, up the stairs, through the second floor hallway, and up the final claustrophobic tunnel to the third floor.

As his head and shoulders passed through the trapdoor, he instantly felt a tingle on the back of his neck. He'd experienced this sensation enough times over the years to know exactly what it was; even before he'd learned about the existence of Odetta Koop, there had been no mistaking that feeling. He was being watched.

But for the first time he wondered whose eyes were on him.

He stepped fully onto the third floor and fixed his own eyes on the half-door, still tight shut, still with that sugary dusting of plaster on the knob. The lock lay in the carpet a few feet from the door where he'd left it this afternoon. That same peach-colored light filtered through the windows from outside.

"Laz?"

A wave of gooseflesh speckled his scalp and forearms. He hadn't meant to speak aloud, and his voice sounded simultaneously loud and flat in the big room. The sensation of being watched grew stronger than ever. An invisible gaze raked him like the hot beam of a searchlight. The half-door gave an almost imperceptible rattle. He probably could have talked himself into believing it had been his imagination, except he distinctly saw several grains of plaster drift down from the knob.

Any other day of his life, he would have fled. But the time for cowardice had passed. Lazarus needed him.

"Laz? Is that you? Come on, man. You asked me to find you. Here I am."

The doorknob twisted slowly, as if cranked by a weak hand on the other side of the door. The ancient springs and mechanisms in the door squeaked, and there was a faint *click* as the door unlatched itself. But it did not open fully. It merely hung ajar on its hinges, still and silent as the rest of the third floor, with a half inch of darkness now visible between the door and the jamb. Very clearly beckoning him forward.

He ran his hands through his hair, which felt like it was standing tall enough to brush the ceiling. But this situation was precisely why he'd come back to New Canaan, wasn't it? The opportunity to square off against Odetta Koop? And that had been before Laz had come into the mix.

"You asked for it," he muttered, unsure whether he was speaking to Odetta or himself. He marched briskly forward, grasped the plaster-covered knob, and wrenched the door open. The hanging papers rustled as they'd done in his dream.

He squatted and peered inside. "Laz?"

No answer came. He let his head droop and he blew out a long breath. What had he really expected? He and Autumn had entered the room just this afternoon and it had been empty then too.

His head snapped up. The little room *hadn't* been empty this afternoon. He hunkered and crawled forward, eyes open to their widest extent to cut through the dark...

There it was. The card he'd dropped, resting in the back corner. He stretched out a hand toward it, but just as his fingertips brushed the glossy surface, heavy footsteps pounded across the carpet out in the main room.

Grover Solomon did the only thing that made sense. He spun around and yanked the door closed, plunging himself into complete darkness. The hanging papers fluttered around his head exactly as they had done in the dream.

Here we go again, he thought, and once again applauded his ability think wry thoughts in the middle of a crisis.

But then something happened that had not happened in the dream. The doorknob began creaking again, now from the other side. Grover Solomon seized it, and a brief struggle ensued, with someone on the other side twisting and jostling the knob while he held on as tightly as he could.

The force on the knob vanished suddenly, but Grover Solomon didn't let go. He took several deep breaths, thinking hard. Of everything he had read or heard about fighting spirits in the last few months, the most compelling information had come just this evening from Alice and her story about the *gwishin*. About how people sometimes had to attempt impossible things.

He closed his eyes—not that it mattered in this complete blackness—and pictured the two bright spots he'd seen when Alice had performed the acupuncture on his hands. He imagined every traffic light in the city of Chicago turning green at once. He imagined a whole city's worth of cars rolling smoothly forward toward their destinations. Cars by the millions that surged forward and turned into little pulses of yellow-gold light, coursing not through a city, but through his own body in strong, steady lanes wider than any expressway. He imagined Lazarus crouched next to him, full-grown and weary, but strong. Ready to stand alongside him against whatever waited outside.

Just as he was about to open the door, the knob twisted again, suddenly and violently, slipping out of his grip. The door flew open and he fell backward onto his elbows, only to find himself staring up into the face of—

"Autumn?" he panted.

"Your bed was empty." She squatted outside the door in her nightclothes, silhouetted by dim peach-colored light from the streetlamp outside. "Did she trap you in here?"

He let himself thud backward onto the hard wood floor, heart hammering madly in his chest. "Not exactly."

She offered a hand and he accepted it. She pulled him easily forward out of the crawlspace. She really was strong.

"Did you shut yourself in there?" she asked. She did not release his hand. "Why would you do that? You're sweating like crazy."

He hesitated. But even though he'd only known Autumn for a single day, he knew she wouldn't make fun of him.

"I had a dream that Lazarus was up here. He asked me to find him. He begged me. I had to check."

Autumn squeezed his hand supportively. She was staring up into his face with concern and something like admiration.

"You didn't have to come alone."

He shrugged, starting to feel distinctly hot around the collar now. She was looking at him the way she had looked at Leon after he'd sacrificed his hands to protect her and Grover Solomon this afternoon.

"Look," he said, "I know you guys said you would help, but maybe you were right before. You should get out of here. I already got Leon hurt today, and you have the baby to worry about. I talked to Alice after we left Leon's place, and she made it sound like Odetta could be even more dangerous than we realized. She had a whole story about some ghost her grandmother helped fight back in Korea."

He was babbling, and he knew it. Still Autumn gazed raptly up at him. She stepped closer, clasping his hand between her breasts. "And you came up here, all alone, to keep us out of danger. That's so brave. So selfless." Their faces were only inches apart now. "Do you have a girlfriend, Grover Solomon?"

He tried to pull away, but she gripped him more tightly. His knuckles popped painfully.

"Autumn, what are you—"

"Don't you think I'm beautiful?" she purred, giving him a coy smile.

A movement over her shoulder caught his eye. He looked up and saw Leon's cat leap lightly through the trapdoor onto the third floor. It advanced a few steps and froze, one forepaw raised like a hound on point.

Still holding his hand firmly to her breasts, Autumn reached up and drew his face back down to hers. Her expression had hardened. "I know what you really want. You can't hide it from me."

The hand up by his face drifted to her waist and began pulling down the hem of her shorts.

"*What are you doing?*" he yelped, leaping away from her. But she jerked him back and held him fast. He felt a tickle at his ankle and looked down, expecting to see the cat. Instead he saw something long and pale dangling between Autumn's legs, limp as a dead python.

The part of Grover Solomon's mind responsible for rational thought broke with an almost audible snap, and suddenly he was fighting like a wolverine in a hunter's trap. He kicked out and clawed at her his free hand while struggling to yank his other one out of her grip. Autumn staggered backward against the assault, nearly tripping over the thing still swinging grotesquely between her legs. It was the opening he needed. He grabbed her full in the face and shoved as hard as he could. Bits of her skin came away in flimsy tatters like old, wet newspaper. He flung them to the carpet in shock and horror.

Over by the trapdoor, the cat was backing away, hackles raised, tail curled upward like a scorpion's sting. It hissed twice before scampering down the stairs out of sight.

The creature masquerading as Autumn recovered its balance and slowly lifted its visage toward him. It no longer resembled Autumn at all, but was growing into a monstrous, shadowy figure wearing a mouldering black cape dress and a ruined mask of Autumn's face, torn across the bridge of its nose. In place of Autumn's green eyes were two uneven lines of black stitches shaped like X's.

The figure glared blindly up from a half-crouch. The Autumn mask rippled strangely as it opened its mouth to speak. "I always wanted better for you." Without another word it spun away to follow the cat down the stairs.

Grover Solomon stood immobilized. Half of his mind shrieked that he was *done* here. Done forever and ever, amen. And forget going back to Chicago; he would only be far enough from New Canaan when he was lying on the beach in Sydney frigging Australia.

But the other half—the half that had carried him up to the crawlspace to hunt for Lazarus after his dream—wondered dazedly if he had just stood toe to toe with Odetta Koop and come out ahead. Had Alice really given him some kind of weapon after all?

The idea propelled him through the trapdoor. He would not get another chance like this.

The Voice in the Closet

The second floor hallway flashed past him, full of shadows but seemingly empty. Odetta had escaped. *The cedar closet!* he thought. If she couldn't hide in her crawlspace, that would surely be her second choice.

But he didn't make it to the first floor. He slid to a halt at the end of the hall, nearly slamming into Autumn. She was climbing the steps, wide-eyed with concern.

"What happened?" she asked. "We heard you shouting."

Grover Solomon instinctively retreated a step. He stared wildly at Autumn, searching for any small sign that might betray a disguise. "Did you see anyone run past here?"

"What do you mean? There's no one else here. Look, what's going on?" she demanded, mounting the last riser onto the second floor landing. "You saw someone up here?"

"Yeah," he breathed, struggling against a suffocating feeling of *déjà vu.* "I dreamed...I don't know. Odetta, she..."

"Hey, calm down. It's okay." She reached for his arm. "We're togeth—"

"*Get back!*" Grover Solomon snarled, and before he knew what he was doing, he charged forward and shoved her with every bit of strength he possessed.

Autumn was fast, all right. She threw out her hand and caught the bannister as she toppled backward. But even her lightning reflexes could not overcome the momentum and gravity working against her. She spun sideways and hit the railing hard enough to shake the walls before pitching head-first the rest of the way down the stairs. Her belly caught most of her weight as she landed hard on the sharp edge of the bottom step.

There was a distressed cry from the living room. An instant later Leon was beside her. "Autumn?" he whispered feverishly. "Come on, honey, you okay? Please be okay."

Odetta Koop, Lazarus, and everything else Grover Solomon had experienced in the last hour fled his mind as the reality of what he had just done crashed over him. What if the fall had snapped Autumn's neck? What if she was already dead or paralyzed? He clutched at his throat, unable to breathe. He tried to descend the stairs but his knees shook so badly he had to sit down or risk toppling over himself and landing on her.

Even as these panicked thoughts raced through his mind, Autumn stirred. "I'm fine," she wheezed. "Just...winded."

Grover Solomon sagged against the handrail in relief.

With Leon's help she managed to stand, which seemed to confirm that she'd suffered no lasting damage.

"Sure you're okay?" Leon asked gently. "You want to lay down until you catch your breath?"

She was clutching her stomach. "Bathroom."

"Here, I'll take you."

But she shrugged him off and shuffled toward the bathroom, still holding her stomach. Leon watched her anxiously until she turned into the bathroom. A bright shaft of light fell across the floor, then narrowed and disappeared as she swung the door closed.

Leon turned up to Grover Solomon. "What happened? Did she just trip or—"

Grover Solomon couldn't answer. His mouth worked to form words, but his throat was still little more than a pinhole.

The bathroom door crashed open. Autumn stumbled out and threw herself into Leon's arms. Tears streamed down her cheeks in bright tracks. "I'm spotting! Oh God, Leon, what if the baby…" She lost control completely and began to sob into his chest.

"It's going to be okay," he said, though he sounded hollow and shocked. "Grover Solomon, give me your car keys, now!"

Grover Solomon didn't waste time asking questions. He dashed down past them to the living room, fished his keys out of his shorts, and returned to Leon, who was whispering inaudible comforts to the still sobbing Autumn. "You sure you don't want me to call an ambulance or something?"

"No, I can get her to the hospital faster than an ambulance could get here. Just go to my house tell my parents what happened. Tell them we've gone to the emergency room, and I'll call them as soon as…" He glanced down at the top of Autumn's head. "When we know something."

He took the keys and swept Autumn out of the house, one arm curled protectively around her shoulders. Grover Solomon considered calling after him to make sure he knew how to drive a manual transmission but thought better of it. If the only available vehicle had been a helicopter, Leon simply would have set his jaw and done his damnedest to fly it to the hospital.

Grover Solomon covered his face with his hands and took several deep breaths. Already, he wanted desperately to do something to make up for endangering Autumn so badly, as if he could reverse what he'd done by simply being helpful. It was a childish and impossible urge, but the alternative would be to sit down right here at the base of the stairs and let himself fall apart completely. Better to be doing something. Anything.

He could start by following's Leon instructions to relay Autumn's injury to Kurt and Cynthia. He hurried back to the living room, pulled on his shorts, and checked the time on his phone one more time—less than twenty minutes had passed since he'd woken from his dream of Lazarus—before jamming it into his pocket.

There was also the question of what to do about the Martins' cat, which had gone MIA after taking off down the stairs from the third floor. He felt guilty for leaving it, but he also couldn't waste time investigating every corner of the house. Cats could take care of themselves, couldn't they? Nine lives and all that? And if it took a dump on the floor or something while he was gone, he had plenty of time to clean up the mess before Monday morning.

He'd just laid his hand on the doorknob to exit the house when he felt a familiar tingle at the back of his neck. He twisted around and felt a terrible thrill like he'd grabbed an electric fence. The cedar closet stood ajar, though it had definitely been closed a minute ago when he'd gone to retrieve his clothes from the living room.

"I know why you're here," a flat, harsh woman's voice announced from the closet. It sounded completely different than the thing that had impersonated Autumn. This was the voice of a strict, old-fashioned teacher accustomed to being obeyed. Odetta Koop's true voice. "You're here for *him.*"

Grover Solomon's breath came in ragged hitches, but he stood his ground. This was the moment he had hoped for and dreaded since he had agreed to come back to this house one last time. "I'm here b-because you shouldn't be," he said shakily. "I'm here to kick you out of this house."

Silence greeted this pronouncement. Outrage radiated from the closet like heat from a furnace.

"I saved you," the voice spat.

Grover Solomon blinked. This comment was so far out of left field, so completely nuts, that for a moment his curiosity outweighed his fear. "Saved me?"

"With two little words, that boy taught you a lust which nearly set you on a straight and narrow path to hell."

Grover Solomon decided he might be hallucinating after all. This made no sense. "*Show me,*" the voice drawled from the closet.

And all of a sudden something Autumn said earlier flashed into his mind. *Religious people and sex! You think you and Lazarus were the first boys ever to huddle around pictures of naked women or play strip poker and compare each other's boners?*

"You have got to be kidding," he said indignantly. "*That's* the big mystery? That's why you murdered an abused child? Because he was the first person who showed me a naked lady when I was a kid?"

All the uncertainty, all the loneliness and tragedy of his life seemed to be fusing with his rage, sharpening it into something like the blade of a weapon. And he knew exactly where to point it.

"Was Autumn right about your husbands too? Did you bump them off because they weren't pure enough for your sick little abstinence school? Did you hang all those Bible verses about sex upstairs so you could feel all righteous about becoming a murderer?"

He advanced on the cedar closet, his voice rising in pitch and volume. The room around him seemed to ring with the sound of his voice, as if he had discovered some magical harmonic that could make all the wood in the room vibrate. The clarity that had followed Alice's treatment returned, bringing a great and terrible sense of power, of possibility. Darkness seemed to fall away around him.

"You murdered my best friend. You terrorized my mother. You made me afraid to live. And now I want you out!"

He reached for the doorknob and noted, without surprise, that his whole arm seemed to be emitting a soft bluish glow. Oh, this was *right*. This was the end. He'd cornered Odetta and now he would grab her by the scruff of her neck with his magic glowing hand and heave her out the door like a bouncer tossing a disorderly drunk from a nightclub.

"That boy did teach you lust," Odetta's flat voice declared grimly. "But not for any woman."

Grover Solomon halted with his hand inches from the door. He stopped so suddenly and completely that he might have been a clockwork toy whose spring had just unwound itself.

"Ask yourself," Odetta coaxed. "When you watch your new friends cling to one another and exchange their long, lusty gazes, of whom are you truly jealous? Him? Or *her?*" She drew out the last word in a long, throaty growl.

His mind flashed to the image of Leon and Autumn lying side by side on their makeshift bed in the living room, fingers interlaced. And he wondered whether Leon's hands were rough or smooth.

"I was right to worry, wasn't I?" Odetta Koop went on, and now there was something like satisfaction in her voice. "The mere memory of your foul little boyfriend has drawn you back here after all this time. Did you enjoy embracing him in the dark of your dream? What do you hope will happen if you manage to free him?"

Grover Solomon shook his head. Where had that weird thought about Leon's hands come from?

"So…" he stammered. If only he could regain that feeling of power from before. "How do you know about that dream? Does that mean Laz really is here? Are you keeping him prisoner somehow?"

Her voice went on as if he had not spoken. "I see how it is. You return now, full of a young man's bile against the only one who has ever tried to protect you from your own unnatural desire."

Silence filled the room like a poison gas. Grover Solomon's hand fell to his side, powerless and mundane.

"You can still recover," Odetta whispered. There was a flutter of movement in the cracked doorway, as if she were leaning forward to deliver a secret. "There is a point from which there can be no return, a moment at which you become forever abhorrent to God. I have seen that moment come and go for other men. But not for you. You can yet be saved. You—"

Her voice broke off at a loud creak from the second floor landing. Grover Solomon jumped away from the closet, staring wildly up the stairs for this new threat. Could Odetta be in two places at once now? Had she thrown her voice to distract him like some ghastly ventriloquist?

But the figure walking down the steps toward him was not Odetta Koop. It was Lazarus. A heavy shadow obscured him like a cloud of smoke, but there could be no doubt it was the fully grown man Grover Solomon had seen on the Joker playing card and then met in his dream. As in the dream, Lazarus wore nothing. He made his way carefully down the stairs, stark naked and—Grover Solomon could not suppress the thought—absolutely gorgeous.

The cedar closet snapped shut. Grover Solomon barely noticed. "Laz?" he croaked.

Despite the gloomy shadow surrounding him, Lazarus looked delighted. "Dude, check me out. Nude descending a staircase." His old belly laugh came rolling down the stairs.

The sound lifted the hairs on Grover Solomon's arms. He had never expected to hear that laugh in a grown man's voice.

The cedar closet door rattled violently. A loud thud echoed from overhead and Grover Solomon thought he could hear a distant ticking.

Laz glanced upward as he reached the ground floor. He stood half a head taller than Grover Solomon. "She's so predictable," he sighed. "No imagination at all. Sometimes I worry the magic is gone from our relationship."

Grover Solomon shuffled backward from this new apparition. No matter how much it looked and sounded like Lazarus, he wasn't going to be taken in by another disguise. "It's still you, isn't it?" he blurted. "I mean, you're still her. Are these sick games your way of 'saving' me? First it was Autumn with a three-foot penis, so what's the gag this time? You going to give Laz a vagina full of shark teeth or poisoned tentacles or something?"

Laz's grin faded. "That's messed up, Grover Solomon. A healthy mind doesn't imagine that kind of stuff. Not that I blame you," he added kindly. "But we don't have time to discuss it, do we?" He gestured at the ceiling, from which a definite ticking could now be heard. "So let me just tell you. You're changing things here, man. I've never gotten out like this before."

"Gotten out of what?"

"I don't exactly know," Laz admitted. "Even she might not know the answer to that. But I do know that this place, where we are now, is still just the surface—the outer boundary of her fortress. You have to be prepared for anything."

"Wait, I don't—"

Laz twisted around to look at something behind him. When he turned back again he began speaking urgently, but inaudibly. The shadowy bag surrounding him solidified, turned opaque. After a moment it disappeared completely, taking the ticking sound with it.

"Laz? Please come back!" Grover Solomon stared desperately into the empty space where Lazarus's face had been. "I love you!"

He clapped his hands over his mouth. But the truth of those words ricocheted through his mind like a bullet inside a bank vault, shredding everything he had always thought he knew about himself, casting every memory of Laz in a new and terrifying light.

A tear spilled onto his cheek. Lazarus had been correct, it seemed. Odetta Koop had already started springing traps, and Grover Solomon was not prepared for them. He exited the house in unmolested silence.

Odetta's Worst Memory

The studentry of New Canaan Mennonite Academy sit at two long tables in the dining hall, boys in black plain coats and girls in black cape dresses. The darkness outside has turned the room's high windows into mirrors fogged with fragrant vapor from the cooking pots. No one speaks as roast beef, potatoes, and carrots cool, uneaten, in round iron pots at the center of each long table. The grandfather clock in the dining hall hammers away the seconds, each tick like a jab from an icepick behind Odetta's left eye. It is the fifth time this month that Zebulon has ignored the dinner bell.

An 11-year-old girl named Hannah with sharply parted blonde hair visible under her lace head covering surreptitiously slides her finger into her nose and digs around in there. Dorcas, the 17-year-old Head Girl, gently pulls Hannah's hand back into her lap. Odetta knows that Dorcas could singlehandedly keep the entire school, not just the girls, straight-backed and silent for the next hour while beef broth turns to cold jelly in the pots if that was what the situation required.

And it is this knowledge—the knowledge that Odetta has finally established the sort of school and student behavior that she and her beloved first husband Eli set out to establish all those long years ago—that drives her to do something she has never done before.

"Dorcas," she calls softly.

The Head Girl rises at once. "Yes, Headmistress?"

"Please help Hannah deliver tonight's blessing."

The younger girl, whose finger has been surreptitiously edging up the front of her dress toward her nose once more, starts horribly at the sound of her name. The ever imperturbable Dorcas nods and continues standing silently until Hannah follows suit. There is a rustle of cloth and a creak of wood as several of the students shift their weight on the benches to glance at one another in surprise before closing their eyes. This happens mostly at the boys table, where even the Head Boy, an obedient if rather dim young man named Daniel, exchanges uneasy looks with some of the older boys.

Surely they won't begin eating without the Headmaster…

"God is great…" Dorcas begins, tipping her head down to encourage Hannah.

"…and God is good," Hannah says, picking up the familiar prayer.

"And we thank Him for our food," intone the rest of the students. "By His hands we all are fed. Give us, Lord, our daily bread."

Odetta speaks along with everyone else, striving to center her mind and spirit on the words. She wants nothing more than to rush out to the woodshop where Zebulon must even now be working, lost in his own fool mind, and drag him into the dining hall to apologize yet again for his tardiness. But leaving the hall in the middle of prayer would set a poor example for the students, and Odetta Koop leads by example. Such was the foremost philosophy when she and dear Eli created their school, and it remains so to this day.

And if she ever begins to doubt whether leading by example works, all she needs to do is look at Dorcas, who after six years at New Canaan

Mennonite Academy could probably run the school as well as Odetta herself. And better than Zebulon.

It would of course crush Odetta to learn that her beloved Dorcas, just last night, spent a very enthusiastic twenty minutes necking with the Head Boy, Daniel, in her cot after lights out, even allowing him to cup her breast through the rough cotton shift all of the female students wear to sleep. Odetta will find out about their relationship—everything that happens in her school comes back to her in the end—but for the moment Dorcas has her complete trust.

"Amen," say twenty-nine voices that should be thirty.

"I must excuse myself," Odetta says. This time it's not just the boys who glance at each other. She waits until everyone is still. "If I do not return before the end of dinner, please fill two plates and leave them in the kitchen. I trust that clean up, evening devotions, and lights out will occur at their normal times?"

"Yes, Headmistress," says Dorcas at once, demonstrating her only failing as Head Girl. Really, the Head Boy should respond first, followed by the Head Girl. However, Daniel seems as content as ever to take his cues from Dorcas, and echoes her a moment later. Honestly, he can hardly be blamed for his inattention, looking forward as he is to another episode with Dorcas tonight after lights out.

Odetta considers reprimanding Dorcas's impropriety, but then, Odetta has only herself to blame for it. Zebulon's vague and distracted turn as Headmaster has forced her to take command of all school matters besides construction and grounds. The students cannot help but notice.

Lead by example, thinks Odetta grimly.

Her devotion to this rule has created a school she loves nearly as much as she loved her late husband, as well as bright shiners like Dorcas. But it has also saddled her with Eli's brother, Zebulon. Not that Zebulon is a bad man. He is quiet and gentle and shy, particularly with Odetta. It cannot be easy, after all, to marry your brother's widow.

In one of Eli's final moments of clarity before the pneumonia plunged him into his final fever and beyond, he had begged his brother and his wife to follow the laws laid down in Leviticus and Deuteronomy for the practice known as Levirate marriage. Childless as Eli and Odetta were—having lost one child to whooping cough in its first year and another three to miscarriages—the Bible was indeed clear about how to proceed after Eli died. The widow was to marry her husband's brother in the hope of producing a male heir.

Not only would this ensure that the academy would carry on after Odetta eventually stepped down as Headmistress, Eli stressed as rills of sweat dampened his deathbed pillow, but Zebulon's presence as Headmaster would also serve as a daily reminder to the students that the heads of their school followed the Bible to the letter. That they led by example.

As Odetta and Zebulon huddled at Eli's deathbed, contemplating a marriage neither of them wanted and listening to the ever present grandfather clock run down the seconds of Eli's life, neither of them could have predicted that the marriage would not only be benign and loveless, but fruitless as well. For while Zebulon is kind to Odetta, he will never provide her an heir.

The night of the wedding ceremony, on her back in the marriage bed she and Eli shared for over a decade, Odetta learned that Zebulon—to employ a crass metaphor she had heard from railway workers she had grudgingly boarded for extra money in the early days of the academy—could not produce iron before the forge. Only once, weeks into their marriage, did she and Zebulon manage the sexual act. He wept afterward, the bed shaking with sobs while Odetta despaired next to him, grief and rage at Eli's dying coursing through her like venom.

However, the students did indeed notice their Headmistress's devotion to the Bible, as Eli had predicted. How could they not, when only five weeks separated Eli's death and the remarriage of their Headmistress to the school's former groundskeeper? Questions came from the younger students in particular, and Odetta took the opportunity to answer them. To teach. To show that trusting God's laws and wishes with complete faith would always lead to a better place.

It has taken almost two years, but Odetta and Zebulon have indeed arrived at a better place. After those early dark weeks, they came to a silent agreement that no heir would be necessary. Their marriage is convenient to both of them and to the school. Zebulon, freed from the pressure of sexual performance, has reemerged as the gentle and supportive man Odetta knew him to be when they were in-laws. He also shares her desire to expand the school, having thrown his energies over the spring months into constructing a new woodshop, garden, and livestock paddock, where he will shoulder some of the teaching load, instructing the students in carpentry, agriculture, and animal husbandry.

Husbandry, Odetta thinks now, snorting to herself as she stalks through the kitchen. She had hoped that Zebulon's enthusiasm for the academy's construction projects and eventual new curriculum would carry over into the duties of Headmaster, but the opposite seems to be happening. He is spending ever more of his days in the woodshop, and it is time to remind him of the responsibilities his brother left him. Out of the view of the students, of course. She must remember her own duties as a proper wife too. It would not do to reprimand her husband in public, no matter how irresponsible he is becoming.

She pushes through the screen door into a dark, balmy night. Midges hover in the glow of the cast iron lamp hanging on a pole outside the door. Odetta lifts the lantern's wooden handle off its hook without breaking stride, holding the light out before her as she follows the worn dirt path from the house to the woodshop at the edge of the grounds. Cicadas drone in the elms overhead. The sound drives some of the new students crazy until they learn to block it out, but to Odetta it is a soothing sound, redolent of the approaching summer. Of warm, clear nights when God's endless Creation wraps the sky in a sparkling blanket.

Trust in the Lord, *she thinks, allowing the night to calm her as she approaches the woodshop.* Lead by example.

And perhaps, in his own way, Zebulon is trying to lead by example. The Lord loves a working man, and Zebulon works tirelessly for the academy, which was not after all his dream. Zebulon never shared his brother's ambition to instruct young people in the ways of the Lord.

It is this realization that makes Odetta pause outside the door to the woodshop. She wonders belatedly whether her students would have been better served by her presence during the meal than by her rash and unprecedented departure from it. The combination of fresh summer air and the calming, tidal drone of the cicadas has robbed her of any desire to confront Zebulon tonight.

Yet she is still curious about what project is keeping him in the shop recently, and she decides—tragically, it will turn out—to see for herself.

Around the side of the shop, dim, orange light filters out of the building's only window onto the knobbly trunk of an elm. The window is as much a vent for disposing of wood shavings as it is a source of light and fresh air, and a mound of sawdust below it rises like a monstrous anthill, five feet high and eight feet across. No one else at the academy would be able to see through the window without a stool or ladder, but Odetta is so tall she could rest her nose on the sill if she stood on tiptoe. She sets her lantern on the ground at her feet, well away from the saw-dust pile, and eases up to the window to peer inside.

The large interior of the shop is lit by only a single lantern like the one Odetta brought with her, but she can make out two people inside. Zebulon is leaning over the central work table, his brow furrowed in something like pain. His construction foreman, John Barnaby stands behind him, with his hand on Zebulon's back. The two are moving oddly together, as if straining against something heavy, but Odetta sees no tools or construction materials. It is only when Zebulon lifts his torso up from the table and curls one arm around John's neck—a slow gesture filled with gentle intimacy that Odetta has never received from her second husband—that she realizes what is happening.

Instinctively, she throws herself backward, colliding hard with the trunk of the elm. It is suddenly, terribly clear why Zebulon cannot make iron before the forge, why he wept after the first and only time he made love to the wife he never wanted.

Odetta's next thought cleaves into her mind like the blade of a hatchet, breaking it completely: Eli knew. He knew about Zebulon's unnatural desires. What if his insistence that Odetta marry Zebulon was only a misguided effort to save his younger brother's soul?

"No," she whispers.

The spoken denial seems to dull her shock, so she repeats it. She is still repeating it when a groan drifts from the window. Odetta squeezes her eyes shut and carries on vocally negating what she has seen. Soon she hears more voices from the window. Quiet voices. Lovers' voices.

Odetta's heart pounds hard enough to make her vision quake. The rage is returning now. She believes—must believe—that her dear Eli did not know the truth about his brother. It would kill him all over again to learn how Zebulon has betrayed them, how he has made an abhorrent mockery of their marriage vows. Because Zebulon didn't just make a promise to Odetta the day they got married; he also made one to his brother's memory.

And there are examples in the Bible for this situation too, aren't there? The necessary fate of men who lay with men is abundantly clear. But even sodomy is not the end of Zebulon's treachery. Odetta thinks of the brothers Er and Onan in Genesis. Er died, leaving a childless wife, and thus it was down to Onan to provide Er's widow with a child. Yet Onan purposely failed his duty, taking sexual pleasure from his new wife without allowing her to become pregnant. And he died for it, as per the will of God.

As Odetta understands the Bible—and she has studied it her whole life, cover to blessed cover—Zebulon Koop is thrice condemned.

The men in the woodshop are still murmuring their pillow talk when Odetta draws herself up, refusing to cower any longer against the tree. She retrieves her lantern and treads slowly across the sawdust-strewn ground to the woodshop's only door. A heavy padlock hangs open and loose in its fixture on the side of the door. Odetta considers reaching up and simply clicking the lock home, but a new righteous clarity has come to her, and she understands that the door being locked from outside would raise questions later on.

So she leans over, playing the lantern's orange light across the grass and dirt around the shop until she finds what she wants: a broken elm branch about six inches long and as big around as her thumb. Back at the door, she slips the heavy iron padlock into the front pocket of her apron and rams the elm branch into the lock fixture instead.

Next she returns to the side of the building, about ten paces from sawdust pile. She rears back and, with the strength of ten thousand avenging angels, hurls her lantern against the side of the woodshop. The inner globe shatters, peppering the wall with glass shards and oily flames that drop eagerly into the sawdust.

For a second the sparks threaten to gutter out. Then the sawdust pile shakes with a puff of what seems to be wind, and the entire thing ignites with a thunderous whoomp! like a giant's cough. The concussion knocks Odetta flat on her butt, singeing her eyebrows and strands of loose hair into tiny black curls of ash. Her brow and cheeks will be shiny and red and tight for the next five days. A single pillar of black smoke and orange flame rushes up the side of the woodshop, licking at the eaves with lively hunger.

Odetta makes certain that the roof and at least two sides of the woodshop have caught before turning her back on what she has done. She no longer carries her lantern, of course, but the path before her is illuminated as if by a noonday sun. She makes her way slowly back to the house, where she will send Dorcas to rouse the fire brigade. After all, it wouldn't do to lose all of the beautiful trees that grow around the shop. They have done nothing to offend God.

"Lead by example," Odetta reminds herself in a voice that sounds nothing like her regular one.

The woodshop door rattles behind her. Panicked fists thud almost inaudibly over the tornadic roar of fire. Odetta hears and does not turn around. The inferno behind her is nothing to the one inside her.

An Unexpected Party

The Martins' porch light snapped on after the fifth ring of the doorbell and Kurt appeared, blinking and stubbly in a blue-checked robe. "Grover Solomon?" he asked blearily.

Cynthia materialized behind him a moment later. "What's the matter? What happened?" she asked at once. She had obviously been sleeping too, but she seemed much more alert than her husband.

"Leon took Autumn to the hospital. She fell down the stairs." Bracing himself, he added, "Actually, I—"

"The hospital?" Kurt interrupted. He no longer looked remotely sleepy either. "Is she okay? Did she break anything?"

Cynthia clutched her husband's shoulder, face suddenly drawn and lined. "The baby?"

"I'm not sure," Grover Solomon admitted. "Autumn said she was 'spotting,' but I don't really know what that—"

Cynthia paled and vanished into the house. Kurt peered urgently over Grover Solomon's shoulder at the street. "Did you walk here? Did they take your car?"

"Yes, sir. Leon asked me to come tell you what happened."

"Thank you. Give me a second to throw on some clothes and you can ride with us."

"Ride with you?"

But Kurt hurried inside after his wife, and five minutes later Grover Solomon found himself sliding into the back seat of an old but well maintained Toyota in the Martins' garage. Cynthia backed the car out of the driveway while Kurt twisted around in his seat to address Grover Solomon. "So what happened? How did she fall?"

He steeled himself. "It was my fault. I mean, it was an accident, but I…I sort of…pushed her."

"What?" Cynthia demanded, her eyes flicking up to him in the rearview mirror.

"I swear it was an accident. I had gone upstairs to—to have a look around, and Autumn was coming up when I was going down."

"So you collided on the staircase and she fell?" Kurt clarified.

Grover Solomon fingered his forehead. Sweat burned in his papercuts. "No, sir," he said. "Pastor Martin, I am going to be completely honest with you now. Odetta Koop appeared and attacked me, disguised as Autumn. Leon and Autumn—the real Autumn—heard us fighting. They came running to help and I thought she was Odetta Koop again. I never meant to hurt her."

Cynthia gaped at him through the rearview mirror with undisguised distrust. Kurt's expression was much more clinical, but no more comforting. He plainly thought Grover Solomon was insane.

"I see," he said at last. He turned around and said no more. Cynthia remained silent too, though her gaze continued to land on him over and over through the rearview mirror, as if she were worried he might suddenly attempt to yank the wheel out of her grip and steer the car into a lamppost. He wished she would just stop the car and let him out.

The ride took less than ten minutes. In the last few years, a new hospital had been built outside the city limits. The facility comprised a series of massive, angular buildings surrounded by farmland. To Grover Solomon it looked like some giant kid had dropped a pile of white Legos in a cornfield. Tall streetlamps littered the mostly empty parking lot, casting the expanse of new asphalt in perpetual blue-white daylight.

Cynthia parked beside Grover Solomon's car near the main entrance and they all rushed inside. Kurt inquired after Autumn and Leon at the front desk.

"Family?" the nurse asked.

Cynthia threw another glance at Grover Solomon, lips pursed, but did not object. The nurse performed a quick search on her computer and directed them to the Obstetrics Ward on the second floor.

"How is she?" Cynthia asked.

The nurse invited them to ask the attending nurse up in OB. They made their way to the nearest elevator, which deposited them in a wide, white hall as brightly lit as the parking lot. They passed through a pair of steel double doors so thick that they might have been designed to keep out rampaging dinosaurs, and followed several signs to the Obstetrics Ward. Cynthia reached the desk first and once again gave Autumn's and Leon's names.

"And you are…?" the nurse asked, peering up from her computer monitor.

"The grandparents," Cynthia said. Kurt slipped his hand into hers.

The nurse's keyboard clacked for several seconds and then she laid out three visitors' passes on the counter. "Room two-eleven," she said, standing and leaning over her desk to gesture down the long hallway to the right. "The doctor is with them now, but you should be able to go in shortly."

Cynthia snatched up her pass, thanked the nurse, and set off down the hall at a fast walk, still holding her husband's hand.

"Can't be too bad if they're letting us see her," Kurt murmured encouragingly.

Grover Solomon accepted his visitor's pass but did not follow them. They didn't seem to notice. He loitered by the main desk until the nurse rather pointedly suggested that he might be more comfortable waiting in the nearby lounge.

He slunk down the hall to the lounge, imagining a harshly lit room with yellowing copies of *Time* featuring predictions about the Reagan/Mondale elections or the love life of Farrah Fawcett. Would he be expected to converse with fretful husbands in their shirtsleeves, smoking cigarettes and pacing while their wives labored alone?

But the lounge turned out to be populated only by sterile white furniture straight out of an Ikea catalog. Two round tables stood side by side in the center with molded plastic chairs scooted underneath them. Vending machines lined one wall, supplying snacks and either hot or cold drinks. Grover Solomon plunked a few coins into the hot beverage machine and pressed the button for black coffee, below which was another button for vegetable soup. All of the liquids seemed to dispense from a single tube, which explained why the coffee tasted vaguely of onions when he took his first sip. A packaged cheese Danish completed his breakfast. It was stale, but at least it didn't taste like old soup. He wolfed the whole thing in three bites.

He approached a little shelf in one corner of the room and sifted disconsolately through a stack of mostly current publications. No Walter Mondale or Farrah Fawcett in sight. The most dog-eared magazine featured photos of models in bathing suits. He wondered how women in the throes of childbirth would feel about their husbands and fathers leafing through pages and pages of half-naked supermodels.

However, he too selected the bathing suit magazine, sat at one of the tables with his onion flavored coffee, and began flipping pages. The first thing that struck him, having never viewed a magazine like this one before, was that the models wore even fewer clothes than the ones on Lazarus's old burlesque cards. Most of the women in the photos were dressed in garments that could technically be called bathing suits, but they were also tugging suggestively at their bikini straps or writhing around in the sand with their butts in the air.

One blonde woman stared up at him from a two-page spread, pouty lips parted. The photographer had draped her in a slimy-looking wreath of seaweed and a pair of stringy underpants. Goose-flesh pebbled her arms, and her hair was plastered across her scalp and face as if someone had upended several buckets of icy water over her before they started snapping pictures. She looked miserable.

With each new picture, Grover Solomon found himself increasingly obsessed with how uncomfortable all of the women must have been during their photo shoots—how the sand must have gritted beneath the elastic of their ludicrous outfits. He found himself laughing harder and harder with each page he turned, until tear drops splashed onto the photos and he wasn't laughing anymore.

Playing Show Me with the burlesque playing cards had been so thrilling. How could this atrocious magazine, whose models were much less successful in hiding their nudity, not affect him in a similar way? Why didn't he want that poor blonde woman to rip the seaweed necklace from her body and show him the goods?

Furthermore, now that he thought about it, could it really be true that he'd never looked at a gentlemen's magazine before? Sure, his parents hadn't exactly left them lying around the house, but he'd spent four years in a college dormitory where such "literature" had been as plentiful as old pizza boxes. How had he never picked one up and flipped through it out of plain old curiosity?

That boy did teach you lust, Odetta's flat voice spat in his mind. *But not for any woman.*

He thought back to his first glimpse of Autumn, Alice, and Leon yesterday morning. He had of course registered Autumn's good looks—undoubtedly the publisher of this fine magazine would have been delighted to devote several pages to her—but he'd had eyes only for Leon. For those slim, tanned features and the exotic scar running up his forehead.

As if summoned by the thought, Leon strode into the lounge. Grover Solomon gave a guilty start and slammed the magazine closed with such force that he tore one of the staples out of the spine. Leon didn't seem to notice. He dropped into the chair opposite Grover Solomon, shoulders slumping with exhaustion.

"Hey," he said unenthusiastically.

"How is she?" Grover Solomon asked at once, trying to ignore the extreme heat in his cheeks.

"They're both going to be fine," Leon said, rubbing his face. "The doctor wants to monitor them for another few hours to be sure, but..." He let out a long, shaky breath.

"Wonderful news," said Grover Solomon, trying to smile.

Leon didn't smile back. "Autumn told me what happened. She said you pushed her. What the hell, man? She could have died."

Grover Solomon leaned forward, nearly tipping over his coffee. "I'm really sorry. Please believe me that I never would have done that to Autumn on purpose."

"You threw her down a staircase," Leon said flatly. "That doesn't count as an accident."

Grover Solomon made himself meet Leon's brown eyes. "I didn't think she was Autumn. I...saw something upstairs."

"I thought we'd lost the baby," said Leon, gazing down at the table and looking much too young to be a father.

"I—I'm really sorry," Grover Solomon repeated.

Leon rose from his seat, his expression unreadable. "Autumn wants you to come back to the room now."

"Oh. Uh, okay."

Not entirely sure it was a good idea but seeing no alternative, he followed Leon past the central desk down a wide corridor lined with closed doors leading into birthing suites. Pink and blue pages hung next to some doors, labeled with what he assumed were the names of the rooms' newest occupants. In less than half a year Leon and Autumn would be the proud parents of one of those little slips of paper.

Except—Grover Solomon's stomach gave an unpleasant swoop—they almost hadn't been, because of him.

The door to Autumn's suite stood open to reveal a huge single room at least as large as Grover Solomon's apartment in Chicago, decorated with tasteful furniture and floor lamps. Kurt reclined on a long sofa against one wall while Cynthia sat in a desk chair beside Autumn's bed in the opposite corner. Autumn wore a pink and white patterned hospital gown, under which ran a series of tubes and cables, as if she were an android the doctors hadn't finished building. All around her, monitors hummed and clucked softly to themselves, showing readouts in soothing blues and greens.

The last time Grover Solomon had seen Autumn, she'd been sobbing hysterically, which in itself had been nearly as alarming as anything else that had happened tonight. He was therefore pleased to see her speaking calmly with Cynthia. They both glanced up when he walked in.

"Autumn, I am so, *so* sorry about what I did," he gushed at once. "Leon says you're going to be okay?"

"It looks that way," she agreed evenly, and then turned back to Cynthia.

Hadn't Leon just said she wanted to see him? It sure didn't seem that way now. Or maybe ignoring him was some punishment for knocking her down the steps. And if so, he realized, he would be very lucky indeed. He deserved so much worse.

On top of this thought came an even simpler realization: Autumn's conversation with Cynthia, whatever it was about, had begun before he came into the room. Why should it stop just because he had arrived? The fact that he had put Autumn in that hospital bed didn't exactly make him the guest of honor.

He lowered himself cautiously onto the far end of Kurt's sofa while Leon took a big armchair next to the restroom door.

"You're sure you don't want us to call your dad and let him know what happened?" Cynthia was asking.

Autumn smiled humorlessly. "Is this how you would want to

find out your daughter is pregnant? Not that the way I told you guys was much better," she admitted. Cynthia gave her forearm a reassuring squeeze.

Kurt pointed at the coffee cup in Grover Solomon's hand. "Did you find that on this floor?"

"Yes, sir. Down past the nurse's station."

"Is it any good?"

"No, sir."

Kurt snorted. "Shame. I'm supposed to deliver a sermon in—" He glanced at his watch. "—five hours."

"Let one of the assistant pastors preach today," Cynthia said impatiently. "We're staying right here." She glanced nervously at Autumn. "I mean, we *can* stay. If you would like us to."

This was not the first occasion on which Grover Solomon had detected some uneasy currents between Autumn and her future mother-in-law, but she looked genuinely touched at the offer. "Honestly, if you guys weren't here, Leon and I would just be sitting around panicking that something might still go wrong."

Leon shifted in his seat. He did not argue.

"And in the interest of not panicking," continued Autumn, resettling the gown over her stomach and turning to Grover Solomon, "how about you tell us what happened tonight. Kurt already mentioned something about Odetta impersonating me?"

"Um," said Grover Solomon, startled. "Maybe this isn't the best time—"

"Oh, yes it is," Autumn countered. "I'm covered in suction cups and hospital goo, and I can't get up for the next three hours except to pee. There's no better time than now."

Cracks in the Wall

The retelling of Grover Solomon's troubled night took longer than he would have thought, partly due to his frequent pauses to decide how best to proceed. He began with the dream in which Lazarus had begged for freedom, and he continued speaking for at least twenty minutes, rushing through most of it so he wouldn't stop. After what he'd done, he owed Autumn the truth. All of it. Despite exchanging frequent unreadable looks, the Martins and Autumn listened to the entire story without interrupting. They seemed to understand that his nerve would only last if he kept talking.

Even so, he faltered when he reached the part about the conversation with Odetta in the cedar closet. "She..." He swallowed. "She implied that she killed Lazarus because she thought I was... in love with him, and she wanted to save me from..." He was blushing violently, but he had come much too far to beat around the bush now. He swallowed again. "She thinks I'm gay. Or, in her words, 'abhorrent to God.'"

Kurt's frown deepened.

"What's more," Grover Solomon continued doggedly, his heart thudding away somewhere around his eardrums, "I think she might be right."

Autumn was watching him with a curiously pained expression, as if she couldn't decide whether roll her eyes or shout at him. "*God,* Grover Solomon," she groaned. "Are you telling us you were outed by someone hiding in a closet?"

Leon gave a loud snort that might have started as laughter but turned into a vigorous sort of throat clearing. "Autumn, come on," he chided.

But Grover Solomon felt a reluctant grin spreading across his own face as a completely unfamiliar and exhilarating sense of relief welled inside him. None of them, not even Cynthia, seemed embarrassed or disapproving of what he'd told them. Indeed, Kurt was leaning forward with an expression of encouragement akin to that of a father watching a child take his first wobbly turn on a bicycle.

Something else too: no one seemed terribly surprised. What did *that* mean? He shook his head. He could worry about it later.

"Right before I left to come to your house," he told Kurt, picking up his story, "I saw Laz again. Just like in the dream, he told me Odetta had trapped him somehow, but he'd escaped. He was telling jokes and acting like his old self. But he said Odetta was coming for him and disappeared almost right away, like she snatched him up. Have you heard of anything like that?"

Kurt's frown returned in full force, carving his already lined forehead into a landscape of craggy shadows. "No," he said slowly. He glanced first at his wife, then at Leon, as if gauging his audience. "I'm sorry, you probably won't want to hear this, but I must say it. Has it occurred to you that you might be facing a psychological issue rather than a spiritual one? You have already mentioned multiple times a belief that homosexuality is evil or sinful, and you admitted that your parents' church took a rather conservative view on human sexuality."

Grover Solomon's mouth went suddenly dry. "I am not making these things up. Leon and Autumn heard the footsteps. They—"

Everyone was watching him.

"Or what about the door? Autumn and I didn't slam it on Leon's hands. Guys?" he added, appealing to Leon and Autumn.

"I don't know what's in that house," said Leon slowly. "There's an energy or something. And we definitely heard somebody stamping around on the upper floors more than once. And," he added, sounding almost reluctant, "I'm not just saying that because Autumn believes you didn't hurt her on purpose, Grover Solomon."

Kurt nodded, but it seemed like a nod of sympathy rather than agreement. "I believe you. All of you. But hearing a floorboard creak simply is not the same thing as seeing a ghost walk and talk. Did anyone else see Odetta Koop or Lazarus in the way Grover Solomon just described? As physical manifestations?" He turned to Autumn. "She must have retreated down the hallway right past you."

"Not past me," said Autumn.

Kurt leaned toward Grover Solomon and spoke softly. "Losing a close friend at such a young age and then, years later, coming to terms with the fact that you evidently had feelings for him as well…" He sighed. "You have built some very thick walls in your mind to hold in these emotions, and now it sounds like those walls are starting to flex and crumble. The apparition you saw as Lazarus could simply be a mental personification of your own latent homosexuality, at last emerging from the prison you created in your mind, desperate for freedom."

He fell silent, looking apologetic but determined. No one else spoke. The machines connected to Autumn and her unborn baby beeped and clicked in the stillness.

Grover Solomon pushed himself off the couch, the paper coffee cup quaking in his hand. "You think this is my fault? All a misunderstanding in my mind?"

"I said you wouldn't want to hear—"

"Stop," said Grover Solomon. He didn't know whether to feel mortified, enraged, or just plain exhausted. "Just stop, okay? I thought you could help me, and I was wrong. Guess it runs in my family."

Kurt closed his mouth as bade, his face an unreadable mask.

Grover Solomon held out his hand to Leon. "May I have my car keys?"

Leon stood as well. "Look, man, you don't have to—"

"*Please.*"

Leon fished in his pocket and drew out the keys, which Grover Solomon accepted but nearly dropped again. "Autumn, once again, I am very sorry about what I did to you. I'm so glad you're safe, and I hope you can forgive me."

He didn't wait for her to respond. He barely made it out the door before he had to press his lips together against a rising lump in his throat. He tossed his visitor's pass in the general direction of the nurse's station as he rushed out of the ward, down the stairs, and into the parking lot.

The sky was lightening over the eastern cornfields, which were unusually high for this early in the summer. The stalks waved blackly against the rose backdrop of predawn.

He leapt into his car, started the engine, and roared out of the lot, nearly ramming into another little Honda driven by a young woman in colorful nurse's scrubs. She would have been very cute if—

If I thought girls were cute, Grover Solomon thought savagely, recalling the woman in the swimsuit magazine whose bikini had been so distractingly full of sand.

Yes, he probably should have realized a long time ago that women did not appeal to him in *that way.* And yes, the realization that Laz had essentially been his first childhood crush had come as rather a shock to his already troubled mind. And *yes,* maybe he should have put these feelings together with the symbolism of the closet.

But whatever his emotional failings might be, he had not imagined speaking with Odetta or Lazarus. He knew it. Even if the others hadn't witnessed Odetta's flight through the second floor, the stinking cat had seen her, hadn't it? It had bristled like a porcupine when she'd approached.

Then again, what if the cat had simply been hissing at him, Grover Solomon, for bursting out of the crawlspace and startling it? Without even the cat to corroborate his story, how could he be sure Kurt Martin wasn't right about Laz and Odetta after all? The brief treatment he'd received from Alice had certainly altered his perception, both sensory and mental. What if her needles had acted like tiny chisels on the "wall" he had built around the part of himself that had been in love with Lazarus?

No.

Kurt Martin was wrong. If the ordeal with Grover Solomon's mother had been the greatest mistake of the pastor's career, then this was his second.

Which, Grover Solomon had to admit, was no comfort at all. He still needed to confront Odetta Koop, now with the added challenge of freeing Lazarus from her. And he no longer had even Leon and Autumn to stand with him.

These long thoughts accompanied him from the hospital and cornfields outside New Canaan into town. He considered trying to meet up with Alice again, but he had no idea where she lived, and the chiropractor would not be open at dawn on a Sunday morning.

So he returned, helplessly it seemed, to the senile old mansion where he had spent most of his life, to pick at the scab that was his relationship with his former home. If nothing else, he owed it to Leon to track down Biff, or whatever that cat's name was, and clean up any messes it might have made now that daylight had returned.

But when he pulled up the curb, another car already occupied the spot where he'd parked yesterday. An old Ford with new Georgia plates.

He whipped out his phone and scrolled through the call records again. Another eight calls had come through since he'd last checked. Even as he sat panicking behind the wheel of his still running car, the front doors of the Ford swung open, disgorging the last two people he had expected to see this morning.

His parents had come back to New Canaan.

PART III: REBELLION

The Parent Trap

The most recent Yoder family gathering had occurred the previous Christmas, only a few weeks before Ethyl and Annette moved to Atlanta. Looking at them now, the change in location seemed to suit them. Despite the purplish emotional storm clouds roiling over Ethyl Yoder's head as he stalked toward Grover Solomon's car, he looked as healthy and fit as ever, bronzed from the Georgia sun.

Annette, however, was nearly unrecognizable. She looked so different than she had in December that for a moment Grover Solomon forgot why any of them were here. Annette had always described herself as "mousy" and "bookish." Ungenerous descriptors, perhaps, but vanity was a sin, after all. The only part of her appearance in which she had ever taken any pride was her hair. As a boy, Grover Solomon had learned his numbers all the way up to one hundred by helping her count brush strokes each night before bed. She would perch on the edge of the bathtub and brush down as far as her arm could reach. When she sat down, the straight sheet of her hair hung almost to the floor.

But as the Bible warns, even minor pride can herald a fall. Annette's hair had gone completely gray before she turned 30. And it had happened quickly. Her nightly brushing ritual began to include several minutes of plucking gray hairs with a tweezers as she leaned into the mirror. Grover Solomon remembered asking once if it hurt. "Not as bad as keeping them," Annette had answered.

Yet she *had* kept the gray in the end, because the alternative would have been shaving her head. More than one new acquaintance had assumed she was his grandmother rather than his mother. Laz had started calling her "Granny Yoder" when she was out of earshot until Grover Solomon had asked him to stop. It was one of the few times Laz had ever listened to him.

Soon enough Annette had laid aside the tweezers and gone back to her faithful hundred strokes per night. Grover Solomon continued counting with her, too. In fact, his job became even more important. With the change in color, her hair grew coarse and unruly. The brush caught in snarls as she dragged it down from her scalp. Some nights she trailed off after only ten or twelve strokes and his voice was the only one keeping count.

All of these memories rushed through his mind as he slid out of the car to get a better look at her. The sheet of hair that had once hung almost the entire length of her body now swooped in a sassy little Gidget flip around her ears, and—

"Mom, did you dye your hair?" he asked, an unbelieving smile tugging at one corner of his mouth.

But the smile died half-formed. His mother hardly seemed to notice him. Her eyes were fixed on the third floor windows. She wore an arrested expression that suggested something monstrous and slavering was bounding toward her, claws out for the kill.

Ethyl, on the other hand, only had eyes for his son. He spared no time for pleasantries. "We've been calling all night," he barked.

"Y—Yes, sir," Grover Solomon stammered. "I'm—" *Sorry,* he nearly said. Except that would have been a lie. He wasn't sorry at all. He didn't know how to articulate such a treasonous idea, so he turned back to his mother and said, "Mom, you look wonderful. Your hair just…" But she still didn't seem to hear him. Something hard and cold settled in the pit of his stomach. "You look really great."

At last she tore her attention from the house, blinking several times. It made her look even younger, girlish and unsure. Grover Solomon wondered if anyone in Atlanta had taken Annette to be Ethyl's daughter instead of the other way around.

"Why did you ignore our calls, Grover Solomon? Why would you make us worry like that?"

Now he would apologize. He knew it. No one could abash him the way his mother could. His lips parted to make room for the apology. But before it could come, Autumn's voice spoke in his mind: *Make* them *worry? They're the ones who sent you back here to deal with the house alone. And why do you think that is?*

"That's a good question," he murmured.

"Excuse me?" said Ethyl, hands rising to his hips.

"I'm just wondering why you asked me to inspect the house instead of doing it yourself."

"I beg your pardon?" Ethyl's version of this phrase sounded nothing like the way Kurt Martin had spoken it yesterday afternoon. It sounded like a threat.

"You know what this place does to me." Grover Solomon's own voice was rising too. "What it has done to me my whole life. And if you don't remember, then Mom does. It's doing exactly the same thing to her right now. Look at her."

Annette jumped guiltily. She had indeed been staring at the house again. She ripped her gaze away and focused on a spot on the ground.

Ethyl drew himself up. The storm clouds over his head crackled with lightning. "You don't answer your phone, you make us drive all night, you ask impertinent questions. Is this how the big city teaches a boy to treat his father and mother? After a lifetime of providing for you, we ask you to drive a measly three hours so we don't have to drive twelve—"

"Don't pretend you care about driving here from Georgia," Grover Solomon snapped. He could hardly believe his own daring, but a new part of him, the one that had spoken in Autumn's voice, cheered him on like a fan at a football game. "You hopped in the car and drove all night just because I told you I wanted to talk to Kurt Martin. Why might that be?"

Ethyl's cheeks went a nasty purple color. His jowls quivered like blackberry gelatin. But these old weapons of bluster and shame weren't going to cow Grover Solomon any more today than they had on the phone yesterday afternoon. He had faced much worse over the last twenty-four hours.

"You weren't answering your phone," said Annette in her meekest, most disarming voice. "What if something had happened to you sweetheart?"

That knee-jerk guilt rose in him again. He had to struggle even harder to keep an apology down this time. "To be honest, several things have happened to me, but I'm fine. Mostly I would love to know why you are so desperate to keep me from talking to Kurt Martin. Any reason at all?"

His parents were goggling at him as if they'd never seen anything quite like him before. Maybe they hadn't.

"Okay, if that question is too hard," he said, doing his best not to shout at them, "then let's talk about the house. Dad, when we talked yesterday you said Mom rewrote and hung all the strips of paper in the crawlspace after the fire."

This piece of information finally seemed to distract Annette fully from the house. She stared at her husband, who had reddened so much that he looked like he'd dunked his head in a pot of boiling water.

"But that's obviously a lie," Grover Solomon went on. "Those papers are just as old and yellow as they were when I was a kid. Which means there couldn't have been a fire. You didn't find my best friend's burned corpse. You only found his clothes. You both knew his parents abused him, so you assumed he ran away and staged his death. I don't know how you could think such a thing, but I suppose it was easier than believing the house ate him or something. Then, when Laz's mom offered to beat the truth out of me, you guys stopped being friends. Any of this ring a bell? Feel free to jump in anytime."

"Who told you?" Ethyl asked at last. His voice carried no shame. Just a resigned curiosity that told Grover Solomon all he needed to know. The adult Lazarus—whatever kind of ghost or spirit or manifestation he might be—had been right. More importantly, he had been real. There went Kurt Martin's stupid theories. Grover Solomon wasn't going crazy after all.

He mashed his palms into his eyes. "This is so messed up. God, what is happ—"

Something struck him hard across the left side of his face and he went sprawling, barely catching himself before his mouth collided with the cement curb.

"How *dare* you?" Ethyl croaked above him. "How dare you add blasphemy to your list of sins today?"

Grover Solomon slowly lifted his face toward his father, left ear ringing. His whole body pulsed with a hatred he would not have believed himself capable of. Never before had he felt such a strong urge to attack another human being.

All the green lights Alice had switched on last night were popping back to red, the traffic screeching to a halt, and the resulting emotional momentum would have to be released somewhere. What better target than the strutting, self-righteous rooster of a man looming over him now?

Something of this must have shown on his face because Ethyl took several shambling steps backward. Annette leapt between her husband and son, arms upraised.

"Nice one, Dad," Grover Solomon growled, lips peeled back in an involuntary snarl. "You learn that move from the Beachys? Or is that just how the big city teaches a man to treat his son?"

Ethyl continued backing away until he stood in the middle of the street.

"Let's all calm down, okay?" Annette begged. "Maybe we should go inside and start over. Grover Solomon? Please?"

She sounded so close to hysteria that the venom began to drain out of him. Annette didn't want to be back under the oppressive shadow of this house any more than he did, but she was willing to go inside if it meant avoiding a family brawl in the street.

Throwing one last disgusted look at his father, he lifted himself off the pavement and slouched up the sidewalk toward the house. His parents exchanged heated whispers behind his back. By the time he stilled his quaking hands long enough to unlock the front door, his mother had joined him.

"Your father is going to stay outside for a bit. Give you both a chance to cool down."

"Yeah, gee, I'd hate for this to turn violent," said Grover Solomon, not bothering to keep his voice down. "Hey! What's he doing?" Ethyl had just pulled out his cell phone.

"Please just get inside," Annette hissed shrilly, herding him through the door.

A quick study of the room in daylight revealed a closed cedar closet door and a staircase free of apparitions. But the room kept swimming out of focus. His left eye watered from his father's blow. He wiped it gingerly on the collar of his t-shirt.

"What's that smell?" Annette asked suddenly. "Is there an anim—" The end of her question dissolved into a horrified squeal as the Martins' orange tabby padded into sight from the living room, meowing rather urgently.

"It's fine," Grover Solomon soothed. He hunkered to scratch the cat between the ears the way he'd seen Autumn do. "Sorry, uh…Skip. Didn't mean to leave you here all night."

It nosed enthusiastically at his fingertips, purring loudly, then wheeled around and trotted toward the back door with its tail in the air.

Grover Solomon straightened up to follow. "Probably needs to go to the bathroom. I bet he wants breakfast too. Leon brought some food along."

For a moment it seemed Annette would not be able to overcome the shock of encountering a live animal in the home she had so meticulously maintained. But eventually she got herself moving again. She was waiting in the living room when Grover Solomon returned from putting the cat out.

"You slept here last night," she said, gesturing at the sleeping bags, luggage, and books strewn across the floor. "And there were others here too. Can you tell me what's happening, Grover Solomon?"

"You know exactly what's happening," he said irritably. "Just look at the books on the floor. Read the titles."

"I don't understand."

"That's enough, Mom. You don't need to play dumb anymore. I know she killed Lazarus. She tormented me for years, and I'm starting to think she did it to you too."

"Lazarus?" repeated Annette with obvious concern. "Honey, no one killed your friend. Why would you say something so horrible? And who is this woman who is supposed to have tormented us? Is it—" She lowered her voice. "Do you mean Lazarus's mother?"

"What? No. Hang on," he said cautiously. "You really didn't hang up all those Bible verses on third, right?"

"No. I don't know why your father said that."

"Never mind what Dad said. Who do you think hung them up if you didn't?"

"This house was a Christian school a long time ago. The school closed decades before we moved in, but we still found lots of old books. Bibles, hymnals, even some documents pertaining to the school curriculum."

"Yeah, I know about the academy."

"Well, the Bible verses were hanging in that room when we moved in. They might have been decoration or a memorization tool for the students, like flash cards or—"

"Why are you lying?" he demanded. His head was throbbing now, whether from anger or the pain of getting hit he could not tell. "For once just tell me the truth."

Her eyes flashed. "For once? When have we ever lied to you?"

Out in the entry room the front door opened and closed. Grover Solomon's ear gave an especially painful throb, as if in response to his father's proximity. "I'm going to see if the cat needs back in."

He spun around stomped out of the room, fuming. When had his parents lied to him? Seriously? Well, let's see. There was the one about finding Laz's body when there had been no body to find. Then there was the fact that his mother had been sexually assaulted at church.

But if those examples were too far in the past, how about *right now?* Annette knew exactly who put those verses up, and he suspected she knew that Odetta Koop continued to dwell right here in this house too. So, really, the question seemed to be when *hadn't* he been lied to?

Outside on the porch, the cat was batting lightly at the glass. It slunk inside before he'd opened the door more than a crack.

"You want some food?" he asked it unenthusiastically. "Let's go see what your daddy brought you."

His parents were whispering violently again but stopped when he reentered the living room. He ignored them and set about searching Leon's backpack for cat food. Both side pockets bulged with several tins. How much did this stupid animal eat?

Ethyl cleared his throat. "Son, I'm sorry I lost my temper outside."

"That's funny, so am I."

He selected two of the cans of food at random and carried them to the kitchen. After several seconds of silence in which he could almost feel his father repressing his anger, Ethyl and Annette both joined him. They didn't seem to know what to say. He let them stew.

The cat sniffed hopefully at the back of his hand while he peeled back the lid on a tin of food. When he set it down the cat dug in immediately, chewing and slurping obscenely. Bits of brown sludge clung to its whiskers and flecked the linoleum. Annette gave a little involuntary moan.

"I admit," Ethyl attempted once more, "that we—ah, *I* didn't realize just how deeply your troubles with this house have run in the past. And I think it might be a good idea to talk to someone about it."

Grover Solomon laughed mirthlessly. "You're still doing it. You still think the problem is my own imagination, don't you? Well, you and Kurt Martin would finally have something to agree on."

"Please, Grover Solomon," Annette said. "We can tell you're hurting terribly."

Yet again, his anger seemed to drain away under the assault of his mother's pleading. Standing up to his father was turning out to be easy—laughably so—but his mother was a different story. A lifetime of guilting and manipulation couldn't be undone in a space of minutes.

"Who do you think I should talk to?"

She swallowed, but she did not look down this time. "A doctor. He's someone I went to after—" She swallowed again. "—after a man hurt me."

Grover Solomon watched her for several moments. "Dad, is that who you were calling outside? This doctor?"

"That's right." Ethyl pulled a small piece of paper out of his pocket and passed it over. "That's his address. He can meet with you this morning. His name is Dr. Shepherd."

Of course it is, Grover Solomon thought morosely.

"Just give me the key to the house and—"

"No, sir. The key stays with me until tomorrow morning."

Ethyl colored again. The fragile peace between them wavered like thin glass in a high wind. In the end Ethyl simply nodded. "Come back when you're through."

Therapy

Given his current mood, it was perhaps inevitable that Grover Solomon would dislike Dr. Shepherd. Except "dislike" didn't quite cut it. Something about the man put Grover Solomon instantly on edge, made him feel like he was chewing tin foil. At first glance Dr. Shepherd looked like an unremarkable man of middling age and equally middling fashion sense, from his stringy blonde comb over and patchy beard, moist with sweat, to his leather sandals, rimed with ancient oil and salt deposits. A gold stud glinted in his left earlobe as he waved Grover Solomon in with a pale, rubbery hand.

Grover Solomon stepped inside and wiped his feet automatically on the welcome mat. Dr. Shepherd's home could not have been more different than the angular, wood-choked house in which Grover Solomon had grown up. Thick white carpet covered the floors. The walls and windows were draped with quilted hangings and velvet curtains, as if the person who lived here suffered constant hypothermia. The very air in the house felt thicker than normal, stale and swampy.

Despite his father's suggestion that he dress up for the appointment, Grover Solomon had elected to stay in his shorts and t-shirt. He'd made the right choice. The doctor, on the other hand, was dressed poorly for the heat of his own home. He wore a mustard yellow cardigan over a button-down shirt and a pair of dark green corduroy pants. Everything was several sizes too large, suggesting that he had once been a much stouter man. Although he could not be called overweight, he looked bloated and tender, like an overfilled water balloon. Grover Solomon half expected to hear squelching noises from his sandals as the doctor stepped forward to close the door.

"Grover Solomon Yoder, as I live and breathe," he said in a melodious tenor voice. He offered a coquettish little smile full of straight, healthy white teeth. The smile was well practiced and clearly meant to put visitors—or patients—at ease. But in Dr. Shepherd's doughy, whiskery face, it skewed indecent, almost lewd. "It's been years."

As Grover Solomon could not honestly remember meeting Dr. Shepherd prior to this moment, he merely nodded.

The man's smile softened into something more fatherly and understanding. "Would you like a cold drink before we talk? Lemonade? Diet cola? The day hasn't rightly begun and I'm already perspiring." In a practiced motion, he swept the back of his smooth hand across his forehead, down his cheek, and into his neck stubble, the way a window washer might wipe a wet squeegee on a dry cloth.

"No, thank you."

"Well, I'm going to have a tiny snort of diet cola if you don't mind." Dr. Shepherd laid a finger to his wet lips in a conspiratorial, it'll-be-our-little-secret kind of gesture. If there had been a large, spinning fan or airplane propeller behind the doctor at that moment, Grover Solomon might have shoved him into it.

He took a deep breath. He was being unfair. His father was the true target of his anger right now, and misdirecting that anger wouldn't help anyone.

"No, sir, I don't mind. I'll just wait in your office."

"Last door on the right, my boy," said the doctor, already drawing a soda bottle out of the refrigerator.

Grover Solomon trudged off down the hall, passing a carpeted bathroom that reeked of potpourri and burned matches. The next door revealed a fussy little bedroom containing a canopy bed with four thick wooden corner posts and a lace skirt that—

He stopped midstride, the flesh on his neck and shoulders crawling. He knew the pattern on that lace. His eyes raked the musty, yellowing fabric. A hundred smug old monkey kings grinned back up at him.

"A gift," Dr. Shepherd said happily. He had materialized at Grover Solomon's side, clutching a fizzing glass tumbler.

"I don't understand."

Dr. Shepherd took a swig of soda and emitted a dainty little belch. "From your parents. They didn't have much money back when—" He paused, throwing Grover Solomon a calculating look. "But of course, you *do* know about—"

"Yes. Mom said she met with you after she was molested. I assume my parents couldn't afford to pay you, so Dad built you this bed in exchange for therapy for Mom?"

"Correct," said Dr. Shepherd, taking another swig of soda and sounding happy again. "Made from one of the elm trees that lived on your property. Solid wood, beautiful grain, and your mother sewed the lace. You recognize their handiwork, I'll wager?"

"Yes."

"The materials alone were worth much more than the cost of the few sessions your mother spent with me," the doctor continued. "I actually attempted to pay the difference, but your parents wouldn't hear of it. Proud people. Well, should we get to it, then?"

With an effort, Grover Solomon turned away from the monstrous bed and faced Dr. Shepherd. "I know my dad made this appointment, but I have money of my own. Whatever you charge, I'll pay for it."

"We're just talking today, my boy." Dr. Shepherd favored him with another of those understanding, fatherly smiles. It was his only expression so far that didn't seem to be a theatrical contrivance, and the only one that didn't make Grover Solomon instinctively want to hurl him off the edge of a cliff.

They walked the last several paces to the office in silence. The only sound came from the ice clinking in Dr. Shepherd's glass. Grover Solomon had expected the office to be another stuffy little room with more thick carpet, perhaps a big desk and a poofy couch. Instead he found a sparsely decorated space with a golden brown hardwood floor, high bookshelves, and impressionist art on the walls. Soft yellow light emanated from several lamps spaced around the room. Two leather arm chairs faced each other in one corner of the room. A low coffee table sat between them.

Almost against his will, Grover Solomon felt himself begin to relax. Whereas the rest of the house had put him in mind of an asylum's padded cell, this room allowed him space to breathe. He took the armchair in the corner and waited while Dr. Shepherd settled himself in the other.

The doctor sucked contentedly at his straw again before setting the glass on one of the coasters sitting on the coffee table. The sleeker, more muted environs of his office suited him, conferred upon him an aura of quiet competence far removed from the squishy, simpering gnome who had answered the door a few minutes ago.

"Do you know why your father called me today, Grover Solomon?"

"No," he said automatically. But then he thought back to the moment when his father had struck him. The expression of shock and terror on Ethyl's face when he realized Grover Solomon might hit him back. "Because I grew up."

"That might be one way to look at it," Dr. Shepherd agreed. "Your father seems to think you are expressing some kind of rebellion."

"Rebellion," repeated Grover Solomon.

The doctor gazed shrewdly over tented fingertips. "Your father possesses many admirable qualities. But he is, forgive me, not terribly perceptive when it comes to other people's emotions. That much was clear back when I was meeting with your mother. Not that I can discuss that," he added with a sanctimonious little bow. "Patient confidentiality, my boy."

Grover Solomon felt his jaw clench. Did the doctor think he wanted to hear details about the terrible thing that had happened to his mother? "So what *are* we going to discuss?" he asked pointedly.

If Dr. Shepherd found the question impertinent, he gave no sign. "Let's start with you. Your father mentioned that you live in Chicago. So how do you fill your days in the Windy City? Career? Hobbies? Social life?" He wagged his scraggly blonde eyebrows like Groucho Marx. "Girlfriend?"

Over the last twenty-four hours a cold, alien anger had risen inside Grover Solomon like a cobra from a fakir's basket. It slithered through him again now, and he had to fight an urge to leap forward and sink his fingers into the wobbly flesh at Dr. Shepherd's throat.

"City planning," he answered in a voice that was as far from a growl as he could manage. "Book collecting. None, and none."

"Come now," chided Dr. Shepherd. "A handsome, intelligent, and dare I say brooding young man like yourself? You must have a few friends. Friends your own age, I mean."

"I have three," said Grover Solomon automatically. And once he said it, he found it was true. He sat a little straighter.

"You see? Tell me about them. Are they males? Females? What do you like about them?"

"One guy, two girls. Or women, I guess. None of us are boys and girls anymore, are we?"

"Only in our hearts," Dr. Shepherd sighed.

"The first one is Leon Martin. We used to play together a long time ago, but our families drifted apart."

"Of course," Dr. Shepherd said knowingly. "Children can

hardly remain close when there is such nasty business between their parents."

"Leon and I sort of reconnected yesterday. And he introduced me to his fiancé and another friend of theirs."

The doctor drained the last of his soda and emitted a little belch, followed by much satisfied lip smacking. "These are your three friends? People you met yesterday?" His high voice was laced with surprise and something that sounded an awful lot like mockery.

"Yes," said Grover Solomon defiantly. "And would you like to know how I can tell they're my friends?"

Dr. Shepherd's cheeks ballooned with an even deeper belch, which he blew into his sweaty fist. The sour scent of old digested garlic wafted across the table. "Very much."

"They respect me. They…" He searched for the correct word. "They empower me. One of them, Alice, showed me—"

"Alice?" Dr. Shepherd cut him off tartly. "I presume you mean Alice Shin? Yes, I know all about the Chinese girl the Martins have adopted as their pet foreigner. I feel obliged to tell you that she is not your friend, no matter how she may have, ah, *empowered* you."

This was such an odd reaction that Grover Solomon felt sure he must have misheard or miscommunicated something, though he didn't see how.

"Alice isn't from China," he began slowly. "She's—"

"Tell me," the doctor interrupted once more, "did she touch you, by any chance? Stick you with those little pins she carries around?"

Grover Solomon frowned. "Yes, actually, but—"

"I thought so." The doctor resettled himself in his chair, looking satisfied once more. "She has brought this town nothing but trouble since she arrived five years ago. Pricks a few people with those tainted needles, and suddenly she's got everyone believing fanciful nonsense about mystical body energies."

"Tainted needles?"

"Of course, my boy. Some kind of Chinese opiate is my guess, and if I could prove it, she would already be on a plane back to her own country to be publicly caned or beheaded or whatever they do to criminals where she comes from. Regardless, I can tell you she's lured more than one of my patients away from crucial psychological treatment."

Grover Solomon's mind traveled back to the previous night—the way the needles had burned white-hot like suns in his knuckles, the way he had literally seen the song of the cicadas and felt the rotation of the earth, the seizure-like reaction he had suffered in his car afterward. Could all of those things have been brought about by drug induced hallucination? Nothing more than a "bad trip"?

"No," he said aloud.

Dr. Shepherd reached across the coffee table and gave Grover Solomon's forearm a damp, fleshy pat with the hand that had only moments before contained his burp. "It's okay, my boy. You've done nothing wrong. She is the one who is lying to people."

"She's not—"

But Dr. Shepherd overrode him prissily. "If we may dismiss the unpleasant topic of Ms. Shin, I would like to advance a theory. Examine your life, my boy. You have selected an occupation that requires intense organization and control." He lifted a finger as if to begin counting points of data. "You live in one of the world's largest cities, where you may exist in complete isolation and anonymity. Your hobby as a bibliophile suggests a strong connection to the past. What are books if not physical records of historical events and ideas? And finally," he added with the air of a lawyer providing a final piece of incontrovertible evidence to a jury, "you selected the more defensible seat when you sat down for our discussion."

Grover Solomon looked down at his chair in bewilderment.

"With your back in a corner and a clear view of the door," Dr. Shepherd clarified. "I did not tell you where to sit, did I? My point, dear boy, is that your lifestyle more closely resembles that of someone in the witness protection program than a single man in his twenties."

"You're saying I live in fear?" Grover Solomon slumped backward. All Dr. Shepherd's training and expertise had led him to this? What profound truth was the doctor going to reveal next—that Grover Solomon had brown hair?

"We all live in fear of something," said Dr. Shepherd dismissively. "No, what I'm saying is that you are *hiding*." He leaned forward, eliciting a high squeak from somewhere near his bottom. Neither he nor Grover Solomon acknowledged the sound. "Would you like to tell me what you are hiding from?"

The answer came almost without thought. In what might have been the most poignant moment of his life—or maybe just the corniest—he said, "Love," and burst into tears.

The Seduction of Grover Solomon, Part 2

"Dear, dear me," Dr. Shepherd clucked sympathetically. "How like your mother you are."

He did not seem especially perturbed by Grover Solomon's sudden breakdown. He rummaged an ice cube out of his glass and popped it into his mouth, rolling it obscenely with his tongue while Grover Solomon labored to pull himself together. After a few moments the doctor swiveled in his chair to retrieve a box of tissues and set it on the coffee table.

Grover Solomon swiped a tissue from the box and blew his nose. "I'm sorry. That came out of nowhere."

"Nonsense," chuckled Dr. Shepherd.

"Fine," said Grover Solomon, balling up the tissue and chucking it irritably at the wastebasket. "Then why don't you just tell me what I'm feeling and I'll get out of your hair. I've got work to do anyway."

Dr. Shepherd wagged a finger. "Tut, tut. First I want to hear your explanation. Why might you be hiding from love? Think, now. Distill your truth. Purify it into something sharp and bright so that together we may drink of it and gain knowledge."

"God," Grover Solomon complained.

Dr. Shepherd waited, his tongue positively wrestling with the ice cube in his mouth.

At least I didn't get slapped this time, he thought. "Do you know the Beachys?" he sighed at last.

The doctor squinted as if in remembrance. "I knew of them. During our sessions, your mother spoke of them as being close with your family. Their son—Lazarus, I believe he was called—was your friend when you were boys."

"Yes, sir."

"And he ran away from home shortly before his father committed suicide."

"What? Laz's dad killed himself?"

Dr. Shepherd wrinkled his nose. "Shotgun in a cornfield. Nasty business. Your parents never told you?"

"No, sir," said Grover Solomon numbly. "But why?"

"Perhaps they believed it too gruesome a tale to tell a troubled boy." Dr. Shepherd shrugged. "All of that occurred after I had finished meeting with your mother, so I could not ask her about it."

"That's not what I meant," he said vaguely.

His shocked and fatigued brain fumbled with yet another new piece of information that had been withheld from him for most of his life. If the Beachys believed Laz had simply run away, then perhaps they also believed he would tell someone about the abuse he had suffered. Ruthless parents though they were, Mr. and Mrs. Beachy had been quiet and withdrawn people, even within their tightknit church family. The idea of their son airing their dirty laundry in public might have been enough to drive Mr. Beachy to suicide.

Finally he shook his head. "You know what? It doesn't matter."

"I agree." Dr. Shepherd was watching him with tremendous interest. His wooly eyebrows rose solicitously. "So let's focus on what does matter. I, for one, am dying to know what a truant child and his broken family might have to do with you hiding from love."

Grover Solomon steeled himself, but he suspected the doctor already knew exactly what he was going to say. After all, the Martins and Autumn hadn't been surprised when he'd revealed himself to be gay. The only one so far who had been shocked by the news was Grover Solomon himself.

And with that realization, a new thought floated to the surface of his mind like a garbage bag drifting in the ocean: what if his parents already knew, too? Was that why their sermons had centered so often on the sin of homosexuality? To drive it out of him like Odetta claimed she wanted to do?

Focus on what matters, he instructed himself. "Okay, well, coming home has forced me to realize some things about myself. Laz wasn't just my best friend. He was the first person I loved."

Dr. Shepherd offered a simpering little smile. "Surely your mother was the first person you loved."

Grover Solomon's eye twitched. "I think I just figured out why some of your patients would rather get stuck by needles than talk to you."

The doctor's eyes widened in genuine hurt. "Oh, Grover Solomon, that was unkind. So, so unkind. Why would you say such a cruel thing?"

Grover Solomon didn't answer. At that instant he would have paid real money to be back in his house, arguing with the murderous ghost of Odetta Koop instead of spending another second in the presence of this sweaty, smelly, manipulative bearded slug of a man-baby.

"It is my job," the doctor said with a sniff that conveyed his gravely wounded pride, "to help you articulate what you mean rather than speaking in riddles or metaphors."

"Then let me be plain. I had a romantic crush on my best friend, and I was too young to understand what my feelings meant. It took me another fifteen years to figure it out."

"Say what you *mean*," Dr. Shepherd urged. Bubbles of spittle collected at the corners of his shiny lips.

"I'm gay. I always have been, and I'm just now figuring it out. Is that clear enough for you?"

"Let us be sure now, before we get too excited," cautioned Dr. Shepherd, though he seemed almost painfully excited himself. Gone was the injured expression from a few moments before. His cheeks and neck flushed raspberry red under his beard and he was breathing like he'd just climbed a long staircase. "Did you have sex with Lazarus Beachy?"

Grover Solomon recoiled. "What? No! We were kids. He disappeared before we were ten, for God's sake."

"Have you ever had sex with a man?"

"Are you even listening to me? All of this is new to me. I'm just now realizing these things about myself. Like, just today."

Dr. Shepherd flopped backward and made his little dismissive wave. "Then you are not gay. It's no wonder children get confused, though."

Grover Solomon gawped at him. "I am not a ch—"

"All of this media nonsense glamorizing the notion that gayness is something inside you. That it's unchangeable, that it's 'who you are,'" the doctor made sarcastic little air quotes, "rather than something you do. Poppycock!" he barked, pounding the arm of his chair with a rubbery palm. "You haven't had sex with a man, so you are not gay."

"That's—But—"

"You are simply dealing with some grown-up questions of identity, and I am delighted to tell you there is a solution."

"A solution," Grover Solomon repeated. "What, like a dating service?"

Dr. Shepherd gave a shrill little giggle that made the hair on Grover Solomon's forearms stand on end. "That is so like your generation, isn't it? People your age have a most unusual psychological trait. I have witnessed it over and over. You seem to believe you must experience something firsthand before you can form an opinion about it. For example, you see your favorite television star or athlete declare he is a homosexual on national television, and you say to yourself, 'I admire that person. I wonder if I am like him.'"

"I don't really watch telev—"

"And so you believe you must try out homosexuality for yourself. Well, you are in luck, because experiential therapy is the very the solution I spoke of. Just not—" he added, holding his hands up to preempt argument, "—in the form of a dating service. For several years I served as a supervising counselor at a retreat for confused teenage boys like yourself."

"I'm twenty-four."

"That particular retreat is now defunct, but it was successful in its time, and I do not think it would be too boastful to share that I designed much of the curriculum." Dr. Shepherd laid a hand to his chest in a gesture of false modesty. "We facilitated situations in which our boys could experience certain aspects of homosexuality without the risk of entering into confusing or damaging relationships. Under carefully controlled conditions, our simulations produced some truly stirring results."

Grover Solomon's ears were ringing again, but it had nothing to do with his father taking a swing at him earlier. At some point in the last several minutes this meeting had gone off the tracks. The atmosphere in this office had soured in some fundamental way. But even so, *surely* Dr. Shepherd could not be suggesting what it sounded like.

"I'm still not sure I understand you," said Grover Solomon slowly.

Dr. Shepherd stood and wicked sweat from his forehead into his beard with that practiced little wipe of his. "Now who's being cagey?"

He leaned over with a grunt and shoved the coffee table off to one side. He had started wheezing again, and not from the minor exertion of moving the table. He planted himself before Grover

Solomon, whiskery jowls aquiver. "From the moment you entered my home I perceived that you were likely struggling with issues of sexuality. I just want you to know that this is a safe place."

Grover Solomon pressed himself instinctively backward against the leather cushions of his chair. If this was a safe place, then why did his "defensible" seat suddenly feel so much like a trap? "Please sit back down, Dr. Shepherd." His voice sounded tinny and distant to his own ears. "I thought we were just talking today."

"The time for talking has passed," said Dr. Shepherd. He twisted around and eased himself into Grover Solomon's lap. "Place your arms around me."

Grover Solomon didn't move. Every muscle in his body seemed to tense at once. His hands involuntarily curled into claws on the arms of his chair. He squeezed his eyes shut, willing himself to wake up. Surely this was another hyper-realistic nightmare like the one in which Odetta had trapped him and Lazarus inside a paper cage.

Dr. Shepherd's head lolled backward so that his cheek smeared sweat across Grover Solomon's temple. His fleshy backside ground into Grover Solomon's lap.

"You needn't fight it," the doctor moaned. "Embrace the experience so that you may know your unhealthy desire and draw it from yourself as the poison it is. Let me save you from yourself."

Without warning the doctor grabbed Grover Solomon's hand and pressed it, groaning, into his crotch.

Grover Solomon's paralysis broke. His whole body snapped like a rubber band, and suddenly he was on his feet. Dr. Shepherd toppled forward and went sprawling. Before he could even try to get up, Grover Solomon stepped forward and swung his foot viciously into the exposed vee between the doctor's legs. And once he'd done it, he discovered that one time wasn't nearly enough. Again and again he kicked at the pulsing, squishy thing he had felt through the doctor's pants. He kicked until Dr. Shepherd managed to curl himself into a tight ball on the floor, hand cupped protectively over his groin. The man's eyes, wide and terrified, fixed on Grover Solomon. He looked like a little boy who had just discovered monsters were real after all.

"What is wrong with you?" he whimpered. Tears leaked from the corners of his eyes and dripped onto the wood floor. "I only wanted to help." It was not an act, either. Sincerity and a sort of hurt astonishment shone clearly in the doctor's watery eyes. His head settled gently to the floor. "Get out of my house before I call the police."

Grover Solomon almost told him to go right ahead. He had a little story of his own that he would love to tell the cops.

Yet even through his revulsion, he understood that Dr. Shepherd's threat carried weight. If the police did come here, a single glance would tell them who had attacked whom, whereas Dr. Shepherd's assault had left no marks at all.

The injustice of it all made him want to start kicking things again. But instead, as ever—as he had done ceaselessly over the course of his entire miserable life—he obeyed in silence, and he left.

The Last Power Struggle

When he returned to his house, his first thought was that Dr. Shepherd must have called the cops anyway. A single police cruiser sat parked behind his parents' Ford. No siren, no flashing lights, but a police car nonetheless.

But as he drew further up the street toward his house, two people came into view on the front porch: Grover Solomon's father and the New Canaan chief of police, a burly, black haired man named Mallard Hook. It was one of the worst kept secrets in town that most locals referred to the chief as "Ducky" behind his back. This nickname had less to do with the chief's unusual first name and much more to do with the fact that he spoke in an oddly high-pitched, reedy voice that sounded like a duck's quack.

But if New Canaanites poked a bit of fun at the police chief's voice, the man himself enjoyed unanimous approval. In the twelve years since he'd risen to the rank of chief, he had shown nothing but respect and care for townies and tourists alike. He was the kind of man who gave warnings rather than tickets for all but the most egregious traffic violations; the kind of man who remembered the names of people he pulled over so he could offer a friendly hello the next time he saw them around town; the kind of man who insisted all of his officers wear cameras in their lapels in case of accusations of illegal or abusive behavior.

Ducky was the kind of man, in other words, who would show up on a Sunday morning to help out a former New Canaan citizen like Ethyl Yoder, who needed discreet, authoritative assistance in dealing with a wayward child. It probably didn't hurt that Ethyl and a few of his brothers had teamed to up to rebuild the first floor of the chief's home free of charge after the river flooded eight years ago.

Both Ducky and Ethyl turned to watch as Grover Solomon parked, exited his car, and made his way, sweating, up the front walk. "Chief Hook," he said, nodding in what he hoped was a masculine and comradely sort of way.

"Grover Solomon," greeted Ducky in his squirrely little voice. He reached up to scratch one side of his mustache. "Your father seems to think we have a problem here."

"Yes, sir, we do," said Grover Solomon. "Do you know Dr. Shepherd?"

Here was his chance, and sooner than he could have hoped. A giftwrapped opportunity to turn in that simpering troll of a psychiatrist who had…had…

But words failed him. How could he begin to describe what had happened? Something had been taken from him. Something tiny and fragile and deeply personal that he couldn't even really identify except by its new absence. How could he express the shame, violation, and inexplicable sadness he felt at having that man's soggy, unwanted weight writhing in his lap? And if he did manage to explain it, could his explanation ever justify the violence of his reaction?

"Dr. Shepherd also thought we had a problem, sir," he said at last. "I've just been to see him. My father insisted."

If the two men heard the bitterness or accusation in his voice, they either didn't understand it or chose to ignore it. His mother would have heard. She would have listened. The same thing had happened to her, after all. Yet where was she? Choosing to remain inside the house, possibly listening at the door but not showing her face because she never stood up for anything.

Except that wasn't quite true, was it? *Your mother fought back,* Kurt Martin had told him. She had stood up for herself, at least once.

And so did I, thought Grover Solomon, taking unexpected courage from the idea.

Ducky and Ethyl exchanged a look that plainly expressed how poorly they felt this conversation to be progressing. Ducky scratched his mustache again. It looked like he had taped a wad of steel wool to his upper lip. "Grover Solomon, it can be hard to give up a piece of your childhood as important as a home, but the deal is done. The owners move in tomorrow. I've met them. Lovely people."

"I don't care about the house, sir," said Grover Solomon. "But there *is* a piece of my childhood in there."

"There's *nothing* in there!" Ethyl practically shouted in exasperation. "Except that darn cat you saw fit to let caper around alone all night. Annette tried to pick it up and the darn thing tried to claw her to death."

Grover Solomon managed not to laugh by pretending to cough. He could only remember his father saying "darn" this often when he fell into one of his frequent streaks of smacking his thumbnail with a hammer.

"You need to return the key you stole, son," said Ducky in his gravest, reediest drone.

"I didn't steal the key, sir. Dad sent it to me with a request to inspect the house before the new family moves in. My inspection isn't finished, so I can't return the key yet."

Ethyl actually stamped his foot in impotent indignation, and

Grover Solomon had to cough even harder to cover another attack of the giggles. What was wrong with him? He'd landed himself in real trouble here, and he wouldn't exactly dig himself out by openly laughing at the two people who could make his trouble even worse.

Sure enough, Ducky seemed unconvinced by the fake coughing. Patient and benign patriarch though he might be, he would obviously tolerate no more direct disobedience today. "I'm afraid this is a legal matter now, son," he said in a growl that would not have sounded out of place coming from a Chihuahua. "That key, this house, none of it belongs to you."

Grover Solomon drew the key out of his pocket and studied, turning it this way and that as if to enjoy the sparkle it made in the sunlight. "I'm finishing what I started."

Ducky's voice rose to a mosquito-like whine. "Son, I'm only going to ask you one more t—"

But too late. Both men's eyes widened in comical unison as Grover Solomon popped the key into his mouth and swallowed it.

Completing the necessary paperwork to process the arrest required two full hours. A uniformed woman about Grover Solomon's own age escorted him deep into the bowels of City Hall and deposited him in a sterile white holding cell. The bed, sink and toilet were all bolted to the floor. The charge of misdemeanor larceny and corresponding $2,500 bail with which he had been slapped would vanish, Ducky promised, if he produced the key before sundown. A stainless steel basin and a pair of rubber gloves rested on the floor beside the toilet, awaiting the moment of "production."

After being been deposited in this cell, exhaustion had finally overtaken him, and he had drifted fitfully in and out of sleep for a period of time. He woke up confused. His brain felt like it had been packed with wool. Since the cell contained no clock or window, he couldn't be sure how long he'd been out. All he knew was that he was enormously hungry, and he had the beginning of a cramp twisting his lower back from lying on the lumpy cot.

At some point a little food tray had been shoved through the flap in his cell door. The tray bore individually packaged apple slices, carrot slices, and a rather tragic tuna salad sandwich on in one of those triangular plastic containers that came out of vending machines. He could not have said whether it was supposed to be breakfast, lunch, or dinner. He ate every bit of the food and washed it down with a few gulps of metallic tasting water from the basin. All in all, it was no worse than his previous meal in the hospital lounge.

And when it was gone, he reclined on his cot once more and glared at the painted cement ceiling with nothing to do but re-live the arrest over and over in his mind. As he'd suspected, his mother had indeed been listening through the front door. She only emerged when Ducky clapped Grover Solomon in handcuffs—af-ter it was too late for her to do anything useful.

She had begged, of course. Begging had always been her first, last and fiercest weapon. And as Ducky shoved Grover Solomon into the back of his cruiser, she'd wielded it at both the chief and her husband, begging them to be reasonable. But they were too busy being men, too busy strutting and posturing and harrumph-ing about respect to give her any.

As for Grover Solomon, he had dismissed "reasonable" as an option the moment he gulped down that key.

He squirmed on the cot, massaging his stomach, where the key must even now be resting. He still couldn't figure out why he'd done it. In addition to being a rather stupid and dangerous little stunt—what if the key snagged somewhere in his digestive tract or, worse, tore a hole inside him as it passed through?—swallowing the key conferred upon him no more freedom to explore the house and save Lazarus. Far less freedom, in fact.

Everything was just happening so quickly. He'd only arrived in town yesterday, for heaven's sake, and he had hardly stopped moving except to sleep. If any of his adventures last night could be called "sleep."

Still, those adventures had unveiled Lazarus, as well as other reverberating truths about himself and his family. Maybe that was why he'd swallowed the key. Maybe too much upsetting information had come whizzing out of the ether of the past, and some part of him decided enough was enough. Maybe he needed to go on personal lockdown until he could organize all of the new information—sort out which parts of it mattered in the short term and which did not.

If so, he thought, staring gloomily around his cell, what better lockdown than a literal one?

He closed his eyes, wishing Alice were here to perform another acupuncture treatment. Between the encounters with his parents, Dr. Shepherd, and Ducky, he doubted any of those metaphorical traffic lights in his body remained green. Then again, as Alice herself had noted, Grover Solomon was a city planner. Who better to get traffic moving again after a series of natural disasters?

Or *un*natural disasters, like getting molested by a psychiatrist who was supposed to be helping him. Yes, Dr. Shepherd's attack had to come first. There would be little point in hunting down individual blocked intersections when half the city had just been trampled by Godzilla. The monster itself might be gone now but the scar of its passage remained, and it would take years, if not a lifetime, to clear away all the rubble.

But in the meantime, traffic still had to get from one side of town to the other. Grover Solomon's *qi* needed access to the whole grid, transporting the emotional equivalent of clean food and water to even the most devastated parts of his psyche.

He laced his fingers together and pressed his thumbs into the spot between his eyes where Autumn had first touched him, willing the pathways to open. Several deep, calming breaths later, he actually felt a little better. Nothing so life altering as what Alice had done with her needles, but he did feel some lessening of pressure.

He grunted. Pressure valves and green lights. It actually helped to think in those mechanical terms rather than investigating emotions or feelings, which probably wasn't terribly healthy. But never mind that now. He could sort out his other miscellaneous emotional problems when all of this was over.

Which led back to his current task of sorting out what mattered to his current situation and what did not. First, he had no intention of waiting around in this cell for his body to evacuate the key. Ducky's offer to drop the criminal charges had been presented as a magnanimous show of good faith, but in reality the charge was a scare tactic that would not hold up under even the most minor legal scrutiny. Would Ducky have tossed him in the town drunk tank if he had simply lost the key, or if it had accidentally fallen out of his pocket into a sewer grate? Of course not. At the very worst, he would be obliged to pay some locksmith ten bucks to make a new key. Problem solved.

No, he was stuck in this cell because after twenty-four years Ethyl Yoder had lost his absolute authority over his son. Unfortunately, Ethyl also still carried enough good ol' boy influence with the town constabulary to throw this tantrum.

Regardless, whatever was happening with his parents could be placed squarely in the "doesn't matter" pile for the moment. As soon as he figured out his next move, he'd post bail and be on his way. The question remained: what, if anything, would be worth emptying most of his savings account in order to get out of this cell a few hours early?

As he lay on the lumpy cot, thumbs pressed once more between his brows, the answer swam up out of the background murk of his mind in the form of Lazarus's pinched, stubbly face.

Find me. I don't want to be here anymore.

Lazarus, half consumed by shadow and ash, caged in some horrific purgatory for fifteen years. Not allowed to live properly yet still forced to grow up in isolation, seemingly aware of the years he had lost. The idea of Laz even now stuck in that hellish nightmare gnawed at Grover Solomon's insides like a nest of hungry rats. It hurt even worse than the pain of losing Laz the first time, and he thought he knew why. This time his horror carried a tinge of hope.

Dr. Shepherd, for all his vileness, had revealed one true thing: Grover Solomon had been hiding from love for as long as he could remember. But no more. He loved Lazarus—he always had—and maybe, just maybe...

Please find me.

It was a child's hope, to be sure. A slay-the-dragon-and-live-happily-ever-after hope. But hope nonetheless.

How could he find Lazarus, though? Both times he'd encountered Laz so far, his old friend had come to him. This time it would need to work the other direction. Obviously the gateway to Lazarus's prison was the little room on third. That's where Odetta Koop had killed him all those years ago; that's where he had appeared in Grover Solomon's dream. Everything led back to that room.

Except...that room was just a room. Even when Grover Solomon had shut himself in there last night, it had been a regular, mundane space with wooden walls and floor. The hanging papers were creepy, but didn't seem to be supernatural. So how could Grover Solomon open the door—the figurative door—that blocked him from meeting Lazarus in person?

His mind flashed back to his conversation with Alice last night. *The tools my grandmother gave that man enabled him to see and confront the* gwishin *in a manner he could not have accomplished on his own.*

Yes, he would have to go back to Alice and ask—or beg, if it came to that—for those "tools" and advice about how to use them. She probably wouldn't be very impressed that he had returned to the house after she had expressly told him not to, but he also thought she would assist him if he asked.

He also needed a better idea of what was really going on inside the crawlspace up on third. Lazarus had hinted that Odetta possessed a whole fortress of traps and weaponry, and Grover Solomon couldn't argue with that. Each time he'd gotten close to that room in the last two days something terrible had happened.

He balled up a fist and smacked his thigh in temper. Obviously, he needed to talk to Lazarus again. Laz had spent fifteen years in the crawlspace, and probably knew every corner, every floorboard, every scrap of paper hanging from that ceiling. But with no reliable way to contact Laz again, how could he find out anything? It wasn't like anyone else had spent years of their life huddled alone in there with—

His eyes snapped open. His mother had done *exactly* that.

He bolted upright and leapt off the bunk. "Guard!" he called through the square pocket of wire grating that served as a window in the cell door. "I'm ready to make my phone call!"

The Women of the Cave

In the strange days following Zebulon Koop's death, the students of New Canaan Mennonite Academy spread throughout the dormitory house, cleaning under every bed, sweeping out every corner, dusting every ledge—a cleansing ritual performed as part of the mourning period for their second departed Headmaster. Classes have been suspended for the summer a week early, and Odetta has imposed a rule of silence. The students are to eat, sleep, and clean without making a sound for one full week's time. This type of silence is of course impossible for thirty people living under one roof; doubly so when most of those people are children. If Odetta had remained in charge during the week of mourning, more than one student would have gone to bed hungry and with a stinging rump to boot. But she has cloistered herself to the third floor of the dormitory, leaving the ever trustworthy Dorcas in charge.

Thank God for Dorcas. The girl may have a face like a shovel and hips that could birth a steer, but she's whip-smart, and Odetta hopes she'll stay on after graduation. She's counting on it, in fact. Odetta has been grooming Dorcas to be the future Headmistress ever since she arrived at the academy at the age of 11, able to repeat whole chapters of the Bible verbatim after only a single reading. Dorcas can also teach. The younger students look up to her in a way that they will never look up to the Head Boy, Daniel. And who can blame them? Daniel may be the oldest boy in the school, but he still receives assistance with his studies from students three and four years younger than he. Yes, opposite poles of the compass are Dorcas and Daniel.

Or so Odetta thinks until partway through the week of mourning, when she is roused from sleep by the rhythmic thump of Daniel's knee on the floor by Dorcas's bed. Odetta descends to the Head Girl's sleeping quarters and discovers, for the second time in less than a week, two people in the throes of forbidden lovemaking. It is a good thing Odetta has no fire to hand. She yanks Daniel out from under Dorcas's sheets by a fistful his hair, hauls him—squealing like a scalded piglet, his stupid prick jutting for all the world to see—through the dormitory, and tosses him out the front door.

Still squealing stupidly, Daniel plunges into the tall prairie grasses at the edge of the academy's property. There he hides, enduring mosquito and chigger bites until Odetta and the handful of students drawn outside by the commotion have all retired into the dormitory. He steals a pair of pants and a shirt off the academy clothesline and spends the rest of the night walking the eighteen miles back to his family's home. He informs his parents, who are no brighter than he is, that he graduated early.

That very day he begins working for his dad on the farm, which is what he would have done even if he truly had graduated from the academy. Sometimes during the long, dusty days on the tractor he will daydream about Dorcas. Sometimes he will think about her in his bed at night and pleasure himself before sleep. This will go on until he turns 19 and marries the neighbors' daughter, Clara, who is only 17 but already bakes the best bread in the county. Daniel will be a kind, *docile husband and father who provides for his kids but can't help them with their homework.*

He will succumb to heart disease at the age of 53, beloved by his family, fat with decades of delicious bread. In his final moments he will feel vaguely satisfied that he'd experienced just about all life had to offer.

Dorcas, on the other hand, gets the Cave. Three days of it—the same amount of time the Lord Jesus spent in His tomb—during which she must scour her perfect memory for Bible verses condemning sexual uncleanliness. She copies them in blocky longhand by the light of a single candle onto long slips of paper to be hung from the ceiling of the little room. Odetta commands several of the boys to carry the ancient grandfather clock up to the third floor, where it bangs out Dorcas's sentence, second by second.

Odetta sits outside the Cave, rising twice daily—once to provide Dorcas with bread and water, and once to empty and return her chamber pot. Odetta consumes the same meager diet as her imprisoned protégé, listens to the same thunderous countdown from the clock. Above all, she begs God to show her why it all went wrong.

But for three days God remains infuriatingly silent, and at last Dorcas is released. Not to redemption or salvation, but to expulsion and disgrace. She is not asked to consider a career as future Headmistress of New Canaan Mennonite Academy. With only the clothes she has worn for three straight days in the Cave, she is escorted out the front door and made to walk a gauntlet comprising the entire student body of the academy (minus Daniel, of course), boys on the left, girls on the right. Wide, troubled eyes follow her passage. Some of the younger children cry.

Little nose-picking Hannah stands near the end of the line of girls, lips pressed together in a white line, chin quivering. Not because she loves Dorcas in any particular way—Dorcas was still very strict, even if she was friendlier than Odetta—but because she, Hannah, doesn't get it. None of the little ones get it. Odetta has announced only that Dorcas has failed them. All of them. Dorcas has failed herself, the students, the school, and Odetta. She has failed God Himself, and the only recourse is exile. Daniel's name never comes up.

Halfway down the line of her former peers, Dorcas begins to cry too. Bright and mature though she may be, she is still only 17, and she is hurt and confused and humiliated. Odetta hasn't explained much to her, either. Has not, in fact, spoken to her at all since imprisoning her in the Cave three days ago. She knows she is being punished because of her relations with Daniel, but has no idea what Odetta has told the students about her. She half-expects her peers to spit on her as she passes, or perhaps hurl small rocks in the symbolic stoning of an adulterer. Yet she shoulders this final humiliation handed down to her by her Headmistress because, even now, she remembers her lessons of the last seven years. She will show the other students what it looks like to accept responsibility for her mistakes, tears and all. She will lead by example, to the end.

Perhaps unsurprisingly, her noble effort is lost on most of the students. But nothing is lost on Odetta Koop. In this terrible moment she is so proud of Dorcas that she wants to scream. And scream she will, but that comes later.

For now, Dorcas walks the gauntlet of staring students, her bare feet swishing through wild grasses and weeds, tears drying on her cheeks in the hot summer breeze. When she reaches the main road she turns on her heel and continues on toward her home, four miles away. She does not look back. Lot's wife looked back at the dying city of Sodom, and we all know how God rewarded her sentimentality, don't we?

So Dorcas, who in another age could have been an educator, a philosopher, an astronaut, returns to her parents' horse farm with every single Bible verse she copied and hung seared into her perfect memory. Like Daniel, she lies to her parents and tells them she graduated from the academy. Five days after her return, a letter addressed to her parents arrives from Odetta Koop. Panicked, Dorcas shreds the letter, unopened. She stirs the pieces into the manure pile outside the horse barn. But the consequences of her escapades with Daniel have not finished with her. She misses one menstruation cycle, then another. For the better part of the summer, she vomits up her breakfast behind the barn during morning chores.

Near the end of August she will nearly bleed to death in an empty horse stall as she struggles to pull the baby she and Daniel made out of her with a baling hook before she starts to show. The horses in the stalls around her stomp and whicker, eyes bulging, nostrils flaring. Dorcas's daddy investigates the source of their distress and comes upon his daughter sprawled in a pile of hay black and sticky with her blood.

The Lord may not have blessed Dorcas's father with any more smarts than He gave Daniel, but the man is as strong as any two of his horses. He looses an anguished roar, cradles Dorcas to his chest, and sprints half a mile down the road to Pat Goering's place, where he can phone a doctor. So Dorcas will live, and a lot longer than poor, dumb, happy Daniel.

But all that is in the future. The other students also return to their homes the day of Dorcas's expulsion. Many of the younger ones spend their first evening back home crying, though they can't articulate why to their bemused parents.

The children's tears are nothing to Odetta's. Not even when her beloved Eli died did she weep like this. In the Cave, she prostrates herself below the strips of paper Dorcas wrote and so carefully hung, and her misery crashes through the little room like a stormy ocean tide ravaging an underwater cove. Her eyes roll under swollen lids, the cords in her neck stand out like pencils, and her teeth—her teeth! They snap and grind and rip at the air as if Odetta is trying to chew through the darkness itself. She bites her tongue and her lower lip deeply enough to draw blood, though she will not notice until morning.

The problem is not Dorcas's betrayal, or even Zebulon's. It is Eli's.

Just as the students purged the lower dormitories of all dust and un-cleanliness, Odetta has performed the same ritual in her living space on the third floor now that she is alone. And she has discovered a letter from her first husband—the one whom she has repeatedly thought of as "the good one." But she will never again think of him that way. Now, finally, she understands that there was *no good one. Maybe there are no good ones at all, not in the entire world. Look at Daniel. So obedient, so stupid. He should have been harmless. But he wasn't. Never harm-less, no.*

Odetta has given herself wholly to two men—yes, even to the sod-omite Zebulon she gave herself—and in return they spat on her oath. On her body, on her soul, on her sex. Oh, they appeared to give her full consideration in front of the students and to the public. They led by example, God damn them. But in the darkest, most rotten chambers of their hearts, they pursued only their own wants and allowed her be dragged into the undertow of their selfishness.

The letter from Eli, now crushed in the same hand that dragged Daniel down a flight of stairs by his hair, bears his last confession. The penmanship is barely legible, and not all of it makes sense. He must have written it in the deepest part of his fever, perhaps even as she slept next to him on the floor. But she understands it well enough to know that her first instinct, the one which flashed into her mind outside the academy woodshop moments before she set it ablaze, was correct.

Eli knew about Zebulon.

He knew Zebulon had lain with John Barnaby, the man who be-came his foreman. And Eli's last act had been to coerce Zebulon to marry and lay with Odetta as well. To force Zebulon to invade her with the part of him that had invaded John Barnaby over and over until the two men had burned for it.

And Odetta hopes in the darkest chambers of her *heart that Eli burns for it too. She hopes his undying bones crackle and char over the devil's spit for eternity. Otherwise, what is Hell for?*

She unfolds the letter again. The sweat of her palm has caused the ink to run, smearing Eli's treasonous words across the page. It doesn't matter. Odetta intends never to read it again anyway. She smooths the page against her breast and then tears off a long, vertical strip. This she stuffs into her mouth, tasting the ink, tasting her sweat, tasting her own blood. Those gnashing teeth finally have something to occupy them. When that first strip becomes pulpy enough to swallow, down it goes. Six strips later, the whole letter is gone. Whatever nutrients her body can glean from the paper and ink will be absorbed into her body—will make her stronger.

This notion appeals so much to Odetta that, even as she swallows the last of Eli's letter, she rips one of the hanging Bible verses off its string and folds it into her mouth like a stick of Wrigley's chewing gum. She continues to eat for the rest of the afternoon and into the evening. By the time she gulps down the last of Dorcas's Bible verses, her jaws and neck ache, and her tongue is sleeved in a sticky white residue like wallpaper glue. Yet she feels better. Not just a little better, either. The consumption of scripture has calmed the beast of her anger.

She lifts herself into a half crouch and waddles out of the little room into her living area. Night has fallen outside, but the larger room, illuminated by bluish summer moonlight filtering through the uncovered windows, looks almost day-bright compared to the Cave. Odetta needs no lantern to guide her through her home (nor would she think much of the synthetic peach glow of the streetlamps to which Grover Solomon later grows so accustomed). She navigates by moonlight and memory and instinct.

And goodness, she feels better. Doesn't she just! She feels righteous and whole in a way that she has not felt since she and Eli first broke ground on her school. Yes, her *school. Not Eli's or Zebulon's, or even Dorcas's. Poor Dorcas, who came so far only to be tripped up at the finish line by the idiot Daniel and his stupid jutting prick.*

Then again, hasn't Odetta herself been tripped up in a similar way? Twice, no less? For the briefest moment she regrets her treatment of Dorcas. But the regret passes before it can even fully form. Dorcas must deal with the consequence of her failures, just as Odetta must.

First, though, she feels compelled to replace the verses that Dorcas hung in the Cave. A rolltop desk built by the sodomite Zebulon sits in one corner of the living area. Another woman might have sold or destroyed the desk so she would not have to look at it and be reminded of her husband's betrayal. But Odetta is unlike other women in so many ways, and she honestly never considers getting rid of the desk. It is a fine and sturdy piece of chattel. Still operating by moonlight, she retrieves a fountain pen and a bottle of ink from the back edge of the desk, then draws ten or so sheets of paper from the top drawer. Last she lifts a candlestick with a book of matches sitting in its brass rim and carries all of these items back to the Cave.

Odetta kneels and strikes a match. Orange light flares inside the tiny room, causing her shadow to wobble strangely against the slanted ceiling. She touches the flame to the candle's wick and, without fuss or preamble, begins copying down the same Bible verses Dorcas spent three days writing. Odetta does not need to consult her Bible to remember the precise wording or the chapter and verse. Dorcas was not the only person at the academy with a perfect memory.

When she has filled one page, she folds it into long segments, moistens the folded edges with her tongue, and carefully tears each verse from the page until they lay in strips at her crossed feet. She pokes a single hole into each with the sharp tip of her pen and ties them, one by one, onto strings still hanging from the ceiling. In this manner, Odetta works her way through the whole stack of paper. She does not stop to consider why she is doing it any more than she questioned why she spent the better part of a day eating paper. That righteous surety still fills her, and she knows that what she is doing is correct. Holy, even. The exercise lasts three days—once again, that powerfully symbolic duration of time that Christ spent in His tomb—enhancing her sense of holiness to a kind of pitched spiritual ecstasy. And at the end, she feels truly, wholly cleansed.

Nor is it the last time she acts out this cleansing rite. Year after year, at the beginning of every summer for the rest of her life, Odetta Koop will persist in her ritual of consumption and reproduction. Of reaping and sewing. Throughout the school year, Odetta prays inside her Cave each day, and after twelve months, the papers have absorbed the energy of her prayers the way a cornstalk absorb water and sunlight.

Seventeen years later, when Odetta suffers a stroke in late May and passes away at the age of 61, a crop of hanging verses remains in the Cave from the previous summer, ripe and swollen with eleven months of her spiritual fertilization.

A couple by the name of Clemmer purchases the dormitory after Odetta's death, not because they need such a gigantic home to live in—their own children are grown—but because there is talk in town of tearing the place down and dividing the property for sale. The Clemmers are academy alumni (they attended before the school took its asexual turn in the early thirties, and so were able to marry without guilt), and they faithfully maintain the dormitory more or less in its original state.

The crawlspace on third they leave alone entirely. They understand that only Odetta Koop could have written out and displayed all of those Bible verses in such a way, and Mrs. Clemmer tells her husband it would only be respectful to their former Headmistress's memory to leave them up. "How in the world would we use such a tiny room, anyway?" she asks, and Mr. Clemmer agrees.

Mrs. Clemmer does not mention what happened the day they moved in, when she opened the half door on third and shoved a box inside to store until she was ready to unpack it properly. She does not tell her husband about the sudden rustling sound from the hanging slips of paper or the way the box came shooting back out of the room and scooted three feet across the carpet as if being yanked by an invisible cord. Why would she tell him about that when nothing similar has happened since? Well, not unless you count the occasional footsteps audible overhead when Mr. and Mrs. Clemmer sit together in the living room or lie in bed at night. But this is an old house, and old houses settle, don't they?

The Clemmers learn pretty quickly to conduct most of their daily matters on the first and second floors of the old dormitory. Like the subsequent owners, Ethyl and Annette Yoder, they use the third floor mainly for storage.

But not the crawlspace. That stays empty. Out of respect for their departed Headmistress, who has not so much "departed" as she has clung with fevered desperation to the house, anchored there by the weedy spiritual briar patch she planted, reaped, and sewed every summer for nearly two decades of her life.

Yet even her precious Cave might not have been strong enough to keep Odetta in the house forever. A generation after her death, along comes Annette Yoder, mother of Grover Solomon. Annette is attacked, groped, violated by a human stain of a man who owns a law firm, a bank, and a realty office in town. She escapes the man physically intact, but mentally and emotionally shattered. A bomb has exploded her heart. She is afraid, furious, guilty, ashamed, and afraid again. She retreats to the little room once known at New Canaan Mennonite Academy as the Cave. It is small, warm, dark. Annette is comforted there, and why wouldn't she be? Partly it is the scriptures which hang in that room, condemning the abuses of sex. She reads the verses with a pocket flashlight and assumes they are relics of the era when the house was a religious dormitory.

There is more comfort to be had here, too. The little room...understands Annette. She knows that is a crazy idea, but she also knows it's true. She feels a kinship with the room that she will never feel from poor Ethyl. He will never fully understand what happened to her, though he will try. So in her terrible vulnerability and hurt she returns to the room again and again—eventually switching from the flashlight to a candle for reasons she can't explain, even to herself—never realizing that someone is, once again, taking advantage of her.

Because the room understands nothing. It is, after all, a room. Odetta Koop, on the other hand, understands Annette Yoder perfectly. The two women share many similarities. Both have been gravely wronged by the desires of men and have sought solace in scripture. Both turn away from sexual intimacy after their abuse. Both are capable leaders and trailblazers—it is Annette, not Ethyl, who takes the helm in creating their new church when they leave Kurt Martin's congregation—within a religious patriarchy that demands their subordination.

At first Odetta actually does use her understanding to comfort Annette. But as Annette pours more and more of herself into the Cave, Odetta realizes Annette is making her stronger. She, the spirit that once inhabited Odetta Koop's body, can cling more tightly to mortal life now that Annette is here. The dreadful pulling sensation Odetta feels, which she has resisted every second of every day since the moment her body died, begins to lessen. Annette is a new anchor, and so much more powerful than the fading energy of the Cave.

So Odetta latches onto Annette, burrows into her, a six-and-a-half foot tall parasite crouched grotesquely on Annette's shoulders. Some sharp, thorny part of her spirit not even she fully understands drills ever deeper into Annette's mind like the proboscis of a tick. It happens slowly, organically, so that Annette does not really notice it. Annette never loses herself. You would not call her possessed. But Odetta is nonetheless tethered to her.

As little Grover Solomon grows older, he also becomes more aware of Odetta's mounting strength. His awareness manifests as fear of the house, which has begun to emit noises and odd vibrations that his parents insist are in his mind. Soon, what starts out as vague unease blossoms into constant terror that shadows Grover Solomon much in the way Odetta Koop shadows his mother. Only the presence of Lazarus

Beachy calms him. Grover Solomon believes that Lazarus keeps the fear at bay simply because he is so brave.

But Odetta and Annette know better, and this shared knowledge acts simultaneously as a glue that binds the two woman and a sharp wedge that threatens to drive them apart. They both see plainly that Grover Solomon doesn't feel afraid when he is around Lazarus, because he is in love.

The Untamed Fury
of Althea Gibson

The uniformed woman who had escorted Grover Solomon to his cell earlier answered his summons and showed him to a little desk in the corner of the small station lobby, its surface blank but for a rotary telephone with a cracked handset and phone book. Two bulky desktop computers connected to fat, yellowing monitors wheezed along behind the clerk's counter.

Only one other civilian occupied the lobby, an absolutely ancient woman who sat alone in the waiting area with her hair pinned up under a lace head covering. She clutched the worn leather straps of a small purse in both hands as if she expected muggers to leap at her from every direction. Grover Solomon offered her what he hoped was a reassuring smile. She clutched her purse more tightly and studied him with dark, unsettling, deep-set eyes until he looked away.

On the opposite side of the lobby was the chief's office. The door was closed, but Ducky could be seen through the venetian blinds covering the single window. He was speaking to someone who sat across from his desk, hidden at this angle by the window frame and closed door. The person was apparently saying something of interest, because Ducky kept nodding and pecking at his keyboard with his index fingers. As if sensing Grover Solomon's gaze on him, Ducky glanced up and peered out the window, but immediately returned his attention to the keyboard with an expression that suggested he had curds of sour milk stuck in his mustache.

Grover Solomon sighed and turned back down to the telephone. A laminated sheet of instructions about how to make a collect call was taped to the chipped formica surface of the desk. He lifted the handset and dialed as per the instructions. The rotary dial whirred after each number, and soon enough he was speaking to an operator who connected him to his mother's cell phone.

"Hello?" his mother's voice asked uncertainly.

"Ma'am," the operator began. "Will you accept a collect call from a Grover Solomon Yoder?"

There was such a long pause that Grover Solomon thought the connection had been lost. The operator must have thought so too, because she asked, "Ma'am? Can you hear me? Are you willing to—"

"No," Annette's voice said in a whisper. "I'm sorry. No."

"Mom, what are you doing?" blurted Grover Solomon reflexively. Did she not understand what was happening?

"I'm sorry," she repeated.

The line died with a tiny, almost inaudible click that sounded as loud to Grover Solomon as someone slamming a door in his ear. His face went numb with shock. His whole body suddenly seemed filled with ice. If he'd thought his parents had reached the limit of how far they would go to preserve their authority over him, it seemed he had been tremendously, desperately mistaken.

The operator was asking if he wanted to try to connect to another party now. He let the handset slide down from his ear and fall back into its cradle. He had no one now. The few allies he had gathered in the last twenty-four hours were used up, driven away by his single-minded and dangerous obsession with Odetta Koop. And his mother, the only person who might possibly understand that obsession—the only other person he knew who had lived under Odetta Koop's oppressive shadow—had cut him off too.

His own mother.

Sure, she didn't hug him when he came home to visit, but he still knew she loved him. However deep she carried her feelings, however faint the signs of affection might be, she still loved him. She must. She was his *mother*, for God's sake!

But now even the simple truth of a mother's love, which he'd taken for granted his entire life, had become another casualty in his corrosive war with a dead woman. Snuffed out like the life of his best friend. What was left? His sanity? His instinctive will to live? Would Odetta Koop just keep chipping away at the foundational stones of his life and mind until he went crazy and threw himself off a cliff like the poor fool who had fought the *gwishin* in that Korean village?

No, Annette's voice echoed in his head. *I'm sorry. No. I'm sorry.*

Without warning the door to Ducky's office burst open.

"—strenuously object to this course of action," Ducky was bleating. "The boy is unreasonable, possibly unhinged. You didn't see—"

"Give it a rest, Mallard," a woman's voice interrupted sharply. "Plenty of people did see, and thank God they called me. You should be ashamed of yourself. You're a public servant, not a hired jailor."

Grover Solomon swiveled around to see Althea Gibson, the town librarian, storming out of Ducky's office in a towering rage. Her hollow cheeks were flushed. Her tiny bosoms heaved beneath her homespun wool top. Ferocious energy baked from her every pore like ripples in a heat mirage. She was at least a foot shorter than Ducky and probably a hundred pounds lighter, but next to her the police chief looked diminished somehow. His barrel chest seemed to deflate inside his starched black uniform. The golden shield pinned over his heart appeared dim and tarnished in the sterile glow of the lobby's flourescent lights.

Gone was the wispy, whispering librarian Grover Solomon had known his whole life. In her place was a fierce, proud lioness of a woman making the New Canaan chief of police shrink back against his own office door like a cornered gazelle.

"I suppose I should be grateful you didn't pull your gun on him," Thea snarled up at Ducky, her face contorted and red. "You coward."

Ducky swelled. "You go too far. You can't talk to—"

"Enough," Thea snapped, and the word cracked like ice covering a frozen lake. "I will be bringing this matter to the next city council meeting. Until then, we have nothing more to discuss. Now where is—" Her eyes fell on Grover Solomon, still sitting mutely at the call desk. An unreadable expression drifted across her face like a fast-moving cloud. "Have they returned your belongings, Grover Solomon?"

"No, ma'am," he answered at once. A hundred questions rose to his mind, but he bottled them all. Now did not seem to be the time.

Thea shot a grim look at front counter. "Peggy," she barked.

The officer who had escorted Grover Solomon from his cell leapt to her feet without even glancing at Ducky and fled through a steel door behind her desk. In the momentary silence, Ducky's patent leather shoes creaked as he rose and fell impotently on the balls of his feet. The other officer, Peggy, returned moments later with a plastic tub containing Grover Solomon's personal effects.

Although he didn't completely understand what was happening, two things had become obvious: first, the police were letting him go; and second, somehow the town librarian had made it happen.

Without a glance at Ducky or Peggy, Grover Solomon quickly crossed to the front counter and stuffed his belongings into his pockets. When he turned back around, he saw that the ancient woman with the purse had stood too. Square of body and straight of back, she cut an oddly impressive figure in the stark, empty room. She moved to Thea's side, still clutching her purse as tightly as ever, and Grover Solomon saw that there couldn't be more than an inch of height separating the tops of her and Ducky's heads. Between them, Thea looked as short and slight as an egret between two imposing rhinos.

"Come on, Grover Solomon. Let's get out of here," said Thea in a somewhat gentler voice that more closely matched the way she sounded in the library.

She gestured for him to walk ahead of her, which he did in silence. He felt Ducky's eyes as two hot points on the back of his head all the way down the hall. He pushed through the station door, stepped out into warm, purple-orange twilight, and stopped dead. Forgetting all his other questions, he spun around and asked, "How long have I been in here?"

"Most of the day," answered Thea grimly. She took him by the elbow to get him moving again. "I would have come a lot sooner, but I only heard about it a couple hours ago myself. I was all the way over in Chinook County visiting Miss Hershberger here." She jerked her head to indicate the tall, silent woman shuffling along behind them.

Grover Solomon heard nothing after the word "day." So the light wasn't a trick of his eyes or some terrible mirage. He had lost an entire day—his last day before the Escobars moved in to his old house.

Well, he'd been wondering what else Odetta Koop could take from him before this was all over, and now he had an answer: time. She had stripped away his last and most precious resource.

Because there was no doubt in his exhausted mind that Odetta Koop had somehow caused his imprisonment. All of the obstacles that had sprung up in the last twenty-four hours reeled through his mind like a newsreel of disaster footage. Odetta's impersonation of Autumn, which had caused him to attack the real Autumn and nearly end her pregnancy (hadn't Autumn herself said she thought Odetta wanted to kill her baby?), the white-knuckled trip to the hospital with Kurt and Cynthia Martin, the fight with his parents, Dr. Shepherd's assault, the altercation with his father and Ducky, the endless legal paperwork, the rejection from his mother…How could all of that have happened in a single day if not for Odetta Koop's malignant hand reaching out to hold him back, break him down? Her spirit might not be able to leave the house, but her influence seemed to suffer no boundaries at all.

Grover Solomon allowed himself to be steered into the back seat of a Subaru station wagon. He could feel his exhaustion threatening to drag him under again. What a relief it would be to go back to sleep, to escape this ceaseless nightmare of a weekend. For a moment he actually did close his eyes, suddenly intoxicated by the hope that he would wake up on his apartment futon in Chicago with cheap paperback ghost stories and pizza boxes scattered around him like the trash they were.

The little car rocked from side to side as Thea and her companion entered and slammed their doors. Grover Solomon opened his eyes wearily. "It was really generous of you to bail me out, Mrs. Gibson, but I can't let you waste all that money on me. If you have a pen, I can write you check."

"Pish," said Thea, starting the car. "I didn't pay a dime, and neither will you. If anything, you could sue for wrongful imprisonment. Mallard had no legal standing to hold you at all."

Grover Solomon leaned back and closed his eyes again. "I'm not suing anyone."

"Of course you're not," Thea snapped. "You're a good person." The car lurched backward and forward again as she maneuvered out of her parking space and onto the road.

"You grew up in the New Canaan Mennonite Academy building," said a new voice. It sounded low and gravelly. A hard voice.

Grover Solomon looked up. The old woman who had seemed so distrustful of him in the police station now watched him through the visor mirror above the passenger seat.

"Yes, ma'am," he said uncertainly.

"Thea told me you were asking questions about Odetta Koop."

Grover Solomon sat forward, his desire to sleep momentarily forgotten. Suddenly he recalled something Thea had told him yesterday morning when they had spoken in the library. She said she'd been working on the academy's historical archives with Kurt Martin and a woman who had been a student at the academy. Grover Solomon remembered saying that such a person would have to be over a hundred years old, and this woman looked older than God.

"Yes, ma'am, that's right. Did you know her?"

The woman didn't answer right away. Her dark eyes, sunken in her lined face but still bright and sharp as an eagle's, never left his face in the mirror.

"Grover Solomon," said Thea, and now there was cold satisfaction in her voice. "I'd like you to meet Dorcas Hershberger, former Head Girl of New Canaan Mennonite Academy."

The Road Home

"Head Girl," Grover Solomon repeated. "So, were you some kind of student leader, or—"

"I was," Dorcas Hershberger answered in her gravelly voice. "Why do you want to know about Odetta Koop?"

He swallowed. Whoever this woman was, she cared little for small talk. Well, that was okay, because he had run out of time.

"I grew up in the house that used to be the academy dormitory. My parents sold it recently and the family who bought it moves in tomorrow morning. Did Thea tell you that?"

Dorcas nodded, still watching him in the mirror.

"What she didn't tell you—because she doesn't know—is that Odetta Koop is still there."

There was a sharp intake of breath. "What on earth are you talking about, Grover Solomon?" Thea demanded.

He didn't answer. Dorcas stared at him, and he stared back at the only part of her face he could see in the visor mirror: her eyes.

Something of Autumn lurked in those dark, deep-set eyes. They were smart like Autumn's, but colder. Harsher.

"I don't know what kind of person Odetta Koop was when she was alive, ma'am, but she's gotten mean since she died. She killed my best friend when I was kid."

"Grover Solomon!" Thea braked so hard that Grover Solomon and Dorcas were thrown forward against their seatbelts. She twisted around, her face a white, angry oval in the deepening twilight. "What do you think you're doing? How dare you say these things? Miss Hershberger agreed to come here to help you. I spent my whole day making calls and driving all over the state of Iowa for you. If you are making some kind of joke, it is in very poor taste."

Until ten minutes ago, he never would have believed his old friend capable of uttering anything more aggressive than a friendly whisper, and to hear her shouting at him now stung almost as badly as his mother refusing to talk to him on the telephone.

"I'm not joking. I—I've seen her."

Thea's eyes widened in outraged disbelief. She opened her mouth again, presumably to tell him off. But Dorcas reached up and enclosed Thea's bony forearm in one large, liver-spotted hand.

"What did she look like?" Dorcas asked.

Grover Solomon forced himself to look away from Thea. "Um, she's big. Taller than you, even. She wore a long black dress. Her eyes—" He faltered, remembering how the sticky shreds of the Autumn mask had clung to his fingertips. "Her eyes were sewn shut with black thread. She had dark, curly hair. I didn't get a good look at the rest of her face."

Thea's mouth continued to hang open, but she no longer looked like she wanted to shout. Scream, maybe. Grover Solomon would have been happy to join her at it.

"She talked to me, too," he went on. "She said she's been watching me since I was a kid, and she's been trying to save my soul because I'm gay. That's why she burned my friend. She knew I was in love with him."

"*Burned him?*" Dorcas hissed. At last she turned and faced him directly, pinning him with those deep, hard eyes. She seemed to swell so that suddenly she filled too much of Thea's little car.

For an instant Grover Solomon recoiled from her, startled at the intensity of her reaction. But then he thought he understood something. "You were there," he guessed. "At the first fire. Weren't you?"

Dorcas did not answer. She rotated slowly away from him. Something about the slump of her broad, round shoulders put him in mind of a huge old grizzly bear lumbering away from a fight. "Take us to the academy," she said grimly.

After a moment's hesitation, Thea obliged, pulling back into the center of the road. No other traffic had passed in either direction during this little discussion.

"You know about the fire," Dorcas said.

"Yes, ma'am. Kurt Martin told me about it, but all I know is that two men died. Odetta's second husband, Zebulon, and someone else."

Dorcas grunted. "His name was John Barnaby. He and Zebulon were best friends. Nigh inseparable were Zeb and John. Never saw one without the other. Many a night the woodshop lanterns burned long after lights out came and went for the students."

Grover Solomon watched her reflection, listening hard.

Dorcas grimaced. "How long must I wait for you to take my meaning, young man? Thea tells me you are intelligent."

He frowned, then his mouth fell open. "No way," he said idiotically.

"During my last year I fell into a habit of staying awake late into the night. A matter of weeks before the fire, I saw Zeb and John through a window, returning from the woodshop, walking slow and clasping hands in the moonlight. Fools," she added, not unkindly.

"So wait," said Grover Solomon, still struggling to pick up the mental debris from this bombshell. "You're saying Odetta set the fire and killed those two men because she found out they were gay?"

In the vanity mirror, a strange expression clouded Dorcas's eyes. "I was in the dining hall when the fire started. All the students were. The Headmistress came straight to me and instructed me to contact the fire brigade."

"And you knew she had done it."

Dorcas didn't answer right away. "When she came inside I could tell something was desperately wrong with her. But why wouldn't there be? Her husband was burning to death not fifty yards away from where we sat eating."

"So when did you figure it out?" Grover Solomon persisted. He felt they were very close to something important now.

"I worshipped her," said Dorcas. "I wanted to be her. She was such a smart, hard woman. She expected a great deal from us students. Never more than we could handle. But there was deep cruelty in her that I never suspected. Not until she locked me in the Cave."

A chill ran in an icy line between Grover Solomon's shoulder blades. "The Cave?"

"A little room off her living quarters on the third floor," she said distantly. "If you grew up that house, I'm sure you know it. It would be just the right size for a child's playroom."

Grover Solomon shivered.

"But there was nothing playful about that room when I was a student. Odetta kept me there for three days, writing by candlelight. It was early summer, already hot. The room was a slow oven, filled with candle smoke and the stink of a chamber pot."

She was speaking so softly now that she should have been impossible to hear, but her voice was perfectly audible. Even the car's engine seemed to be whispering so as not to drown out so much as a syllable of her story.

Locked me in the Cave, Grover Solomon thought. *The Cave. Writing by candlelight.*

"What did you write?" he managed at last. He knew the answer, but he couldn't help asking the question anyway.

"Bible verses. The Headmistress instructed me to write out all the verses I could remember about carnal impurity."

"Because of her gay husband?"

"No. I fornicated with a boy in my bed and the headmistress caught us. That's why she imprisoned me. It was my penance."

Another silence filled the car, this time so heavy that it seemed to have actual weight. Grover Solomon almost felt imprisoned himself.

Locked me in the Cave.

An invisible vice seemed to be compressing his chest so that he couldn't draw in enough oxygen no matter how deeply he breathed. The purple twilight outside the car grew dimmer, the night darkening with unnatural rapidity. A new smell filled his nose—a noxious, suffocating miasma of sulfurous smoke and ammonia.

Distantly, he heard Thea shouting, and he hoped she wasn't shouting at him. He was thrown hard into his seatbelt again as the car lurched to a halt. There was a light, anxious tapping at his cheek.

"Grover Solomon!"

Thea's voice, clearer now. She *was* shouting at him.

His eyelids fluttered open and he saw that she had turned around in her seat once more, her expression fearful, one hand upraised and swatting at his cheek. Outside the car, the black veil had lifted on the night, returning the sky to dim purple twilight. He also saw, without surprise, that Thea had stopped the car just up the street from his old house. His little Honda still sat parked behind his parents' Ford, half a block away. Lights blazed from the first floor windows. Clouds of silvery vapor he had first seen last night after Alice's treatment carved out glittering tunnels through the air all around the house. But there were more of them now. Many more, and brighter than before.

They're memories, thought Grover Solomon incoherently. *Mine and Laz's and this poor old woman's, weaving a storm around Odetta Koop.*

"A hurricane of memory, and she's the eye," he murmured.

Thea gave him another of those swift little taps to the cheeks. "Stop that now," she demanded. "You, too, Dorcas. Now are you two going to be okay, or do I need to turn around and head for the hospital?"

Dorcas's broad shoulders were heaving. She too seemed to have suffered a fit of some kind. Had she revisited her imprisonment in the Cave as Grover Solomon had?

He reached up and gently pushed Thea's hand away. "Mrs. Hershb—" he began to say, and then broke into a ratchety spasm of coughing, as though his lungs were still full of that toxic combination of smoke and ammonia. When he got himself under control, he tried again. "Mrs. Hershberger, the Bible verses are still up in that room you called the Cave. My mom used to pray in there after a man from the church tried to rape her."

He had expected Thea to react with horror at this news, perhaps clutch her throat in her bony hands. But her only reaction was a slight thinning of her already thin lips.

She knows, Grover Solomon realized. Perhaps he shouldn't be surprised. This was New Canaan, after all. Maybe a ghost could immolate a forgotten, abused child without anyone finding out, but an attempted rape inside a church building? There must be dozens of people who knew.

He pushed this unwelcome revelation away. His family's increasingly pungent laundry list of problems could wait until after whatever happened tonight. Because he could feel a gathering storm inside himself, too. He could feel it in this car, whipping between him and the two women like gusts of wind on the edge of a cold front.

Dorcas leaned back against her seat's headrest, still wheezing. "I went mad for a time inside the Cave," she said in a choked, impossibly smoke-filled voice. "A single candle flame starts to look as bright as the sun when you live in constant dark. I kept it extinguished whenever I wasn't writing, and during those times without light, I never knew whether I slept or simply lay awake and dreamed with my eyes wide open.

"During one of those times of wakefulness or sleep, I saw something like a curtain fall before me, heavy and blacker than the darkest shadows in the room. God help me, I pulled that curtain aside."

She coughed a deep, barking cough and winced. She drew a handkerchief from her handbag and spat into it. When she spoke again, she sounded younger, slightly wistful. "I'm a hundred and three years old, and I should have died when I was eighteen. For much of my life I've wished I had."

Finally she twisted around again so that both she and Thea were peering into the back seat. "If you want to drive Odetta Koop's spirit away, don't count on succeeding. I've seen what she hides from."

"What?" asked Grover Solomon at once, but Dorcas was already shaking her head again.

"I won't be the one to tell you. You might find out anyway tonight."

Once again Grover Solomon thought of Alice's story, and the man who emerged from the *gwishin's* dwelling only to hurl himself, raving, off the side of a mountain. Had that man learned some terrible truth during his confrontation with the *gwishin?* Had he too pulled back some dreadful curtain and seen something that broke his mind?

Then another thought struck him. "You knew Odetta Koop was still here, in this house. That's why you came."

Dorcas made a low sound that could have been either affirmation or negation.

"Does that mean you'll come inside with me?"

"I will." She reached down to unclasp her seatbelt. "Please pull forward, Thea, dear."

Thea's lips had thinned so much that her mouth was only a

straight black line that looked as if it had been hastily scrawled onto her face with a magic marker.

"You don't have to come," he told her.

"Ha," said Thea simply, and she eased the car forward to park with the others in front of the house.

PART IV: EMANCIPATION

The Taking of Dorcas Hershberger

Outside Thea's car, the phenomena that Grover Solomon now thought of as memory tunnels encircled the house in glittering ribbons, brighter and more solid than they had been even minutes ago. As Grover Solomon, Thea, and Dorcas turned onto the walk leading to the front steps, a fourth vehicle came into view around the other side of the house. It was an old Toyota. Dread splashed heavily into the pit of Grover Solomon's stomach. He glanced at Thea, who was also looking at the car with obvious understanding and more than a little apprehension.

"I called Kurt Martin earlier," she admitted.

He stared at her.

"I knew you went to see him after you stopped at the library," she said defensively. "And the next thing I heard, your parents were suddenly back in town, and you were in jail. I had to know what Kurt told you." She glanced at the car again, chewing her lip. "I didn't expect him to come here, though."

Without responding, Grover Solomon pulled out his phone

and checked the call list. Leon's number was still near the top, and he jabbed it with his finger. He started walking again, the phone mashed to his ear.

Leon picked up after the first ring. "Hey, man. You get out of jail?"

Grover Solomon grimaced. Did the whole town know? How, exactly, had Lazarus's death been kept secret again? "Yeah, I'm out. Listen, where are you?"

"We're—" Leon began, but Grover Solomon let the phone drop from his ear. He had just mounted the bottom step leading up to the porch, and he could hear raised voices inside.

"—think you can come back here after all these years and tell us how to raise our child, after what you've done?" his father roared.

"Uh-oh," said Thea, and she began trotting up the steps more quickly.

"He's not a child, Ethyl!" Cynthia Martin's voice countered. "He's a grown man, and he needs help!"

Grover Solomon lifted the phone again and spoke urgently. "Please get over to my place as soon as you can. Our parents are having some kind of shouting match."

Without waiting for an answer, he stuffed the phone in his pocket, leapt up the last three steps, and yanked open the front door.

In the middle of the entry room, his father stood practically nose to nose with Cynthia Martin, just as red in the face as when Grover Solomon had last seen him. Kurt hovered a few steps behind his wife, his own face a mask of dumb anxiety. All three of them jumped and turned toward the door as Grove Solomon hurried inside with Thea practically stumbling over his heels in her haste to follow.

"Dad?" Grover Solomon said quickly. "Mrs. Martin? What's going on here?"

Cynthia retreated a couple steps from Ethyl, looking guilty. But Ethyl turned toward his son at once and held out a rough hand, palm up. "It's about darn time," he growled. "Give me the key, son."

Grover Solomon's hand rose unconsciously to his belly. He'd forgotten all about the key.

Ethyl noticed the movement, and his face clouded even further. "Chief Hook wasn't supposed to let you out until you had that key in your hand."

Grover Solomon opened his mouth to answer, but Thea strode past him so that she stood next to Cynthia Martin. "Mallard Hook didn't have any right to lock him up in the first place," she said hotly. "Why would—"

"Unless I'm very much mistaken," Ethyl interrupted loudly, "this is a matter for my family to work out and no one else's."

Kurt Martin nodded meekly and laid a hand on his wife's shoulder as if to steer her away. She shook him off. "It's true then?" she demanded of Ethyl. "You actually let your son be locked up?"

"What business is it of yours?" Ethyl practically shrieked. His eyes bulged. He balled his hands into fists on either side of his head as if to keep it from bursting. In that moment he looked utterly insane.

Grover Solomon unthinkingly stepped around Thea and put himself between her and his father. "Come on, Dad, calm do—"

"I will *not* calm down! I didn't raise you to talk back to me any more than I raised you to be a…a *faggot!*"

The word struck Grover Solomon as a physical force. He stumbled backward, nearly knocking Thea over. The room rang with stunned silence.

"You think I didn't know?" Ethyl sneered. "Everyone knows. Your foul little friend Lazarus knew, too. You think he ran away because of his parents? Please. He ran away from *you*. You made him sick, just like you make everyone—" He gestured wildly at the others in the room, nearly whacking Cynthia Martin in the side of the head. "—*sick!*" he finished.

And he spat in Grover Solomon's face.

The spittle slid down the side of Grover Solomon's nose, mingling with shocked tears. No one moved or spoke. Ethyl's shoulders heaved as he glared at each person in turn, apparently waiting for someone to challenge him. At last he noticed Dorcas Hershberger, standing just inside the door with an arrested look on her ancient face.

His chest ballooned and he pointed with a trembling, accusatory finger. "You!" he bawled.

Dorcas's dark eyes narrowed as she looked him up and down. The corners of her mouth turned down in a determined grimace. "Me," she agreed.

In the silence that followed this bizarre exchange, the back door that led off the kitchen could be heard opening and closing softly, three rooms away. "—just getting back home now."

The newcomer's words drifted from the kitchen door and through the long dining room into the entry room, where everyone had stopped to listen.

"No, I'm sure he won't press charges. I'll talk to him. Sorry to get you involved."

Grover Solomon's father appeared in the kitchen doorway with a cell phone pressed to his ear. Upon seeing the host of people staring at him from entry room, he stopped dead. His bewildered eyes traveled across all the different faces until they landed on his own.

Two Ethyl Yoders—the one standing red-faced in the entry room, and the one who had just emerged from the kitchen—goggled at one another with identical expressions of mute surprise. Time slowed and spiraled into a miniature, soundless infinity while everyone present contemplated the impossibility before them.

Then, as if to make up for the slow-down, time leapt forward again, and several things happened at once. Grover Solomon sprang at the nearest Ethyl and wrapped him in a bear hug, pinning his arms down. Immediately all the lights on the first floor began to flicker. The globe light fixture overhead exploded, showering the room with shards of white glass.

Grover Solomon squeezed his eyes shut as glass peppered his hair, but he didn't dare loosen his hold. The thing in his arms squirmed obscenely. There was a wet, tearing sound, and a huge dark shape burst out of his grip, leaving behind a sodden pile of clothes and false, papery skin the way a molting snake sloughs off the empty husk of its scales.

In the confusion, the cedar closet door was wrenched open and slammed shut again. Wall lights that hadn't exploded continued to stutter on and off in their sconces for several more seconds before snapping on again, bright and steady as if nothing had happened.

Still framed in the kitchen doorway, Ethyl—the real Ethyl—collapsed to his knees with a heavy thud that rattled the windows. His cell phone clattered across the dining room floor, the line still active. Ducky's reedy voice broke the silence. "Ethyl? You still there? Hello?"

Grover Solomon, who had, after all, experienced something like this before, recovered first. He gingerly daubed the spit from the side of his nose with his sleeve before crossing into the dining room. He bent, switched off his father's cell phone, and straightened back up.

Behind him, Cynthia Martin said, "Wh—what was that? What just happened?" She sounded close to hysteria.

Grover Solomon, on the other hand, felt as clear-headed as he had since arriving in New Canaan. Difficult though it had been to hear that terrible rant in his father's voice, he also now felt a building exhilaration. Odetta Koop had tipped her hand. She had shown herself, albeit in the form of his father. They had all seen her.

He frowned. They had *all* seen her. Something about that made him uneasy, but he couldn't put his finger on what.

"I'm sorry, Grover Solomon," Kurt Martin said in a husky voice. "I'm sorry I doubted your story. Those things I said to you in the hospital..."

Ethyl was climbing to his feet again. "Kurt?" he asked. There was a tense moment as the two men studied each other.

"Ethyl," said Kurt. He looked like he wanted to say more, but instead he simply nodded.

After a moment Ethyl nodded back and looked away quickly.

"Maybe we can hold off on greetings until we figure who I was just arguing with," Cynthia Martin said loudly. She sounded more angry than hysterical now.

"You know who it was," said Grover Solomon. "I told you this morning."

"Odetta Koop is dead," Cynthia answered in would-be reasonable voice.

"That was her," said Dorcas flatly. "I recognized her, and she recognized me."

She advanced toward the cedar closet door, which quaked briefly on its hinges. A muffled rattling came from the closet like the sound of dry beans in an African rain stick. Broken plaster, perhaps, cascading down the walls onto the wood floor.

"That's the closet where she spoke to you last night?" Kurt asked.

"Yes, sir," said Grover Solomon, but his attention was on Dorcas. She had stopped within several feet of the closet door, as if wary of getting too close. "Ma'am, can you tell me how you recognized her?"

"I saw what's behind her," said Dorcas in a choked voice. "Jesus wept. It must follow her everyw—"

The cedar closet door burst open. A face came thrusting through the opening, but it was like no face Grover Solomon had ever seen. It was seven feet high, filling the doorway from top to bottom. Its skin was a swampy dark gray, the color of rotting leaves. Fleshy cheeks, forehead, and chin dimpled as it pushed and strained against the sides of the doorframe, cracking the surrounding wall as it came. Its lips were two feet across, as black and droopy as a pair of dead eels. They flapped over uneven teeth the size and color of rusty axe heads. The eyes were sewn shut with black, uneven X's of thread as thick as climbing rope. Hidden behind the heavy gray lids, eyes the size of bowling balls rolled and quested.

The room filled with the screams of men and women alike. Exquisite terror, huge and absolute, paralyzed Grover Solomon where he stood. It bubbled downward from his scalp all the way to the tips of his toes as if someone had just shattered a full champagne bottle across the crown of his head.

And in the grip of that fear came a new, detached clarity of vision. He watched, frozen, as thick strands of curling black hair sprout from cracks in the wall around the closet door. They slithered over Cynthia's sandaled feet like octopus tentacles. Kurt yanked her backward so forcefully that the two of them went sprawling.

But the hair showed no interest in Cynthia. It advanced across the floor and crawled up Dorcas's body, coiling around her ankles and wrists. The face's gibbering mouth yawned to an impossible size, revealing multiple rows of those crooked axe-head teeth, all tipped inward like a shark's. The strands of hair binding Dorcas now dragged her toward the open mouth.

Grover Solomon's paralysis broke, and he lunged forward to pull Dorcas back. But before he could lay a hand on her, Dorcas reacted in a most surprising way. She dipped her shoulder forward like a linebacker setting up for a tackle and threw herself at the open mouth, which was now easily large enough to swallow her. Her torso and upper legs vanished into the maw and seemed to get stuck there, the way a ping-pong ball might get stuck in the tube of a working vacuum cleaner. Her ankles and tan SAS shoes poked out, kicking like swimmer's feet between the flabby lips.

The huge face changed. Its dark gray skin turned the purple-black of a ripe plum. An unspeakable tongue caked with slime jutted out and flapped at Dorcas's ankles in distress, spattering the wood floor below with a viscous substance like petroleum jelly. The mouth stretched wider still, and suddenly there was hideous sucking sound. Dorcas's feet shot the rest of the way into the mouth with frightening speed. A roar of hot wind buffeted Grover Solomon, lifting the hem of his t-shirt.

The gigantic face returned to its original gray color, and the mouth broke into a grisly axe-head smile. "*Mine!*" it shrieked, elongating the word in celebration. And in the depths of its cavernous throat Grover Solomon saw, not Dorcas, but two tiny orange pinpricks of light like fiery stars in a midnight sky.

"Laz?" he said, then repeated it more loudly. "*Laz!*"

Instinctively he made to launch himself into the mouth as Dorcas had done, but several pairs of hands seized him from behind and dragged him away.

The face yanked itself backward. The remaining loose strands of hair also retreated into the cracked wall. The closet door swung shut with such force that the hinges bent and broke. The door tipped slowly, almost gracefully outward, and fell to the floor with a crash.

Grover Solomon peeled away the hands restraining him and staggered forward, ignoring the alarmed, wordless cries of the others, to peer into the now doorless closet. "Laz!" he shouted into the swirling plaster. "Dorcas!"

But the closet was just a closet again.

The Taking of Annette Yoder

Sometime during the scuffle with Odetta Koop's outsized head, the ranks of the living within the battered entry room had swollen by three. Leon, Autumn, and Alice stood at the fore of the cluster of people now gaping at Grover Solomon with uniform terror. Leon and Autumn were breathing as hard as he was. Alice's face was a stony mask.

"Glad you guys could make it," Grover Solomon grunted, setting his hands on his knees and letting his head droop while he struggled to catch his breath. When he looked back up he thought he saw a smile flit across Autumn's lips, but it happened too quickly to be sure.

"What the hell was that thing?" Leon wheezed.

"Thing?" Cynthia asked.

Leon pointed, frowning. "Yeah, that enormous effing head sticking out of the closet. What other *thing* would I be talking about, Mom?" He spoke with unnatural good humor which quite plainly announced that he, too, was suffering from shock at what they had all just witnessed. "Was that what Odetta Koop really looks like?"

Cynthia mirrored her son's frown back at him, confusion mingling with residual fright.

Thea gingerly leaned forward and peered at the floor of the closet as if she expected to see a gaping hole there. "What happened to Dorcas? I saw her go through this door. And what on earth was that noise?"

Now Grover Solomon added his own frown to the visual chorus of them. "Noise?"

"It sounded like a..." She groped for the right words. "...like a freight train made of bones. I thought the whole house must be about to collapse on top of us." She shook her head angrily. "Somebody please tell me where Dorcas went. I saw her go into this closet."

"Grover Solomon," interrupted Autumn. She was pointing into the cedar closet.

He followed the line of her finger and saw something the curtain of sifting plaster dust had hidden from view until this moment. Two white playing cards rested side by side at the back of the closet where the floor met the sharp downward slant of the ceiling. He stepped carefully over the ruined door, dropped to his hands and knees, and crawled just far enough inside the closet to be able to tweeze the cards off the floor with two outstretched fingers. He backed out again and brushed chalky dust from the cards while Autumn and Leon gathered at either shoulder to look too.

The first card was the Queen of Spades. It showed a black and white photo of a young woman with a wide, flat face and wider, flatter hips. She wore a white cotton shift with a stark, black stain shaped like an ink blot covering her stomach and crotch. In her hand she carried a bailing hook. Grover Solomon looked from the hook to the black stain in the woman's dress, feeling sick.

"It's Dorcas," said Thea, who had moved beside Leon to look at the cards too. "I recognize her face from her school photos, but..."

She put the back of her hand to her mouth and turned away.

"Show us the other one," Autumn urged.

Grover Solomon understood the anxiety in her voice. She had already appeared on one of these cards this weekend. He slipped the Queen of Spades behind the second card, and immediately gave a startled cry. As with the previous card, symbols in the upper corner gave the card's suit and rank, but he didn't notice or care about that.

The person on the card was his mother. Like the image of Dorcas, this one did not reflect Annette's current appearance, but a previous one. Instead of her sassy new Gidget haircut, she wore her former hairstyle, steel gray and impossibly long. Much longer, in fact, than it had ever been in real life. Every inch of her body was draped in a thick, suffocating mass of hair. She knelt against a black background, head bowed, eyes closed, hands clasped and poking through the curtains of her hair as if through arm holes in a prayer shawl.

Little slips of paper hung down from the top edge of the card on white strings. The papers were longest at the outermost edges of the card and grew progressively shorter as they moved toward the center, forming a saw-toothed, triangular peak above Annette's bowed head. White candles formed an opposing triangle below her knees so that she appeared to be kneeling inside a diamond-shaped cage made of paper above and fire below.

The Queen of Diamonds.

"No, no, no," Grover Solomon moaned. "Dad!" he barked. "Where's Mom? Why isn't she with you?"

Still standing alone in the dining room, Ethyl blinked several times. "Annette? She…" He swallowed. "I went out to buy us a late dinner. She didn't want to come along."

In an instant Grover Solomon realized what had been bothering him after the unmasking of the fake version of his father. "Listen," he demanded of the others, "who saw a giant face sticking out of that closet just now?"

"Me," said Leon at once. Autumn also nodded and held up her hand. After a moment Alice followed suit, looking grim.

"But you're sure you didn't see her last night, when she ran down the hallway past you?" Grover Solomon asked Autumn.

"Positive."

He contemplated the rumpled pile of clothes and the slimy Ethyl mask lying in the middle of the floor, thinking hard. Everyone had seen Odetta wearing the Ethyl disguise, but only some of them had seen the huge face. Complicating matters, Autumn and Leon *had* seen the face, but they'd missed Odetta as she retreated past them last night. Why? What had changed? Was Odetta somehow stronger than she had been before? More present? More *real*? And if so, how?

He looked back down at Queen of Diamonds card and felt his insides go hollow.

"Okay, everyone who could see Odetta's face just now, come upstairs with me. The rest of you get out of h—"

"I saw it, too," interrupted Kurt, stepping purposefully around his wife. "I'm coming with you."

"What are you all talking about?" Cynthia Martin asked with a note of pleading in her voice. "Please tell us what's happening. How did I see Ethyl in two places at once? Who was I arguing with?"

Grover Solomon made himself look her in the eye. He was on the edge of panic, and everything was happening too quickly. But he owed her as much of an explanation as he could give. "Thank you for coming here to defend me, Mrs. Martin. It really means a lot. You too, Thea," he added to his old librarian. "But I think you will both be better off if you leave this house right now. The same goes for you, Dad," he called over his shoulder. "Don't worry about Mom. I'm going to find her."

To the others he said, "Let's go."

Without waiting for a response, he hurried over to the staircase and flung himself upward, taking three steps at a time. The image of his mother framed—imprisoned—inside a diamond made of scripture and flame was seared into his mind, and nothing else mattered. Not Dorcas, not Lazarus, not Odetta Koop herself. He had to rescue his mother, and she could only be in one place.

He didn't pause at the second floor landing but sped down the hallway to the narrow, enclosed staircase leading up to the third floor. The trapdoor at the top of the stairs was closed, although it had been open and hooked to the wall the last time he'd seen it. He set his shoulder against the bottom of the door and heaved upward. The heavy door rose an inch and stopped dead. He reset his legs on the fourth and fifth step down from the top and pushed with all his might. Again it moved that single inch, but no more.

Leon's pale face hovered in the dark doorway below.

"Help me," Grover Solomon begged.

"Not me," said Leon. "Only one other person can fit in there. You need the big guns."

He moved out of the way and Autumn appeared. She walked sedately up beside Grover Solomon and braced her palms on the bottom of the door. "On three," she said. He nodded. "One... two...*three!*"

He shoved upward with all his might. He thought of his mother up in that little room with the half-door, held captive by Odetta Koop. His legs quaked with the strain. The door seemed to give another inch. Autumn's body, pressed against him in that cramped space, hummed like a plucked guitar string. Her thigh muscles rippling in long cords below the hem of her shorts. She emitted a constant stream of soft and extraordinarily creative curses as she pushed.

Suddenly the pressure keeping the door closed let go. Grover Solomon and Autumn popped up into the third floor like targets in a whack-a-mole game. A shape hurtled toward his head in the darkness, rattling as it came. He instinctively let go of the trapdoor and threw out his hands to protect his face. If Autumn had let go too, the door would have fallen shut on their heads.

The rattling shape rebounded off his upraised palms and clattered heavily to the floor. It took several seconds before he could make sense of what he was looking at. The main piece of the object was the ancient cast iron padlock that until lately had hung beside the half-door. Its long locking bar was latched around two rectangular metal pieces. Someone had knotted one end of a long length of white fabric to the lock. The other end of the fabric was tied to the metal ring on the top edge of the trapdoor.

Behind him, Leon clambered up through the door and helped Autumn hook it to the wall. Alice and Kurt joined them a moment later.

"It's a shirt," said Leon, examining the fabric knotted to the ring in the trapdoor.

"It's Mom's," said Grover Solomon, going cold as understanding filled him. When his father had left to buy them supper, his mother must have come upstairs and used her own shirt and the big padlock to jury rig a sort of lock to keep anyone from joining her. The two rectangular pieces of metal that had come loose and nearly whacked Grover Solomon in the nose were the pull handles of the kitchenette cupboard doors. They had been yanked clean out of the cheap plywood when Grover Solomon and Autumn had finally pushed open the door.

But that didn't explain why Annette had wanted to keep away visitors. Unless…she was taking orders from someone else now.

He climbed up the last few steps. The air felt heavy up here, unnaturally hot, even considering the warmth of the early summer evening outside. Several of his ghost books had mentioned that the presence of spirits tended to correspond with a drop in ambient temperature, sometimes to such a degree that it could turn a person's breath to steam. Well, that might be true for some ghosts, but not for Odetta Koop. Her spirit ran hot.

He drew in a deep breath of that hot air and then strode across the boundary of linoleum and carpet that separated the two main rooms of this floor. He half-expected Odetta to leap at him from the shadows at any moment. But he reached the half-door unmolested, and set his hand on the knob.

The others clustered behind him, willing—if not necessarily eager—to lend their support. They weren't "used up" as he had believed before. If nothing else, he could take comfort in the fact that his terrible weekend had given him real friends for the first time since Laz had died.

I'm not alone, he thought, and the simple, profound reality of their presence behind him filled him with courage. He twisted the knob.

He had known since the moment he laid eyes on the Queen of Diamonds downstairs what he would find behind the half-door, but seeing it in person felt like a sock to the gut.

His mother knelt, shirtless, in a pool of flickering orange light, eyes closed, hands clasped as they had been on the card. Unlike the card, her hair did not cover her entire body, though it was longer than it had been this morning, and turning gray again. Her breasts, covered only by an old off-white brassiere, rose and fell in a metronome of breath. Otherwise she might have been carved from marble. And she was far away, much too far away—perhaps twenty feet from the door, despite the fact that crawlspace only measured eight feet at its widest axis.

It's the Cave, Grover Solomon thought. *The real one where I met Laz in my dream.*

Dropping to his hands and knees, he crawled forward toward his mother—

—and cracked his forehead hard enough to make his teeth click together. He shied back and sat on his heels, rubbing a spot above his right eyebrow.

"What happened?" asked Kurt. "Are you okay?"

"Hit my head on the do—" he started to say. The air in the doorway rippled strangely, like the surface of a pond broken by a tossed pebble. The image of his mother distorted and broke as if he were viewing her through deep water.

Grover Solomon reached out and prodded the empty doorway with one index finger. The tip of his finger met a hard, smooth surface as unyielding as polished crystal, generating more ripples. He placed both palms against that hard, invisible surface, shoving at it as if he could simply muscle through, the way he and Autumn had muscled open the trapdoor. But whatever this barrier was made of, it budged not a bit.

"Mom?" He smacked the barrier the way a child might smack a thick glass partition at the zoo in the hopes of attracting an animal's attention. He earned a stinging palm for his effort. His mother didn't so much as twitch.

Except...she *did* seem to be moving. Or...No, not moving. Shrinking. Gliding away from the sealed doorway as if she and her little wedge of candles were resting on a treadmill someone had just switched on.

"Mom!" Now he banged on the barrier with both fists, producing a wild rippling effect. By the time it cleared, Annette Yoder, like Dorcas before her, had disappeared into the blackness.

Odetta's Keep

You have to be prepared for anything. Lazarus's words from the previous night rolled through Grover Solomon's head like distant thunder. But Laz had been wrong. To deal with Odetta Koop, Grover Solomon only needed to be prepared for *one* thing: loss.

During his life she had robbed him of so many qualities and experiences, be they emotional, mental, or physical. All that was left for her to keep taking away the people around him until he was, as he had been for most of his life, utterly alone.

He straightened up and regarded the small knot of companions who had joined him in his final spasm of defiance against the monster who lived in his house. "Go," he told them. "Please."

None of them spoke.

"I can't tell you what it means to me that you came here. The fact that you are all willing to risk your own safety to support me in—" he smiled humorlessly and gestured at the empty room around them "—whatever the heck this is. Odetta can't take that knowledge from me."

"I wasn't *willing* to do any of this!" Alice suddenly exploded, making the rest of them jump. "I told you not to come back here, remember?" She jammed one of her tiny hands into her pocket and advanced on Grover Solomon, her expression mutinous.

He took a single step back from her, then stopped, holding his ground. "I had to."

"I know that!" she snapped. From her pocket she drew the tiny lacquered needle case. It flashed a dull green-gold in the dim light filtering through the windows. "I *also* had to, you jackass!"

Autumn uttered a surprised chirp that turned quickly into high, delighted laughter.

"You're *all* jackasses," Alice muttered, though the corner of her mouth twitched. She snatched up one of his hands, selected a needle from the case, and slid it deftly into that hot spot between his knuckles. From there she worked quickly, probing and adding more needles until his hands looked like pin cushions.

"Something has drawn us all here, Grover Solomon," said Kurt Martin in a voice that strove to be confident and reasonable. "If it is God or some other force, we can't ignore it any more than you can."

"We're here, man," said Leon. "Like it or not."

"Yes, yes, aren't we all so brave," put in Alice irritably as she placed yet more needles. "We have to stay if you want someone to pull you back out."

Grover Solomon heard this last but did not understand. He felt his body becoming lighter. The room around him seemed to be growing simultaneously larger and dimmer. Alice's treatment was already working, it seemed.

"But your baby..." Grover Solomon heard himself say to Autumn.

All traces of amusement were wiped from her face in an instant. "You don't get to say that to me," she said harshly. Her eyes flashed—literally flashed—in that same angry green strobe from last night. Her mouth formed words he could no longer hear.

Suddenly her whole body glowed bright, hot, and fierce in the darkening third floor, which now seemed to have grown to the size of a ballroom. A golden corona sizzled around her.

My God. She's magnificent, Grover Solomon thought deliriously.

Alice had one more needle in her case. She lifted it up to the side of her head like a bar patron preparing to make one last toss at the dartboard. Grover Solomon kept very still as he watched the gleaming needle move toward his face. Something like the toll of an enormous bell clanged through his head as Alice pushed it into the soft mound of skin between his eyebrows. He squeezed his eyes shut against a sudden burning sensation that traveled from his forehead down his arms and legs like an injection of hot cinnamon oil.

The burn faded slowly. That weightless, dizzy feeling from before departed, too. At last he opened his eyes. The others were gone.

Or maybe he was the one who had gone. He still stood a few paces from the half-door, but the room around him had grown alarmingly. The ceiling peaked five stories above his head. The kitchenette was visible as a gleam of linoleum flooring and formica countertops a football field away. He saw the trapdoor angling up from the floor and bolted to the wall. Even at this distance it looked as big as the side of a barn.

He raised his hands to his eyes and saw no needles. He probed cautiously at his forehead, and his fingertips met only smooth skin.

Someone has to pull you back out, Alice had said before she and the others had faded from sight.

He thought he understood. During the last two days he had begun to develop a crude sense of the logic that governed Odetta Koop's existence. And if he was correct, he had crossed into the house as the Odetta herself knew it. This was the same place he had visited in his dream. The place to which Lazarus had begged him to come find him.

Except if he was right, he now had to locate *three* people, not just one, who had been wrongfully imprisoned in this dark, cavernous facsimile of his house.

He turned purposefully, decisively and knelt before the half-door, which was the only part of the third floor whose proportions had not changed. It appeared as a rectangular patch of utter darkness set in the white plaster wall. A glimmering barrier still hung in the doorway. Grover Solomon reached for it, noting as he did so a familiar tracing of hard blue light around his fingertips.

The air in the doorway quivered, almost appearing to shy away from his touch. He reached forward more confidently and pushed through the barrier as easily as if it were cellophane wrap. And as soon as his mind made the comparison, it *became* cellophane, crinkling in his hand. He balled it up and tossed it aside.

A hot, stinking breeze shot out of the little doorway, ruffling his hair. In the same moment, the floor shuddered and bucked under him, first pitching him into the air, then rising up to smack his knees and chest. The earthquake—for what else could it be?—continued for another ten seconds or so and then stopped as suddenly as it had begun.

When the floor stopped moving, he rolled over, body aching, and peered up into the face of Odetta Koop. It was the same face that had burst from the closet downstairs, seven feet high and gray as slate. But now the face was attached to a body that matched its size. Odetta wore a black cape dress so voluminous that it could have covered an entire house—this house, the real one that had earned a plaque from the Iowa Historical Society—from roof to foundation. Had she straightened up to her full height, she would have cracked her head on the fifty-foot ceiling. But she stood hunched over, burdened with the weight of a grandfather clock nearly as tall as she was. It hung off her back like the world's most cumbersome backpack. The clock marked time with deep, resonant booms like distant cannon fire.

But as remarkable as the clock was, something else behind it stole most of Grover Solomon's attention. An oval-shaped smear hung in midair, as if a clumsy painter had smudged reality with a misplaced thumbprint. The smear drew his eye, yet when he tried to look closer, it danced instantly out of his vision. It seemed to be visible only when he wasn't looking directly at it.

Then Odetta Koop spoke, and he forgot all about the dancing smudge and the building-sized grandfather clock. "*How did you get here?*" she boomed down at him in a voice that sounded like the screams of a thousand people dying in a massacre.

The voice struck him with physical force, propelling him several feet backward, toward the half-door. He was overcome with a terror so absolute that he wondered if he would ever be able to think clearly again. He also wondered—in that same small, rational way that had come to him last night after Alice's first treatment—whether he might be pissing his pants without knowing it.

Another blast of hot wind struck him from behind, from the half-door, and he was pitched aside. A dark shape bolted past him toward Odetta Koop, swelling ever larger as it moved. A shape in a black cape dress the size of a circus tent.

There's two of her! his mind brayed, any last rational detachment swept away by fresh panic. *Dear God, there's two of her!*

But the newcomer was younger, her massive body more angular in her black dress. It was Dorcas, young and grim, the way she had appeared on the Queen of Spades playing card.

The two women launched themselves at one another like sumo wrestlers, colliding with a tectonic crash that pitched Grover Solomon across the floor yet again. They scratched and pulled and kicked and bit with wild, animalist ferocity. Dorcas took hold of one of Odetta's arms and spun her around. With Odetta off balance, Dorcas hoisted the giant grandfather clock into the air and hurled it savagely to the floor. The clock shattered into ten thousand fragments of wood, glass, and metal. A brass cog the size of a tractor wheel whickered through the air past Grover Solomon and embedded itself in the wall behind him.

"Go!" bellowed Dorcas back over her shoulder. "Go now!"

He didn't need telling twice. He scrambled backward on his keister, pistoning his arms and legs like a crab fleeing the jabbing beak of a hungry seagull, his mouth a jagged, inarticulate O of fright. He skittered through the open half door into sudden, stifling darkness. The sounds of struggle between the two gargantuan women out in the main room ceased as abruptly as if they had never existed. He felt like he had just been thrust into a sensory deprivation tank. He patted himself down to make sure his body hadn't disappeared as well. He seemed to be fully present, all parts accounted for—and with dry pants to boot.

He stood cautiously, not quite daring to stand up straight lest he crack his skull on the peaked ceiling in the tiny room. But as he stretched slowly up to his full height, countless papers fluttered across his ears and the bridge of his nose.

His assumption from earlier was correct: he had indeed returned to the realm of his dream.

"Mom?" he called. "Laz? Hello?" His voice seemed to fall dead only a few inches away from his mouth. He squinted in every direction, hoping to see the two sparks of light he had seen for the briefest instant in Odetta Koop's terrible mouth downstairs. Empty darkness spiraled out in every direction.

He had a sudden, overwhelming intuition that his time might be short here. However real this space might look and feel, he believed his body must still be with Alice and the others. Hadn't she said that someone would have to "pull him out"? And what if they did so before he had located his mother and Lazarus?

For that matter, would Alice be able to pull out all three of them when he did find them?

He shook his head and attempted to tamp down these pessimistic worries. Any plan that involved infiltrating a ghost's hidden fortress was bound to have some flaws.

With the half-door no longer visible, he made a guess as to which direction he had entered from, rotated his body in the opposite direction, and set out at a jog. The dangling papers continued to brush at his head and face, but they seemed softer now, almost tentative. These were not the same papers that had slashed relentlessly at his hands during his dream. Or maybe they were the same, but *he* was not.

Even as this thought entered his mind, that cool blue light returned to his hands, blooming in the darkness, transforming his pumping fists into beacons against the crushing black of this place.

The Cave Alight

He ran without stumbling or growing tired. Hanging slips of paper parted at his passage like the surface of a calm, upside down sea. Ancient, worn floorboards slid in and out of view below his feet, winking malevolently in the light emanating from his fists. Every step felt the same, seeming neither to bring him closer to his goal nor take him farther from his starting point. Could that be one of the magicks of this place? To hold him in one spot like the track of an unimaginably large treadmill while allowing him to believe he was making progress?

But no. In his dream, Lazarus had heard him somehow. Lazarus had approached him and chased him down over a distance of perhaps a hundred yards. So where could his mother and Lazarus be now, if not in this lightless crypt? Where was Odetta hiding them?

Hiding...

Unbidden, Dr. Shepherd's prissy voice rose in his mind. *You are hiding,* the doctor had declared in his self-satisfied, condescending way. *Would you like to tell me what you are hiding from?*

And when Grover Solomon had answered, *Love,* how had the doctor responded?

How like your mother you are.

At the time, Grover Solomon had been rather too distraught for the doctor's remark to soak in fully. But now, here in this nightmare where everything was *hidden* all the time, those words about his mother took on a new, fearful poignancy.

What if Odetta wasn't hiding his mother at all? What if his mother was hiding from him?

He let himself shuffle to a halt. The papers around his head fluttered, then stilled. Another voice now rose up to replace Dr. Shepherd's—his mother's, when he had tried to call her collect from the police station.

No. I'm sorry.

Had she already been in Odetta Koop's clutches by then? Perhaps Odetta herself had mimicked Annette's voice on the telephone the same way she had impersonated Ethyl at the house later.

Somehow he didn't think so. Because his mother had also neglected, until it was too late, to intervene when Ducky had chucked him into the squad car and carted him off to jail. She had allowed him to be sent to Dr. Shepherd, and she must have known the man's history as a pray-the-gay-away camp director.

His stomach roiled. Was that the reason his parents had sent him to Dr. Shepherd? Did they know he had been in love with Lazarus? Did they know he was gay? Odetta Koop had suggested as much while imitating his father, but she might just have been trying to screw with his mind. Then again, the Martins and Autumn sure hadn't seemed surprised when he'd told them in the hospital.

Maybe…

He tried to stifle the thought and couldn't.

Maybe that's why she never hugs me.

He felt something crawling up from the center of his chest toward his throat like a starved, mind-sick bear emerging from hibernation. He opened his mouth and the crawling bear-thing burst out of him in a roar that was wordless and miserable with grief. But not only grief. Rage came too, sudden and scalding.

He balled up his glowing fists and bellowed, "*I am not hiding from love!*"

This time his voice echoed instead of falling flat. Floorboards vibrated beneath him. The hanging papers around his head rustled in unison. In the hard blue light emanating from his fists, he saw the long strips of paper all draw in toward him like iron shavings toward a magnet.

Then, without warning, they burst into flame. All of them at once, in a twenty-foot radius around his head. They writhed like dying snakes. They spun and twisted, touching the edges of other nearby papers and setting them alight in a furious chain reaction until Grover Solomon seemed to be standing below a sky of endless fire. Torrents of yellow-orange firelight pressed outward in an expanding sphere, extinguishing the darkness.

"That's right!" Grover Solomon shrieked into the frenzy of hot, swirling ash. "I'm coming for you, next, Odetta Koop! You hear me? I'm gonna burn you to the gr—"

A scream of pain and terror rent the Cave. At first Grover Solomon thought it was Odetta Koop herself—that he had wounded her somehow with the destruction of her hanging papers. But as the scream intensified, he realized that he recognized the sound from his past. He had heard it once before, during the worst moment of his life. The scream was coming from Lazarus.

He lunged forward, following Laz's cries through the dim, smoky hellscape. Floating ash clawed at his nose and throat. He began coughing uncontrollably. His eyes and nose streamed. But he kept running.

Not this time, he thought hysterically. *She doesn't get him this time.*

Up ahead, a huge bonfire materialized in the gloom. The screaming seemed to be coming from inside it. Without breaking pace, Grover Solomon drew back his right arm, which now blazed from fingertip to elbow as brightly as a halogen bulb, and pistoned his fist forward into the side of the bonfire. Hard blue light met flickering flame and the whole works exploded outward with the force of a bomb. Burning shrapnel spiraled in every direction. Grover Solomon was hurled backward through the air. He crashed onto the hardwood floor in a heap, but he didn't stay down. He rose, still coughing, and took a quick inventory of himself. By some miracle he didn't seem to be hurt.

Ten feet ahead, a figure huddled amid a shattered circle of still-burning embers. Grover Solomon ran forward again and squatted beside the figure. It was Lazarus, nude and trembling and streaked with ash, but also whole. Laz crouched in the rubble of his erstwhile cage, hugging his knees and shivering. This was the same grown-up Laz who had appeared on the Joker card. The same Laz who had descended with such delight the staircase in the entry room last night. It was really him.

Grover Solomon draped an arm across his back and felt the solid warmth of his body. Beads of sweat carved clean lines through the ash covering Laz's skin. This was real. It had to be. Grover Solomon had found his friend.

"You okay?" he asked.

Laz uttered a choked noise between a sob and a laugh. "I guess so. You probably didn't know this, but I don't like fire very much."

Tears pricked Grover Solomon's eyes, adding their own sting to the irritation from the airborne ash. "No, I guess not," he said. "I'm sorry. I didn't mean to do it."

Laz finally lifted his head sat back heavily, still hugging his knees. He stared momentarily up into the guttering flames that had so recently consumed his cage, eyes over-bright. "Fuck this place, man. Fuck it so hard."

"I'm sorry," Grover Solomon repeated hollowly. Something about Laz's voice just now had brought home the reality—the weight—of fifteen years in this lightless dungeon. "Can you stand?"

Laz closed his eyes. A tear cut down one ashen cheek in a glowing orange track as bright and hot as a lava spill. After a moment he held out a hand. Grover Solomon took it and hoisted him to his feet. They embraced, quickly, perfunctorily, and Grover Solomon suddenly knew something else: Lazarus wasn't coming back with him.

His chin threatened to quiver, and he clenched his jaw to firm it up. Lazarus had been his protector in this house of horrors when they were children, and now it was time to return the favor.

"Let's grab my mom and get out of here. I haven't seen her yet, but I know she's in here."

Lazarus nodded heavily. "Odetta's feeding on her. Using her to—"

"Feeding on her?" Grover Solomon blurted. "Well come on! Where is she?"

Lazarus grimaced. He wouldn't look at Grover Solomon.

"What!" Grover Solomon shouted. "Do you know where she is or not? Or...no." A clammy hand of panic was curling around his neck. "Is she—*Can* she come back or is she...like you?"

Lazarus's orange eyes found his, and Grover Solomon saw something like relief in them. Maybe even gratitude. "Not like me," he said softly. "Your mom came here by choice."

Now Grover Solomon was the one who looked away. "She's ashamed of me."

Lazarus put a companionable hand on his shoulder. "God, you're always so dramatic. She's ashamed of *herself*."

Grover Solomon closed his own eyes and drank in Lazarus's touch. Never before had he felt true adult desire. But how, how, *how* could such a thing come to him now, in this place of fire and darkness, with his mother's very soul suffering nearby?

"She knows I'm gay," he told Lazarus. "Do you know that?"

Lazarus squeezed his shoulder and then let it go. "Yep," he said easily.

"Did you know when we were kids?"

"I don't think so. I mean, did you know yourself?"

Grover Solomon sniffed. "A little while ago Odetta was pretending to be my dad, and she told me that you ran away because you figured out I was gay and didn't want to be my friend anymore."

"Yeah, well, Odetta's an asshole. You can tell her I said that, too. I don't even care."

Grover Solomon looked up desperately. "Are you gay too?" It was a child's question, and he asked it in a voice that sounded more like a child's than a grown man's.

Laz didn't answer right away, and Grover Solomon saw a sad smile on his friend's lips. Laz snapped his fingers like a magician. A playing card suddenly appeared in his hand. He spun the card around and Grover Solomon saw the old Queen of Hearts, fleshy and nude, frozen in her eternal coy pose for the camera.

"My girl," said Lazarus, tapping the side of the card fondly. "I'll love her forever."

The card blurred double in Grover Solomon's vision as tears pooled in his eyes. "I'll luh-love you f-f-forever," he blubbered. He staggered forward and laid his head on Lazarus's bare shoulder.

"I know it, man," Laz said kindly. "I'm sorry."

They stood in the sooty darkness for several moments, Grover Solomon sobbing and Laz giving him time to do so. And then Lazarus's body stiffened.

"Dude."

Grover Solomon wiped his wet cheeks on the sleeves of his t-shirt, gulping. Even though he had never felt so miserable, he still somehow felt lighter. Not a literal lightness of body like when Alice had first treated him with her needles, but a lightness of spirit. When he finally dried his streaming eyes, he saw that his hands weren't the only parts of him that glowed now. Cool blue light illuminated his t-shirt from the inside.

He looked up, mouth open to ask whether Laz could see the glow too. But Laz was staring over his shoulder with a distressed look on his face. Grover Solomon spun around and peered into the emptiness. He saw only swirling embers.

"What?" he asked.

Laz nodded at the darkness ahead, his mouth set in a grim line. "Your mom's coming."

Beyond Odetta's Reach

Grover Solomon squinted in the direction Laz had indicated. He still couldn't see anything, but he could hear...what? A sound like metal being dragged laboriously across a hard surface? It reminded him of a movie that—like most movies he'd watched as a child—had terrified him. When he was six or seven his mother had deemed him old enough to watch one of her favorite Christmas movies, *A Christmas Carol* starring George C. Scott as Ebenezer Scrooge. Grover Solomon, who very rarely got to watch television or movies of any kind, leapt at the chance. He was a very good audience as he snuggled up to his mother on the couch, losing himself completely in the drab, gray Victorian scenery and Scrooge's grouchy barking.

But then the movie took a turn. Jacob Marley's ghost, gray with death, wailing and dragging chains and lockboxes as large as his own head, trudged into Scrooge's bedroom to deliver his famous portents of doom. Or at least he would have done had Annette not switched off the television and carried a nearly hysterical Grover

Solomon up to his bed, where he clung to her hand, twitching at every sound, until he finally collapsed into an unquiet sleep three hours later.

Even as this memory surfaced in Grover Solomon's mind, a crawling shape materialized on the floor twenty paces ahead. It was low and lumpy, trailing long appendages the way a giant jellyfish trails clusters of stinging tentacles through the water behind it. The sound of dragging metal—dragging chains?—grew louder as it approached. Grover Solomon saw a pale arm questing outward from the front of the thing. Saw its hand flatten against the ash-covered wood floor. Saw muscles and tendons tighten in the hand as the thing lugged itself forward a few feet, then repeated the process.

"Not doing so hot, is she?" said Lazarus conversationally as he watched the single, frail arm extend outward and drag the lumpy mass forward another few feet.

"What do you mean? Is that—" Grover Solomon began, but then he recalled the image of his mother as the Queen of Diamonds. She had nearly been drowning in thick, matted locks of gray hair.

The pale hand dragged the body forward yet again. As if in response to this motion, a dozen new snarls of hair were expelled from the mass to land on the wood floor with heavy metallic thunks.

Grover Solomon thought he heard a weak cry from somewhere deep in the tangled pile. "Do something!" he cried at Lazarus.

But Laz shook his head. "What am I supposed to do? You're the one glowing like a Christmas tree over there."

Without warning, everything around them rocked as if an earthquake had struck. The floor buckled and split upward in ragged splinters as long and thick as fence posts.

"Whatever you do, make it fast," urged Laz. He stared upward doubtfully. "Something's happening out there."

The crawling thing was only a few paces away now. Grover Solomon knelt and took up fistfuls of the coarse, wiry hair. Near the spot where the pale arm disappeared into the tangled mess, he could make out one wide, desperate eye peering at him.

"Grover Solomon," husked his mother's voice, nearly inaudible with exhaustion. "I heard your voice just now. I never knew how badly you—"

The cave bucked again. A few unburned paper strips detached from the invisible ceiling and floated down around them like streamers at some disastrous party. More thick cables of hair burst from the pile and forced Annette's head back down out of sight.

"Mom!"

"Faster, dude," Lazarus warned. "This place is coming down and we're nowhere near the door."

Grover Solomon snatched one of the falling streamers out of the air, thinking of the way Lazarus had wielded a hunk of paper like a sword in his dream the other night. He squeezed his eyes shut and imagined the blue light from his hands traveling out into the paper. When he opened his eyes again he was holding what looked like a beam of blue light in his clenched fists.

"Looks like somebody finally saw *Star Wars*," Laz remarked approvingly.

"When I was twelve. Scared me half to death." He raised the shining strip of paper over his head and brought it down with a motion like a lumberjack chopping firewood. Gray tentacles of hair fell away, twisting and convulsing.

A rumbling sound filled the darkness. Debris fell all around them.

"You might want to double-time it with your swashbuckling there, Obi-wan!" Lazarus shouted, raising his hands protectively over his head. "She's going to bring the whole place down on us!"

Grover Solomon's makeshift sword fell again and again until most of the metallic hair lay on the floor and he could no longer make any cuts without risking harm to his mother. He extended a hand toward her. "Can you stand?"

She pushed herself to her knees, nearly toppled over as the floor heaved again, and then managed to climb into an upright position.

"Give it here," she said to Grover Solomon, holding out a shaking hand.

He passed over the glowing paper sword without a word. Annette reached up with her free hand and grasped the remaining ropes of gray in a bunch at the base of her neck. She gingerly swung the paper sword upward. The heavy bunches clunked to the ground and squirmed before they too went completely still.

Annette tossed the paper aside—the blue light died the moment it left her hand—and enfolded her son in an embrace for the first time in fifteen years while the world continued to break apart around them.

"This is super touching and all!" Laz bellowed. "But maybe we ought to get out of here!"

Annette released Grover Solomon and put her arms around Lazarus. Grover Solomon saw her lean into Lazarus's ear and whisper something. Lazarus listened, stony-faced. He did not reciprocate the hug, but after a moment he gave a reluctant nod. When Annette pulled back she was weeping.

Hunks of ceiling rained down around them, shattering in bursts of plaster and rotted lath. Between the collapsing ceiling and the erupting floor, the three of them were completely surrounded by a circle of rising rubble.

Lazarus shouted something. Annette took his hand and squeezed it. Together they looked like children trapped inside a witch's larder, waiting their turn to be made into stew. But perhaps for the first time in his life, Grover Solomon wasn't scared. His body shone so brightly in the gloom that Laz and his mom cast dark shadows against the rubble behind them.

He reached up with one finger and drew a vertical line of blue fire all the way down to the floor. The line hovered in the air. He jammed both hands into it and pulled in opposite directions, as if drawing open a pair of musty old drapes. But instead of drapes, he pulled apart the air itself, revealing a ragged opening that led back into the third floor living area. There was no frame or visible means of support to this new opening, but Grover Solomon didn't waste time puzzling out the physics involved in tearing a hole in reality. He took his mother's free hand and pulled her forward, with Laz bringing up the rear.

All three of them tumbled out onto shag carpet, and Grover Solomon was relieved to see that the living room's proportions had returned to normal. Dorcas and Odetta, tall but person-sized once more, stood several feet apart, wheezing from exertion. Both women's hair hung in lank, sweaty curtains. Their dresses were ripped and blotted with dark patches of sweat.

"You can't keep me away forever," said Dorcas grimly.

"Or me," Lazarus put in, stepping around Annette and planting himself beside Dorcas. "You're just—Listen, you're kind of an asshole, and I don't want to live with you anymore. Funny story, actually. I was telling Grover Solomon this same thing just a minute ago, and then you tried to bury us all in falling rubble and totally proved my point for me."

Odetta hissed at him through her rusty axe-head teeth.

"See?" said Laz, looking back over his shoulder to Grover Solomon. "There's just no talking to her. Terrible roommate."

Grover Solomon moved forward to stand beside his friend. "Odetta Koop, you aren't welcome here."

She turned blindly up to the ceiling and roared like a dying bull. The sound was so animalistic, so full of rage and despair that Grover Solomon finally understood the depths of her madness. Sometime in the years since she had died, Odetta Koop had gone truly, irrevocably insane.

The smeared, blurry shape behind her—was there just one, or could Grover Solomon see two shapes now?—seemed to grow and pulse.

Several things happened very quickly then. Odetta spun around to flee down the trapdoor, as she had done the night she had pretended to be Autumn. Dorcas and Lazarus made to pursue her, but Grover Solomon acted first. He launched himself forward and caught the back of Odetta's mouldering cape dress. She squealed and tried to shy away from him, but he held fast. Unlimited strength seemed to flow through him now, and he lifted her bodily over his head like a father playing airplane with a small child. Odetta shrieked at him, flinging curses in a language no human tongue could ever replicate.

His eyes bored up into her livid face. "You are *not* welcome here!" he repeated. This time the words came out as a command.

He trotted forward, still holding Odetta's body over his head like a soccer player preparing to make an in-bounds pass, and tossed her forward as hard as he could. Still screaming her alien curses, she sailed through the midair doorway he had created between this place and the collapsing Cave. Grover Solomon arrived at doorway an instant later. He grabbed two fistfuls of nothing at either side of the portal and brought his hands together with a clap, sealing it off.

But an instant later, the empty space where the hole had been suddenly bulged outward again. Hand shapes clawed at the air so that it bent and dimpled outward. Behind him he heard Lazarus's jubilant voice: "Hey, thanks, Grover Solomon! You're a good man, Charlie Brown!" And then he called, "I'm coming, baby doll!"

Before Grover Solomon could even begin to guess what these words meant or who Laz might be talking too, he was driven to his knees by a sound that his mind would later insist on calling "singing." It was a sensation, a vibration, of excruciating joy. It brought an ecstasy that ripped like knives. He somehow knew that if he turned around and looked at whatever was making that sound, his body—his very soul—would be ripped to shreds in one jubilant instant. Beside him, his mother screamed with exquisite bliss.

"Don't look at it!" he screamed back. He squeezed his eyes shut and blundered toward her. Her hand found his forearm and gripped down like a vice. "Hold on!" he commanded, quite unnecessarily. She was already holding on so tightly that his arm would probably be covered in bruises tomorrow.

Concentrating harder than he had ever concentrated in his life, he reached blindly above his head and tore another one of those holes in midair. Almost at once, as if they'd been waiting for him, several pairs of hands clutched his and yanked him and his mother upward. Gravity seemed to warp around him so that up suddenly became sideways, and he crashed face-down onto a jumble of bodies and limbs. Someone that was probably his mother fell on top of him. That wonderful, terrible sound, now more distant, continued to wail on and on.

"Close it!" someone begged in a voice that might have been a sob or hysterical laughter. "Grover Solomon, for God's sake, close it!"

He finally opened his eyes and saw the new hole he had made, this time hovering in a patch of shag carpet. Through the hole he could see the room he'd just left—nearly identical to the one he was in now. He looked over his shoulder and glimpsed his mother, Alice, Leon, Autumn, and Kurt Martin strewn around the room. Leon was curled on the floor in a fetal position, clutching his injured hands as if they suddenly pained him again. Autumn was cradling her belly protectively, eyes also squeezed shut. Annette was crawling away from the hole they'd just come out of in an obvious effort to escape the wonderful, terrible sound. Kurt stood frozen like a wax statue of himself, eyes staring glassily into the hole in the floor.

Only Alice was looking back at Grover Solomon. "Close it," she repeated weakly. Her face was covered in tears. "I can hear my grandmother. She says you have to close it."

With one final burst of effort and concentration, Grover Solomon rolled over and grasped the edges of the hole. Down in the room he had just escaped, the first hole he made—the doorway into which he'd thrown Odetta Koop only moments ago—reopened, and Odetta slithered back out of it. Her hair and the fringes of her dress were on fire.

Grover Solomon brought his hands together with another clap, and the rip in the shag carpet closed. The awful, gorgeous sound that was not singing was cut off at once. For a moment Grover Solomon felt a swell of longing so powerful he almost tried to re-open the hole so he could hear the sound again.

But he gave his head a shake and staggered upright. The others were doing likewise, helping each other to stand with groans of exertion and pain. Once everyone was on their feet, he led the way to the trap door and down the stairs. His mother came directly behind him, followed by Alice, then Autumn, then Leon. Kurt Martin remained in the living area, staring down at the patch of carpet that moments before had been a doorway into another dimension.

"Pastor Martin?"

"Dad!" Leon called sharply. "Come on."

Kurt twitched, seeming to come to his senses, and then Grover Solomon lost sight of him as he continued descending the staircase into the second floor hallway. They all hurried in single file, no one speaking, down the hall, then down to the first floor entry room, and out the door into the warm night.

Thea, Cythia Martin, and Ethyl huddled together on the front lawn. When Ethyl saw his wife, he rushed forward to take her in his arms. She clung to him in silence.

"Where's Kurt?" Cynthia asked, studying their haggard faces with mounting panic of her own.

Kurt was nowhere to be seen.

"Dad?" called Leon, looking all around. In an instant he leapt back up the front steps and reached for the door.

Before he got it open again, there was a crash of glass over-head. Kurt Martin sailed out of the third-story window, shrieking a string of words that Grover Solomon couldn't make out. He hit the ground with a complicated *crack* like a bundle of twigs being snapped over a giant's knee and rolled over and over, limbs flopping grotesquely. When he finally came to rest in the grass, his upper and lower body seemed to be facing different directions.

Leon and Cynthia rushed forward. Leon was holding his arms out as if his mind hadn't quite arrived at the notion that it was too late to catch his father out of the air. Cynthia's legs gave out before she reached her husband, and she skidded the last few yards to him through the soft grass on her knees. Her mouth hung open in a silent scream.

Autumn was already speaking rapidly into her cell phone. Six eternal minutes later, paramedics fitted Kurt to a spine board not unlike the one his son had been strapped to five years earlier inside the ruins of a condemned church in western Germany. They loaded him into the back of the ambulance, slammed the heavy doors and roared off down the street, washing the neighborhood in frantic red and blue light.

Epilogue:
Between Heaven and Hell

The Escobars arrive first thing in the morning, gung-ho to start hauling their belongings from the rented moving trailer to their new home. Enrique Escobar stands beside his wife, the former Rebecca Childs of upstate New York. Enrique is five-foot-six, and Rebecca is six-foot-one. They cut a happily lopsided figure on the sidewalk as Enrique slips an arm around her waist and she leans over so that her cheek rests companionably on top of his head. They have been saving money to buy a house for twenty-three years.

Grover Solomon, who has been sitting on the front porch, descends the steps to meet them. He has hardly slept in two days, and he knows he will crash soon. But he has one final job to do before he can be shut of Odetta Koop and this house forever.

The bulk of the day's work is already over. He and his parents left the hospital and returned to the house before sunrise to clean up the aftermath of last night's battles. Ethyl braved the third floor to repair the window through which Kurt Martin made his hasty exit. He also patched the cracked plaster in the wall beside the half-door. Grover Solomon did not go upstairs to inspect his father's work. Instead, he swept up the broken glass from the exploded light fixture in the entry room, and rehung the cedar closet door on new hinges. The clothes and mask Odetta left behind after impersonating Ethyl Yoder puddled into a gray sort of jelly, which Grover Solomon scooped, repulsed, into the dustpan with the shattered glass. Annette, for her part, also elected not to go upstairs. In fact, she refused point blank to go back into the house at all. She spent her time squatting in the yard with her pocket flashlight, rooting through the long grass for sharp fragments of window glass, which she deposited in a canvas bag.

A fourth person, a locksmith whom Grover Solomon called the moment the man's office opened at 5:00 this morning, has already come and gone. The replacement key for the front door is now in Grover Solomon's pocket (the original is still floating somewhere in his internal tubing). He has been waiting alone on the front porch for the Escobars for almost an hour. Ethyl and Annette retired to their hotel room after the cleanup effort.

Grover Solomon introduces himself to the Escobars and shakes hands with each of them. He hands over the new key and warns them about wet paint around one of the windows up on third. "Last-minute repair," he tells them. "Nothing to worry about."

The lie will out, he is sure. Sooner or later, these two lovely people will find out about the local pastor who almost killed himself by leaping from the highest level of their new house last night. Grover Solomon suspects that by the time the story hits the New Canaan Gazette *tomorrow morning, Pastor Martin's "accident" will already be old news in town. Even now, police chief Hook is at the hospital, taking statements from the Martins about Kurt's near-fatal fall while Kurt himself lays in traction, conscious but uncommunicative. The others have already tried to ask him what on earth happened up there, and so far he has ignored their questions.*

Grover Solomon doesn't know what happened either, but he suspects it has more than a little to do with whatever Dorcas Hershberger saw behind that black curtain she pulled aside one feverish moment 85 years ago.

Even as these thoughts blow through his mind like wind through a block of swiss cheese, his attention is drawn to the back of the moving trailer, where a little boy of about seven has just emerged with a clear plastic bag of action figures cradled in the crook of one arm and a handheld video game system in the other. Rebecca and Enrique twist around to watch the boy hop down from the back of the trailer and make his way up the sidewalk.

"Encontraste los juguetes?" Enrique asks. The boy nods.

"I didn't realize you still had children at home," Grover Solomon says, suddenly feeling a bit sick.

"Paulo's our little Catholic blessing," says Rebecca. "Our next youngest is just finishing up her second year of college. She'll be here in a couple weeks to spend the summer with us." She turns back to Grover Solomon with a kind of dopey smile on her face.

She seems to be in a tremendous mood, and Grover Solomon regrets that he will have to bring that mood down. "That's...wonderful."

"Well, Mr. Yoder," Rebecca says with some finality, "it was very kind of you to come out this early on a Monday morning. I'm sure you have work, and we're itching to get inside, so—"

"Actually," he interrupts, "I have to tell you one more thing about this place."

He glances down at the little boy, Paolo, who is struggling to switch on his video game without putting down the bag of action figures. Grover Solomon hesitates, but he's been thinking all morning about how he should pass on this information. The unexpected presence of a child only makes it all the more important that he does so.

"There is a ghost here," he begins, less tactfully than he rehearsed in his mind. "I—Well, I guess I'm pretty sensitive to stuff like that, so

maybe she won't bother you the same way she did me. But I am legally obliged to tell you about her before you move in. I—I tried to get rid of her, but I'm pretty sure she's still around."

Rebecca and Enrique exchange a look. "We already heard about the ghost from the realtor," says Rebecca.

"Me, I'm not so worried," Enrique says easily. "My grandmother believed that ghosts only stay behind so they can pass on hidden treasure to the next generations."

Paulo looks up from his game, grinning. "Dad says if I ever feel scared, I'm supposed to say, 'Dame el tesoro!'"

Grover Solomon glances at Rebecca, bewildered.

"It means 'Give me the treasure.'" She laughs. "Look, we appreciate you sharing this with us, but we've been all through this house, and the only place that felt a bit weird was that room up on third."

"Room?"

She points upward, a crease troubling her forehead for the first time. "That little cubby hole your parents kept as a museum piece for the historical society or something? I didn't really understand what the realtor was saying about it. Just between us, I'm going to gut that place and punch a hole in the wall for a window. Get some light in there and…I don't know." She shrugs. "We'll figure out something to do with it."

"And if things get bad," says Enrique confidently, "two of my uncles are priests."

"I see," says Grover Solomon. "That's—Well. That sounds like a plan." Rebecca and Enrique watch him expectantly. Perhaps a bit impatiently now. He nods. "Okay then. I just wanted to pass that along. It was very nice to meet you."

They all shake again, and Grover Solomon excuses himself to his car. He is practically falling over with exhaustion now. He thinks he should telephone Autumn one more time to see if Kurt has improved at all. And then he will rent himself a room at the hotel out by the *highway where his parents are staying.*

His parents. Boy, oh boy. Aside from a brusque divvying of work this morning, they have not exchanged any meaningful words since before Ducky marched Grover Solomon off to jail yesterday. He shakes his head. His parents can wait. The three of them have days and months and years to sort out their issues. Assuming that's even possible. No matter what, sleep must come first.

He slips behind the wheel of his car. A hysterical, high-pitched giggle erupts from him, as unexpected and violent as a sneeze. "Give me the treasure," he mutters.

And then the bald truth of this weekend settles on him like a lead blanket. He wasn't able to banish Odetta Koop. Although the house was mostly quiet while he and his parents cleaned up this morning, he believes she is still there. Weakened, perhaps, but after what happened to Kurt, there can be no doubt that something of her lingers.

On the other hand, he is pretty certain he freed Lazarus from Odetta's prison, which makes him feel both depressed and exalted in some way he still doesn't fully understand. There is also no sign of Dorcas Hershberger, living or dead, which Grover Solomon takes to mean that she escaped along with Lazarus.

His mind butts up against the memory of those last frantic moments on the third floor again and again like a fly smacking its face stupidly against a closed window. Even now, only hours after the final confrontation with Odetta Koop, the details are starting to grow fuzzy in his mind. Did he really sprout a glowing sword from his hand and rip a hole between dimensions?

Actually, he's pretty sure he did. How does a person move past something like that? How is he supposed to go from tearing his way into a parallel dimension and battling a fifty-foot ghost, to troubleshooting software over the phone with a client in Chicago?

"Sleep," he says aloud. But first he pulls out his phone and dials Autumn's number. It goes to voicemail after a single ring and he hangs

up. *If nothing else, he can ask her and Leon for an update at supper tonight. He starts the car and pulls away from the house for what he very sincerely hopes is the last time in his life.*

The Escobars scarcely notice his departure. Enrique is climbing down from the back of the moving trailer with the first armload of boxes. Paulo, already toting his own cargo, practically dances in anticipation behind his mother as she uses the new key to unlock the front door. Enrique joins them with his boxes just as Rebecca pushes open the door. All three of them pile into the entry room together and breathe in the scent of wood that just two days ago smelled like wilderness to Grover Solomon. High overhead, floorboards pop and creak with something like footsteps.

Enrique and Paulo turn up to the ceiling and shout in perfect unison, "Dame el tesoro!" They burst out laughing, set down their items in a corner, and head back outside for the next load.

Acknowledgments

None of my books would exist without the support, generosity, and insight of my brilliant wife, Kate, so she gets her own paragraph, right here at the beginning.

Second in line is my former editor, Alan Rinzler, a wise, patient, and mildly terrifying mentor without whose help I never would have learned how to write a proper novel. Even though he did not edit this book, he still gets a paragraph to himself, too.

Next come the early readers who gave their time and energy to provide feedback and/or copyediting: Susie, Joanna, and Heidi. I also piloted a very early version of this book's first chapters in a fiction workshop at Bowling Green State University. Thanks go to Dr. Lawrence Coates and my fellow students for helpful criticism during the formative stages of this story.

Lastly I must acknowledge—but never thank—the spirit who may or may not still inhabit the house where I grew up. She taught me fear of the dark, and I hope we never meet again.

About the Author

André Swartley is the award-winning author of four novels, including *Leon Martin and the Fantasy Girl.* He lives with his family in central Kansas, where he teaches English.

www.ingramcontent.com/pod-product-compliance
Lightning Source LLC
Chambersburg PA
CBHW060308260626
47160CB00007B/2540

* 9 7 8 0 9 9 0 5 5 4 5 0 9 *